Stardust Trail

A Nate Ross Novel

STARDUST TRAIL

A Nate Ross Novel

By J. R. Sanders

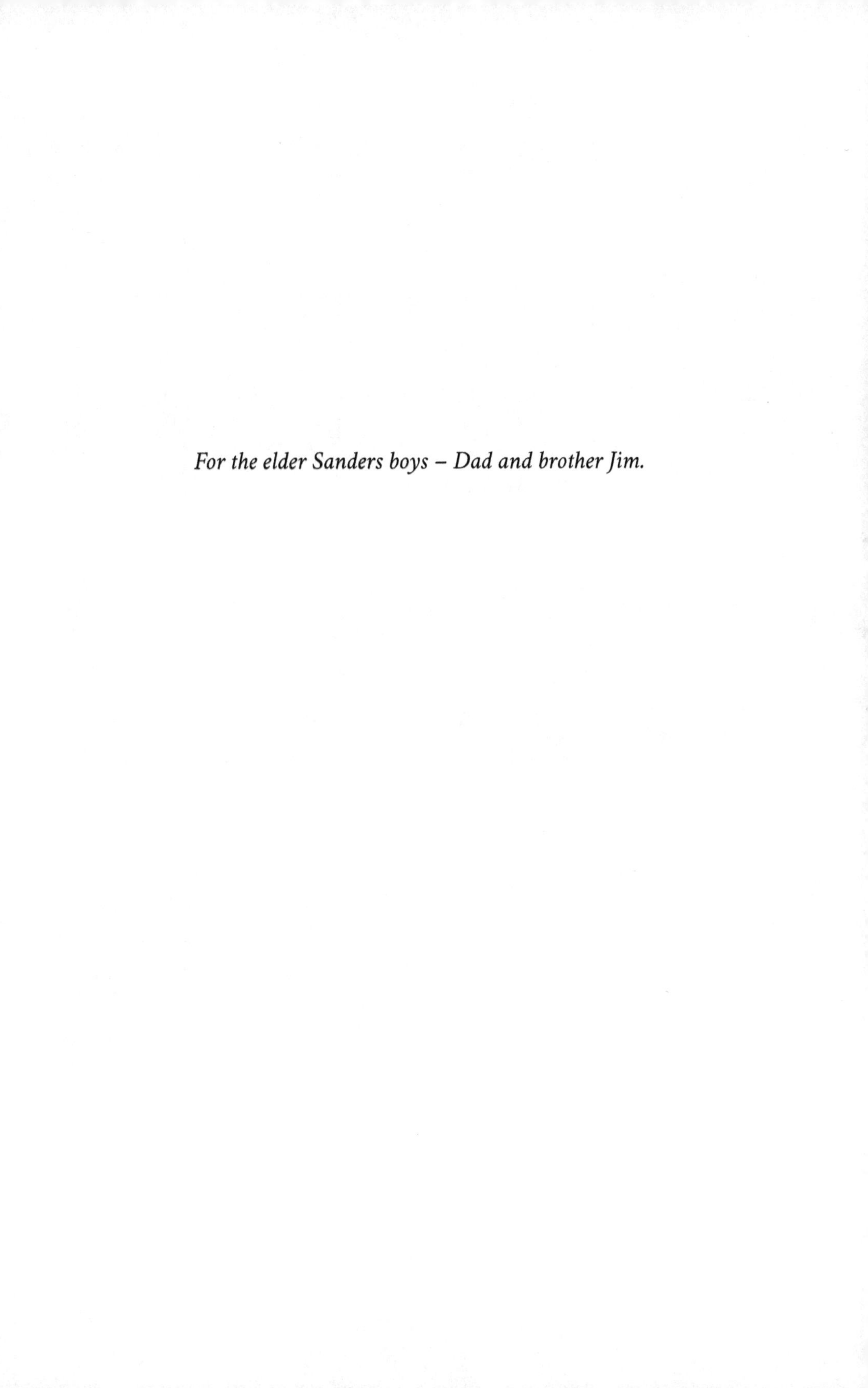

For the elder Sanders boys – Dad and brother Jim.

Chapter One

In Hollywood anything can happen, and usually does. If I'd hunted up a pastrami on my own side of Vermont, maybe none of this would have happened. Maybe it would have happened to someone else. Either way would have been fine by me.

Raindrops drummed on my hat as I stepped off the red car. I'd left my raincoat at the office, advice courtesy of the KNX weatherman. What a pal. Still, it was a small price to pay; the Gotham Deli had the leanest pastrami in L.A. My mind should have been on work—my bankbook was pretty thin—but sometimes a guy needed to let all cares float away and give his full attention to a pile of shaved pastrami on a cloud-soft, mustard-painted bun. That's what a guy needed.

The long, glassed-in carryout counters up front showcased everything from oysters to roasted chickens to shortcake; they made the place look like an edibles museum. It was crowded, even for a Friday, and I didn't much like crowds. I liked pastrami, though, so I steered toward the tables in back. Two cabbies were just leaving a corner booth along a window, and without waiting for service I slid right in. The waitress didn't much like that, but she forced a smile as she took my order. Pastrami and Pickwick Ale, my dear.

In the booth behind me sat three boys who looked as though they should've been torturing their brains in algebra class instead of loitering here over Cokes and milk shakes. The Gotham didn't exactly cater to kids, anyway. I'd have sat elsewhere, given a choice; high school boys could be boisterous, and a Gotham pastrami required quiet solitude to be duly appreciated.

But I worried for nothing; these kids leaned in close over their table and spoke in murmurs, like cons in the yard. I watched them in the wall-to-wall mirror over the bar and figured they were comparing notes on the waitress, who wasn't much older than they were but, if I knew Hollywood waitresses, led them by furlongs in experience. When she breezed over with my lunch and nobody sneaked a peek at her caboose—and it rated a peek—it got my attention. Hollywood had its share of lavender boys, but these three didn't look it. Once a copper always a copper; my twitching antennae told me the boys were capering and, try as I might to ignore it, professional curiosity crowded out my need for a quiet sandwich. I hardly tasted the pastrami and beer as I aimed my ears their way and kept subtle watch in the mirror.

Two of the boys were husky, varsity football types. One had heavy, mooncalf features, and the other did his best to affect the worldly, wary air of a card sharp. The third was a tall, skinny, batfaced kid with twitchy pale green eyes. He tried to look bored and hard but the eyes gave him away. They always did.

Necessity had made me a skilled eavesdropper, and anyway teenagers were always louder than they thought, so I had no trouble catching most of their talk. Batface did the bulk of it while his pals listened with an oddly respectful air, making a quiet comment here and there. If their furtive demeanor hadn't grabbed my notice, the conversation would have. It ran along these lines:

Card Sharp: "How do you know they got your note?"

Batface: "A guy called me at the number I gave them."

Card Sharp: "What number?"

Batface: "Pay phone in the lobby." He pointed out the window to the Roosevelt Hotel, just across Hollywood Boulevard.

Mooncalf: "What if they was watching the phone booths?"

Batface snorted. "I just gave 'em the number, stoop. I didn't tell 'em where the phone was."

Mooncalf gave a bleating laugh. "Jeez, that's good. Like a Jimmy Cagney pitcher."

Card Sharp: "So what'd the guy say?"

Batface: "I did all the talking. Told him if he wanted to see his little buddy again, leave five c-notes in an envelope addressed to 'Mr. Lindy' at the front desk of the Biltmore."

Card Sharp: "You think they're gonna come through?"

Batface: "The guy sounded pretty worried. I said once I had the green I'd call back and tell him where to make the pick-up. I told him if he welshed, or I smelled copper, splash—I'd chuck his blue-eyed pal in the river."

Mooncalf snickered. "I tell ya, this is just like a Cagney pitcher."

Batface: "I gave him twenty-four hours. So by this time tomorrow morning yours truly will be five hundred smacks to the good. The drinks are on me, boys." He saluted with his Coke and drained it in a gulp, like a barfly tossing off gin.

Mooncalf: "Where you got him stashed for now?"

Batface: "Trunk of my heap." He giggled. "Plenty enough air in there for him, I guess."

I looked out the window, ran my eyes along the street for a car that looked like this punk could be driving it. Nada.

They shared a laugh at Batface's remark, then their conversation lapsed into the usual braggartly hooptedoodle of high school boys. Here I tuned them out; I had zero interest in cross-town football rivalries or Ginny Thompson's garter belt. But I kept an eye cocked on the mirror. When Batface reached for the check I scooped mine up, made for the counter, and paid. Outside I stood at the curb and futzed around lighting a cigarette. I watched the rain clouds deliberating overhead, and my three dime-store hoods through the plate glass in the double doors.

They came out together playing grab-ass and paying me no mind. After cheery goodbyes, Card Sharp and Mooncalf sauntered off down the street and Batface headed for a dusty Plymouth coupe parked on the side street not twenty feet from where I stood. He whistled "Pennies from Heaven" and jiggled the keys in his hand, oblivious. I ambled down the sidewalk in his direction.

"Amateur," I muttered around my cigarette. Still, I adjusted my holster a little under my coat. He looked green as hell, but a spooked youngster might just do something dumb. Shooting a kid would be bad for business, but so would a knife between the ribs.

When he reached for the door handle, I tossed my cigarette and closed on him. I grabbed a handful of his right shoulder and torqued his left arm up behind. He gave a little yelp as I crowded him against the car.

"Hello, Mr. Lindy," I growled in his ear. "Keep that right mitt in plain sight." He started to put up a weak struggle, but just as quickly gave it up.

"I ain't done nothing, mister," he whined.

I clicked my tongue. "Wrong answer, bub. An innocent lad would figure this was a heist, and cough up his wallet. But you aren't so innocent, are you?"

He answered with a loud, blubbering sound that almost made me feel sorry for him.

"The bad news is you're not getting any five hundred bucks today," I said. "Good news is if you're lucky you'll only do state time, and not swing."

That buckled his knees. I had to hoist him by his belt to keep from snapping his arm. As I shuffled him around to the trunk, he still gripped the keys in a pale-knuckled right fist.

"Open it," I said next to his ear. "Say a prayer, sonny, and open it." After a couple misses, he got the key in the lock. I backed him up enough to let the lid pop up, and held my breath.

The kid had said "he," but was it a man, or a boy? Alive, or dead? In one piece, or...? The Marion Parker case flitted through my mind; the Hickman kid hadn't been much older than this one. I was ready for nearly anything. Nearly.

The small figure lay sprawled on a greasy tarp, arms akimbo, bent legs tucked to one side. The face wore a frozen look, its too-white teeth bared in a half grimace, half grin. Wide, lifeless blue eyes in a pale, waxy face stared up at me, yet not at me.

"What the hell?" I let go of the kid without realizing it. He melted into a sitting position, shoulder to the car and head between his knees, and bawled like a three-year-old.

The inert figure was lighter than it looked. As I lifted it out, the limbs hung slack and the head swiveled grotesquely. A doll—a damned doll. No, not a doll—a long slit down the back showed a broomstick peg that turned the head from side to side, and a cord that worked the jaw up and down. It was a ventriloquist's dummy, decked out in gaudy cowboy attire—plaid shirt, jeans, two-tone boots and a colorful bandana tied around its neck. Its head was covered with ratty yellowish wool for hair.

The thing didn't look like it was worth five dollars, let alone five hundred. I dropped it back on the tarp. The kid had about cried himself out by now, so I nudged him with a shoe. "Up, Junior."

He wiped his snotty nose on his jacket sleeve and climbed to his feet. I slapped the driver's door.

"Get in." I slid in beside him and motioned for him to start the car and drive.

+++

"Okay, spill it, wise guy," I said as I pointed him back east down Hollywood. "Who—or what—is that thing? And what makes it worth half a grand?"

"It's Elmer," he said, like that should make it plain. "Elmer Sneezeweed." As we angled south toward Sunset, I dragged out of him that Elmer belonged to a cowboy actor named Max Terhune. Max was one of the "Three Mesquiteers," he said. Their cowboy films, especially the ones featuring Elmer, were apparently hot stuff with the younger crowd. They'd put in an appearance at a theater near the kid's house a couple of weekends ago, and he and his two buddies waited in the alley behind, hoping for autographs. On a dare, he'd snatched Elmer from the studio car while the driver was helping lug out the cowboys' other gear.

Like a dumb kid, he hadn't thought beyond that, but once he had Elmer, he began to get ideas. The studio, or Terhune anyway, was sure to want the dummy back. So he sent the studio a ransom note made with letters cut from a magazine—"like they do in pictures," he explained. The note gave directions for calling the pay phone, and threatened curtains for Elmer if the police were notified. He hadn't really expected a call—wasn't even sure the note would get to the right party. He was surprised when a studio rep named Mel Berman called this morning and assured him the studio would comply.

All the kid's earlier swagger and tough-guy talk was gone now. He was just a scared boy, who suddenly looked like he was forty.

"I didn't mean no harm," he said, "Honest, I didn't. My pop's out of work—he's been out for months, and the rent's behind. I was just tryin' to…I figured five hundred dollars was chicken scratch to them big movie guys."

"This your dad's coupe?" I asked. Not much of a car, but this kid didn't look flush enough for an apple crate scooter. He nodded.

"He don't know I have it. He's…" He looked at me sideways. "He got sauced downtown a couple nights ago. Jumped tough with the cops, so they vagged him. He's been in jail ever since."

We hooked north just before Sunset and I pointed out my building. He looked at the dingy diner on the ground floor, the row of windows with their sun-bleached curtains above, and shot me a dubious look.

"You ain't a cop?"

"Private investigator," I said. "Name's Nate Ross." He looked relieved. "Don't start celebrating just yet," I added. "A city copper can afford to take pity on a poor, dumb kid; he gets his salary either way. There's nothing in my pockets right now but fists, and I figure the studio owes me for busting up your little caper. Finder's fee, let's call it. Whether I hand you off to the law afterward—well, that's gonna be up to them."

We parked in the little corner lot next to the diner. As we got out, the kid flicked a glance at the horizon. I recognized that look. He was scenting the wind, like a zebra on the Serengeti.

"I'm quicker than I look," I lied. "Don't get any foolish notions. Anyway, you wouldn't be hard to track down." I pointed at his old man's car and his shoulders sagged. He hadn't thought of that. I had him fetch Elmer and when I opened the stairway door and waved him in, he went up the steps with no fuss.

We halted at my door while I unlocked it. The kid didn't think much of my office. Nobody ever did. But he took the chair I pointed to without looking like I ought to dust it first. I propped Elmer on my spare chair because I had one—I'm that successful—and perched my hat on his woolly head.

The rain had stopped, so I raised both windows to let the place breathe a little. The diner's kitchen was just below me, and the smells of grilled cheese and onion rings filtered right through the floor. I didn't complain. Gus Karavolos, the old Greek who ran the place, was my landlord, and rent was cheap. Thanks to the aroma, clients tended to leave hungry, and generally beelined into Gus's on their way out. If I'd had enough of them to make it worthwhile, I'd have tapped him for a commission.

"First things first," I said, handing the boy a pad and pencil. "Give me your name, parents' names, address, and phone number. Lie to me and I'll know it, and we'll cease to get along."

"Ma's dead," he said. "It's just us two. We got no phone." He wrote down the rest in surprisingly neat handwriting and handed back the pad.

"Michael Floyd Galvin, father Floyd Leroy Galvin," I read aloud. "You go by Michael or Mike?"

"Mikey, mostly."

The address I recognized. One of those cheap, pay-as-you-go flops on Third. Lousy place for anybody to call home, much less a kid.

A quick look through the *Herald*'s movie listings told me Three Mesquiteers was a Republic Pictures property. Not exactly M.G.M., but if they were set to pony up five hundred to my young friend, they had a few bucks in the kitty. The kid had Berman's number scrawled on a piece torn from the yellow pages. Part of me hesitated to call. As a rule, I avoided all dealings with movie studios. I preferred more reputable businesses, like pool halls and whorehouses. But I was in no shape to look this gift horse in the mouth.

I rang the main jail first, and they confirmed that Floyd L. Galvin was locked up on a vagrancy charge. Good boy, Mikey. Then I dialed Republic, and after a minimum of fuss was on the line with Mel Berman. I laid out the story as briefly as I could. After overcoming a little natural suspicion, I got from him that yes, the studio certainly wanted to recover Elmer—Mr. Terhune had been quite upset at the loss. And no, the studio had no desire to press charges. He was confident the young man had learned a valuable lesson. Plus, I thought, he didn't want the publicity of a trial to lose them all those cowboy-crazy kiddies and their ticket money.

Berman didn't commit himself, but hinted that the studio would show its gratitude in the form of legal tender. We arranged that I should drive out to Studio City at three o'clock and deliver Elmer to him personally.

"Ring-a-ding-ding, kid," I said as I hung up. "Looks like it's my lucky day, and yours too." He'd sat silent and stoic so far, but threatened to start blubbering again when I told him Republic wouldn't prosecute.

"Are you gonna tell my pop?"

"I think I'll leave it to you to tell him," I said. "Or not tell him. You're his business, not mine."

He wiped his nose on his sleeve again. "Thanks, Mr. Ross."

I'm not the big-brotherly type, but I felt for the kid. I know what it is to have a bum for a father. I tried to think of what sage advice I could offer him, but came up snake-eyes.

"Listen, bud, I've known my share of crooks and trust me—whatever you're good at, you're not cut out to be one." It wasn't much, but it wasn't nothing. I gave him a wink. "Cheer up, Mr. Lindy, that's good news."

"Mikey," he said with a shy smile. It made him look like a kid again.

"You're always gonna be 'Mr. Lindy' to me." I flipped a business card across the desk. "Your old man's got any questions, have him call me. I'll tell him you took it like a champ." I wouldn't wait by the phone for that call. I jerked my chin toward the door. "Now scram."

He pocketed the card and went out without another word. I listened to the slap of his sneakers as he took the stairs two by two. I didn't need to look out the window; he wasn't going to be stopping at Gus's.

Maybe I should have felt like a heel, putting the arm on a simple kid. It helped a little thinking that he might fly right, for a while at least. Anyway, he was grateful, the studio was happy, Elmer was going home to daddy. I was everybody's pal, and about to pocket some sweet, easy cash. Not a bad day's work, after all.

I didn't give a damn about the pastrami anymore. I lit a celebratory cigar, put my feet up on the desk, and blew smoke rings out the window at the chumps driving down Hillhurst. I pulled the windows down a little as the rain started again.

Elmer Sneezeweed sat at silent attention in my spare chair, with my hat tipped over one eye like a movie gangster. Maybe after I dropped the little guy off and collected my fee, I'd drive by Mikey Galvin's building and slip the landlord a twenty. I blew smoke at Elmer.

"Because that's just the kind of sap I am," I said.

Chapter Two

Phil Okel's office didn't look Hollywood. Not big Hollywood, anyway. Toss in the greasy diner smell and it might have been my own dump, except that Okel had three guest chairs, so maybe I should have worn a tuxedo after all. I was occupying the middle of these chairs, while my hat claimed the one on my right. The one on my left was empty in case Clark Gable dropped by.

Okel squinted at me over steepled fingertips like a banker weighing whether I was a good risk for a five-year loan. He had wiry salt-and-pepper hair and hard, dark, close-set little eyes under wild brows in sore need of pruning. A pointy nose and a bristly gray toothbrush mustache hung over his wide, wet mouth. He looked like a mean little terrier all set to go off on a barking jag.

"Appreciate you coming in on such short notice, Mr. Ross." His brusque, over-loud way of speaking only added to the terrier impression.

"I'll admit, Mr. Okel—" He stopped me to say I should call him Phil. I said I was Nate. Practically family already. "I'm a little puzzled, Phil, about why you wanted to see me. Mel Berman paid me on Friday when I brought the, uh—Elmer—in." I'd liked Berman. I'd liked him two hundred dollars' worth. "He made it clear Republic's got no interest in prosecuting the kid. So what's left to be done on the…matter?" My professional pride wouldn't let me call it a case.

"Oh, this ain't about that." His grin showed off a rack of teeth to keep a dentist's family cozy for generations. "Though I gotta say that was some smooth bit of work. You got no idea the stink that business caused around this farm. Holy hell, you'd have thought it was the Lindbergh baby all over again, not some damn yammerin' puppet."

Mr. Lindy. Only now did I get the kid's moniker. Getting slow on the draw, Nathaniel.

"Anyways," Okel went on, "Berman gave the old man the skinny on that deal, so the old man thought you might be just the boy to help us out with another little problem."

"The old man?"

"Herbert Yates," he said, as though that should explain it. It didn't. "Head of the studio."

"Sorry, I don't spend much time reading *Variety*."

The shaggy eyebrows lowered a fraction, as if he was starting to doubt whether I was just the boy. "Anyways," he went on, "we got a situation on our hands that needs a certain…touch."

"I don't do a lot of studio work, Phil. Hollywood's lousy with private dicks—why not call in one of those guys?"

Okel hissed through his teeth. "Every Hollywood gumshoe's a pipeline to the gossip rags. Yates wants this thing kept on the q.t. No ink."

"Well, you're chief of security," I said. "Why not just use your own staff and keep it all in-house?"

He gave a short, barking laugh. "Now I see you don't know Herb Yates," he said. "That son of a bitch would steal the pennies from his dead granny's eyes and kick her 'cause they weren't dollars. You're looking at my staff, son. And my days and nights are mostly spent keeping rambunctious cowboys out of jail so Yates can get his pictures made. That don't leave me much time for sleuthing."

"What is the job, exactly?" I asked.

His eyes turned foxy. "First I got to know you a little better. The old man left the yea or nay to me. I've asked around a little already—I understand you used to be with the county sheriffs."

"Right," I answered. "Did five years there." He stared at me in silence, waiting for me to volunteer more. "I had to give it up."

He kept staring. When he saw that was all he was getting, he shook his head. "A guy don't walk off from steady work in these times, friend. And a cop job, with a pension—you leave that for three reasons: fired, re-tired, or ex-pired. Now me, I'm retired—old San Francisco copper—but I got twenty years on you. I can see you ain't dead. So what was it got you shown the bricks, you don't mind my asking?"

I minded. I always did. But I also needed the work. "I was honest," I said.

"Honest, like how? You tell old Sheriff Biscailuz his wife was ugly? Refuse to tear up a speeding ticket for a senator's kid? What?"

He was a lousy liar. I could see from the glint in his eyes he'd already heard this story; he just wanted to make me tell it. I wanted to tell him to go piss up a rope instead. But I didn't.

"A couple of my fellow deputies had a racket going. Fake burglaries at jewelry stores, and a few hardware stores for guns. Fence the goods, split the cash—you know the grift. They got burned, and I gave testimony to the grand jury."

"Testified against your own boys? And you, Jimmy Ross's kid."

I let the crack about my father ride, for now. "Call me crazy. I had this goofy notion that guys getting paid to lock up crooks shouldn't be crooks themselves."

Okel's eyes gleamed brighter. He flashed his wolfish grin again. "So then Biscailuz put the skids under you?"

"No, but he was none too happy about the mess I made for him. Particularly after the press got wind, and learned that one of those fenced guns killed a liquor store owner in a holdup."

Okel gave a low whistle through his ragged teeth. "So he just let the rest of the boys turn up the heat on you, eh? Blackballed—persona non grata in your own department."

I nodded. I didn't fill in any details. If he knew already, there was no point rehashing it. And if he didn't, it was none of his damned business.

"And when you had enough, one day you handed the sheriff your badge, is that it?"

"Not literally," I said. "The grease on that bastard's palm, it would have slid right out again. No, I laid it very gently on his desk, said my adios, and left the building by the front door. The civilian's entrance. And that was that. If there was a goodbye party for me, I wasn't invited."

Okel leaned back in his chair and squinted at me for a long moment. "So you're a real white hat, eh?"

My hat was brown, and I reached for it. I'd have bet a C-note this interview was over.

"Yeah" he said, standing. "Grab your lid and let's take a little walk. I'll tell you what we got."

+++

When I was a kid my old man used to take me to Westerns all the time. Tom Mix, Hoot Gibson, Buck Jones. These days I wasn't much of a film fan. Going to pictures took money and spare time, and if I had one I didn't have the other. So as we toured Republic's back lot and Okel pointed out where various films had been made, or mentioned actors whose names I apparently should have known, I was at a loss. Inside the huge sound stage, we wound our way through the dusty streets of a false-fronted, clapboard, Old West town that looked real enough if you could see past the lights and dollies and miles of cables snaking every direction.

"Over there's the saloon that got busted up in Rio Grande Ranger," Okel looked at me for some sign of recognition or appreciation. "And down there's the fence the horses stampeded through in *Barbed Wire Banditos.*" He could see he might as well have been showing a caveman the wheel.

We stopped in front of a half-painted saloon. "This is one of the sets they're sprucing up for *Stardust Trail*," Okel said. "Don't tell me you ain't heard of that one." I didn't need to; he could see it on my face. "Holy hell, son, you don't have to read the trades to know about *Stardust Trail.*"

"Sorry." I wanted to help him out—I really did. He gave me a look like he thought I was ribbing him, but before he could say so a studio flunky interrupted to tell him he had a phone call. He excused himself and told me to feel free to look around. I wasn't sure what to do with myself until he came back. Just try not to step in horse shit, I guessed.

As I waited, wondering if Okel would get around to telling me what the job was much before Christmas, I noticed a tall, wide-shouldered cowboy standing off by himself, leaning against some scenery flats. His face was shaded under a broad-brimmed white Stetson. A cigarette dangled from the corner of his mouth as he bent over and struck a match on his boot sole. When he brought it up to light his smoke, I got a good look at the face and recognized it, though I hadn't seen it in quite some time.

I walked over and stuck out a hand. "Duke? Duke Morrison?"

"Yeah?" He squinted at me through a cloud of smoke and stood up straight. He was even taller than I remembered. Before I could say any more his lazy eyelids snapped open and the bullet gray eyes behind them lost their bored expression. His face split in a wide, friendly grin as he grabbed my hand in a mitt big and hard as an iron skillet. "Well, what do you know—Nate Ross!" he said. "How the hell are you?"

I hadn't been sure he'd recognize me. We'd been pals at Glendale Union High, but that had been a thousand years ago. We played football together three out of four years. He was good at it; I was just a second-string bench jockey, only in it for the girls. Last I'd heard of Duke, he was playing for USC.

"I didn't know you were in the movie trade, Duke. You an actor?"

He shrugged. "The jury's split. It's what they pay me to do, anyway. How about you?" he asked, looking from my hat to my brogues. "Are you workin' in pictures?"

"Not me. I'm—I was a cop."

"Like father, like son?"

"Not exactly." Now wasn't the time. "I do private investigations these days. I did the studio a little favor, so it looks like they may chase some more work my way."

"A private eye—no foolin'? Wait a minute." He hammered a fist into my shoulder. "Are you the guy that got Elmer Sneezeweed back?" He didn't wait for an answer, but strode over to an open fire door and shouted through it "Hey, Max! Come here a minute!"

He returned accompanied by a pudgy, rubber-faced fellow in cowboy duds topped by a black hat. "This is my old high school chum, Nate Ross," Duke said. "Nate, this is Max Terhune, my fellow Mesquiteer." We shook hands while Duke explained that I was Elmer's rescuer.

Max gave me a gap-toothed grin. "I'm awful grateful to you for that, mister. Elmer's been with me since the old vaudeville days. I'd have sure hated to lose him." He actually had tears in his eyes. People could be goofy over the damnedest things.

I told him he was welcome. I didn't know what else I could say. To my relief he excused himself, saying he had to go for a costume change, and something about if he could ever return the favor, and so on. Maybe a little over-sentimental, but he seemed like a nice enough guy.

"Look," Duke said, "I gotta get over there for a change myself. But let's grab a beer one of these days, get good and caught up."

I promised we would, and he ambled off. Just after he left, Phil Okel returned. "Max giving you his thanks in person?"

I nodded.

"And I see you met John Wayne."

John Wayne. That was a name that I had heard, though I never would have connected it to my old classmate. John Wayne had been making pictures for a few years now; word was that he might be the next Tom Mix. I guess I really should go the movies more. I didn't bother explaining to Phil how I knew Duke.

"Anyways," Okel began, "here's the deal. Republic's meat is Westerns. Low budget singin' oaters and shoot 'em ups, ground out like hamburger for the Saturday matinee crowd and the hicks in the sticks. Each one's pretty much like the one before it, you ask me, but the audiences don't care about that. So the pictures make money. Yates divvies up the bulk of 'em between Gene Autry, who does the musicals, and Duke Wayne, who's the action guy."

I knew who Gene Autry was, of course. I owned a radio.

"Well," he went on, "the old man's agreed to loan Wayne out for a big project John Ford's got in the works."

He saw no sign of recognition. "He's a director. The Iron Horse?" Still nothing. "Anyways, Ford's got this high-dollar Western he's planning to shoot out in the Arizona desert or some damned place. Like California ain't half desert. Well, the big studios won't touch it. They all think the Western's played out, and Duke Wayne's not big enough box office to tempt them to take a chance. So Ford—cantankerous bastard he is—drums up his own backing for the thing. They start shooting in the fall, I hear."

"Where's Republic come in?" I asked.

"Now that he's committed to loan 'em Wayne, the old man's having second thoughts. He's scared. If this Ford show pulls in the money, and the rumors all say it will, the major studios may do an about-face and start doing Westerns again. It's all monkey-see, monkey-do in this burg. Yates can't compete with that, long-term, and he risks giving up the biggest slice of the pie. Plus he's already haggling over salary with Autry, and he's worried Wayne might get airs and start bawling for more kale. So the penny-pinching prick's raided the piggy bank and he's shooting his own big-budget picture, *Stardust Trail*, hoping to get out ahead of John Ford and leave him with his drawers around his ankles. Unlike the usual Republic cheapie, this one's got it all: name actors, classy production values, top-notch music, a real pip of a script. He's hired himself a varsity player to write it, guy named David Prince. Grade-A lowlife—has wangled himself out of a couple of stat rape charges—but he's done a couple of top studio pics, writes Western novels under a pen name. 'Kit Rawls,' I think."

"This all sounds peachy, Phil. I hope it works out for the old man and he ends up richer than Bill Hearst. Where do I come in?"

"Here's the thing," he said, dropping his voice to what for him passed for a whisper. "Prince dropped out of sight two weeks ago. Alakazam—gone."

"Two weeks, and you're just now worried?"

"Well, the guy's a rummy, like all writers. He goes on the occasional weekend wingding. But never anything like this before."

"But if he's already written the script, isn't his job done?"

"It would be, if this was the normal Republic job. But on an A-picture there's always last-minute rewrites, high-priced talent that like to monkey with their lines, and so forth. Yates needs Prince around for the whole shootin' match so he can fine-tune as they go."

"So I find this guy, and then what? I'm not interested in a job wet-nursing some Hollywood boozehound."

"Just find him. We'll deal with him from there."

I had to admit it sounded like a milk run, and I was in no shape to sneeze at easy money. I told him I'd take it on.

He pulled out a photo of Prince and a pocket notebook. He gave me the snap and I studied the face. It was thin and dissipated-looking, with a knife-blade nose and an unpleasant mouth. The slick black hair was parted just off center, and the pale eyes had a too-intense gaze, like a schoolyard pervert's. I wasn't going to like David Prince.

I put the unlovely face in my pocket as Okel read off the vitals—description, home address, phone number, car make, model and tag number. No known family. A few friends—all Hollywood, and all already contacted and claiming ignorance. Not much to go on, but for an ace detective like me, it ought to be kid stuff.

Chapter Three

The on-again-off-again rain had finally let up, leaving the air smelling cleaner than normal as I drove over to the apartments on Marmont where Prince lived. The building was one of those beige stucco numbers built after the war, designed to look vaguely Spanish, but it had long since given up trying. Whatever Prince paid in rent, the landlord wasn't wasting any of it on upkeep. I knew places like this, and the people who lived in them. Nothing in common but water-stained ceilings and broken dreams. Everyone minded his own business and expected you to do likewise. I wouldn't count on much help from the neighbors; nobody would have seen a thing.

A door in a flop like this was bound to have a pushover lock, but I went straight to the office. This not being my usual hunting ground, I figured I'd better break as few laws as possible. I rapped on the manager's door. It was answered by a paunchy guy in his forties, slow-moving and slower talking, with one of those thyroid conditions that gave him eyes like a carp. His balding dome was poorly camouflaged under oily hair, and not much of it, combed up and over the top from half an inch above his left ear.

I played the skip tracer—told him I was looking to run Prince down over some unpaid bills. That made him happy to help; a guy who'd welsh on Sears and Roebuck wouldn't flinch at stiffing his landlord. He let me in without a fuss and he didn't insist on sheep-dogging me while I looked around. I have my mother's trustworthy brown eyes.

The building may have been a dump, but Prince's apartment was clean and orderly as a hospital ward. Peculiar, for a drunk. Still, it was plain that I wasn't the first visitor. There was just enough disarray to say that someone had tossed the place before me. A scent of night-blooming jasmine and a couple of cigarette butts with coral lipstick told me a woman had been there. Was she a lady friend, or the mysterious room searcher? Maybe one and the same.

There were no suitcases in the closet. Okel had told me that Prince owned some sort of little ranch getaway out in the Simi foothills. Sounded like just the sort of secluded spot he might hole up in with a bottle, but Okel didn't know exactly where it was, so nobody had been out there to check yet.

The closet was filled with flashy cowboy clothes—shirts with pearl buttons and wild, embroidered designs, ornate boots and big hats. Dave Prince didn't just write about cowboys, he clearly enjoyed dressing the part. In the pockets of a fancy-stitched buckskin jacket I found a matchbook from the Hackamore Club, a local joint where Hollywood's cowboy crowd went to unwind.

I went through his desk but found nothing to tell me where the ranch was. There was a passbook from First Union Bank. Prince was no starving artist; he'd logged deposits of $2,000 around the middle of each month, going back almost a year. I wasn't sure what kind of scratch screenwriters made, but it seemed a bit heavy for a tightwad like Yates. There were a couple more matchbooks from the Hackamore Club—it looked like Prince was a regular. I pocketed one of them.

While I was going through the place, I glanced out the window to where I'd parked across the street. A man was standing next to my car, looking through the side window like he was reading the registration. He was medium-sized and dressed in the uniform of the working Hollywood cowboy: plaid shirt, bandana knotted at the throat, dungarees with a six-inch cuff turned up over high-heeled boots, and a battered, wide-brimmed tan hat. From my angle the hat hid his face, but I was almost sure I'd seen him on the lot at Republic. I started down the stairs, taking two at a time, but when I reached the street, the cowboy had vanished.

I went back up and locked Prince's door. I'd learned all I was going to learn here. Evening was coming on, so I figured I'd have some dinner and try my luck at the Hackamore Club.

Chapter Four

The Hackamore was what the young, clubby crowd would call "a jumping joint," but not in the same way they'd mean. It wasn't quite what I'd pictured, though I wasn't sure what I had pictured. In most ways it was like any other club—hazy with tobacco smoke, and a little rank from too many bodies moving around in not enough space. People who filled it sat in twos and threes, speaking in confidential tones with heads leaned in together like mobsters, or they hung together in boisterous clusters and rattled on at full boozy volume. The music was the big difference. In place of the big band's sassy horns and stuttering drums were the twang of guitars and string bass, the reedy whine of harmonicas and the poink-diddle-oink of banjos.

The main bar was a curious sight, in a city that had long since cornered that market. Forty feet, maybe longer if straightened out, but the whole dingus was bent into a horseshoe. Not just an inverted "u", but an oversized replica of an actual horseshoe. Its zinc top had recessed rectangles at intervals along each side, and these bogus nail holes, six or eight inches deep, were filled to the top with peanuts in the shell. Instead of the plush pile found in uptown joints, the floor was wood plank and carpeted wall-to-wall with a heavy layer of crushed peanut hulls, kept replenished by the obliging patrons. Wagon wheel chandeliers dangled from the ceiling, and the tables—also supplied with heaping bowls of peanuts—were set with kerosene lanterns rigged with electric lights. Centered on each table was a copper ashtray in the shape of a Tom Mix-style cowboy hat. Saddles, branding irons and other cowboy geegaws adorned every inch of space that wasn't spoken for. The walls were painted with striking desert scenes, given depth by the occasional potted cactus, some of them five or six feet high. It must have been fun to watch the drunks navigate those at closing time. The atmosphere was intentionally hokey, but comfortable.

I didn't stand out as much as I'd thought I might; although it was mostly a boots-and-bandana crowd, quite a few patrons wore normal out-on-the-town attire. One of these I spotted sitting near one end of the horseshoe. Duke Morrison had shed his cowboy clothes for gabardine slacks, loafers, a brown shirt, and a light tweed sport coat. Dressed this way he looked more like the Duke I remembered.

"Hey, if it isn't John Wayne," I said as I slid onto the next stool.

He turned and pinned me with those steely eyes, then his face broke into the wide, familiar grin. "Only until the man yells cut, Nate."

"And I heard the big stars didn't hang out here."

"Guess I'll take that as a compliment." He saluted with his beer glass. "I like this place. Nobody comes here to be seen. So what brings you around? You here to take me up on that beer, or are you working a case, like Sam Spade?"

"Somehow I don't picture you reading *Black Mask*."

"A guy's gotta read something when he runs out of Zane Grey." He waved the bartender over and set me up with a beer.

"If I'd known you were here I guess I'd have dropped in anyway," I said. "But you're right—I'm working. Do you know David Prince?"

"Prince, the writer?" His eyebrows inclined a little. "Wouldn't say I know him. We've never worked together. I've read one or two of his books."

"Any good?"

"He can write. Goes all over the West, I hear, talking to whatever old-timers he can find who'll tell him stories from back in the day. Figures it makes his stuff more authentic." He scanned the bar mirror, looking over the crowd. "He's usually in here evenings, decked out in his cowboy rig. Now that I think of it, I haven't seen him the last couple of times I've been in. He in trouble?"

"Not like you're thinking," I said, pausing for a go at my beer. "He's faded out of sight, right in the middle of filming."

"*Stardust Trail*, right? Herb Yates's pet project."

"Right. The studio wants me to find out why he's dropped out, get him back on the job. They tell me he goes on the occasional bender."

Duke nodded. "He's been carried out of here more than once."

"Apparently, he heads off by himself now and then, has a place out in the hills somewhere. You wouldn't know where?"

He shook his head. "Like I say, I hardly know the guy. I can ask around if you want." He turned around and looked over the room. "You could try yourself, but these cowboys can be a pretty tight-lipped bunch. With outsiders anyway. With their own they're as gossipy as a knitting circle."

"That'd help," I told him. I fished out a card. "You can always reach me here. Give me a call if you get anything."

"Sure," he said, with a wry grin. "Anything for Herb Yates." He squinted at my card. "I figured there'd be a magnifying glass, maybe a Sherlock Holmes cap."

"Enough about my job. Last time I saw you, you were headed off for college. How'd you end up in Hollywood?"

"Banged myself up surfing and had to quit playing ball," he said, pocketing my card. "So adios scholarship. I had some buddies doing grunt work at Fox, hauling flats and props around and what not, so I got in on that to make ends meet. Got talked into doing a couple of acting parts because I was a tall guy and they said I had a 'look,' whatever the hell that means. That worked into a couple of studio films—nothing that set the world afire. My first big shot flopped—flopped hard. Couldn't get any work from the big houses after that, but I picked up a few lead parts in cowboy pictures." He paused, smiled. "Between you and me, some of those I only got because I looked enough like Ken Maynard they could cut in stunts from his old films. Anyhow, here I am almost ten years later—no college degree, but a couple dozen pictures behind me. And a handful of 'em aren't half bad. If the one in the pipeline pans out, I just might leave Poverty Row for good."

"Poverty Row?"

"The nickel-and-dime outfits that crank out quickie films—Westerns, mostly. The kind of stuff that only heads the bill in Moose Fart, Montana.

Monogram, Lone Star, and so on."

"What about Republic?"

"Republic's not Poverty Row exactly, but Yates isn't going to parties at Jack Warner's house, either." He paused to order another beer. "I can't complain. Hell, I'm no Gary Cooper, but I'm working. I'm just putting my time in, anyway, hoping maybe down the road I'll get a crack at directing. Meanwhile I'm getting pretty well known to the Saturday afternoon crowd. You don't go to cowboy pictures, I guess?"

"My old man used to take me. Tom Mix, Buck Jones. I haven't been to any movie since before he died."

"I heard about your dad. Sorry," Duke said. It was about all he, or anybody, could or would say. Nobody wanted to talk about it, least of all me.

To break the awkward silence I asked, "You married?"

"Yeah," he said with a smile. "Two kids. You?"

"No kids. I was married." Duke was a friend, or had been once, but I wasn't in the mood to trot out my sad tales. "It's a long story, and not all that interesting."

He took the hint. "Hollywood's full of those," he said with a wink. "They shoot 'em in Technicolor."

As the band on stage finished to whistles and stomping boots, a little old guy in a cowboy hat three sizes too big came out under the spotlight. He glared at the audience until they settled down, then announced in a high, wheezy voice, "Ladies and gents, The Cady Sisters."

The lights dimmed, and the tempo of the place changed. Drunks piped down, cowboys swept their hats off, and everybody made for a seat, orderly as a Sunday school class.

"Come on," Duke said. "You'll like the show." He dropped a couple bills on the bar and led me to a table at the front of the room.

Three ladies came out onto the half-lit stage and took up instruments—string bass, violin and guitar. The one in the middle took a couple of quick cuts at the violin, the others joined in, and the lights came up as they broke into "Don't Fence Me In." They wore identical cowgirl outfits—fringed buckskin skirts over fancy tooled, multi-colored boots, and white silk blouses spangled with red sequin stars. Each had a bright blue scarf tied around her neck. Big white hats sat on the backs of their heads, so as not to hide their faces. The house knew the faces would draw as well as the music.

They were all three lookers, but three women never looked more different. The bass player was a tall bottle-blonde with bright blue eyes slanted like a cat's, and flame-colored lipstick. She was like a brass statue—glittering and golden, but cold and hard. Not nearly my style. The guitar girl was a merry little brunette with short hair done in Betty Boop curls. She looked like the kind who'd laugh at your jokes and give you your way for a drink or two, but not one you could talk books with. At least not the kind with words in them. The one in the middle was a dish. Not too tall, curves where they belonged, hair a shade of blonde you can only be born with. Her eyes had just the right space between them, and whether you called them blue or green you'd be right.

And they weren't just stage dressing. Their playing was clean and sharp, voices smooth and sweet. Their harmonies could cut glass. I hadn't thought this was my kind of music, but I was feeling so good I sprung for the next round of beers.

Duke leaned across the table. "How do you like 'em?"

I nodded my appreciation. "Who's the girl with the violin?" I asked.

"It's a fiddle."

"What's the difference?"

He laughed. "If you've gotta ask that, you're in the wrong house, friend. Her name's Valerie."

The girls finished their tune. Before the cheers and applause faded they slid right into their next number, a quieter tune which started with some fancy bow work by Valerie.

Duke dropped his voice a notch. "You might talk to them," he said. "They're working on *Stardust Trail*. The Texas Bluebonnets, they're calling 'em for the picture. I've seen your boy Prince tomcatting around 'em more than once. Especially," he added with a touch of friendly malice, "your fiddle girl there."

I didn't need an excuse to make her acquaintance, but didn't kick at being handed one. "Are they as shut-mouthed as the cowboys?" I asked.

"Well, I wouldn't bother with Madeline—the tall one—you aren't the type she'll cozy up to."

"Because I'm broke?"

"Because you're sober. And little Jean's sweet, but dumber than a sack of gravel. I'd stick with Val—she'll talk to you. She might even tell you the truth."

The sisters slid into a bright-bouncy number called "Cowboy Moon," which Duke said was written for *Stardust Trail*. They ended their set with a version of "Shenandoah" that had every cowboy in the place dewy-eyed. As they bowed and smiled their way off stage, I got up.

"Thanks for the beer, Duke, and the advice."

"Straighten your tie, Casanova."

"I'm looking for information, that's all."

"All right, then," he said, grinning. "Happy hunting."

Chapter Five

Whatever a club looked like out front, backstage they were all pretty much the same. The money went where the customers would see it. Behind that were always the same half-lit corridors with dingy paint, threadbare carpet, a stale tobacco stink in the air, and a film over everything.

A name card tacked on the door said I had the right dressing room. I was about to knock when I heard a ruckus inside—a man's voice and a woman's, shouting over each other. I couldn't make out the words, but the tone was pure trouble. I was debating whether I should poke my nose in when I heard a scuffle and a gunshot.

That decided me. I plowed through the unlocked door and saw Valerie Cady, one sleeve of her spangled shirt torn loose at the shoulder, struggling with a lanky, greasy-haired guy with a dark, wispy mustache. He was dressed in a black shirt with white stitch work and new dungarees tucked into fancy-stitched boots, and looked like the nameless heavy in every bad cowboy film.

As I cleared the doorway, a little nickel-plated pistol thumped to the floor at their feet, and tall boy backhanded the girl across the mouth. I crossed the room, spun him, and hit him just below the mangy mustache. He fell hard on his ass then sprang back up, mouth twisted in anger and pain, and swept a hand toward his back pocket. I showed him my .380 and the hand froze.

"Who the hell are you?" he snarled.

"Just a fan, come to pay my compliments," I said. I looked at the girl. "Are you hurt?"

She shook her head and he snorted. "Hurt, hell! This crazy bitch tried to shoot me."

"Did she? And you just minding your own business in her dressing room, I guess."

"It ain't how it looks, amigo."

"I guess that depends on how you think I think it looks. Who are you?"

"Ed Jarboe," he said, with meaning. It had none for me, and he didn't like that. "I work here. I'm the house man."

"I see. Is roughing up the talent part of your job?"

"This is what you might call a personal matter."

I looked back at the girl. She didn't deny it. "All right, Mr. Jarboe, should I call the cops?"

"To hell with you. I got work to do." He started to crowd past me then stopped, his face not a foot from mine. He wiped blood off his mouth with the back of a hand. "Boss don't like shooting in here, so I'll settle with you some other time." He showed me a nasty smile, nastier for the blood streaking his teeth. "You don't ever put hands on me, amigo."

Just to be contrary I hit him again. He reeled backward through the still-open door and bounced off the corridor wall. He shook his head and took a half step forward, then changed his mind and stomped off down the hall instead, throwing his best tough-guy sneer over his shoulder.

I shut the door. The girl probed the reddened side of her face with delicate fingers and examined it in the mirror.

"Doesn't look like it'll swell up," she said in a soft, drawling voice. "Or bruise much." She gave me a sidewise smile. "I think you spoiled his aim, coming through the door like that." She turned to face me. "I guess I should thank you, Mr...."

"Nate Ross." I pointed a thumb towards the door. "Boyfriend?"

"Lord, no!" She saw I wanted more answer than that. "It was a—a kind of business dispute."

"What sort of business?" I picked up the little break-top revolver from the carpet. Out of habit I snapped it open. A .32 five shot; four live rounds and one spent.

She frowned at my question. "I don't mean to be rude, but…"

"But it's the kind of business that's none of my business." I closed the .32 with a loud snick. "This yours, or his?"

"Mine."

I laid it on her dressing table. She studied me in the mirror as she fussed with her hair and frowned at her torn blouse.

"Are you a friend of Duke Wayne's, Mr. Ross? I thought I saw you at his table."

I liked that she'd noticed. I pretended it wasn't because I'd been sitting with John Wayne.

"I used to be, anyway. We were pals in high school."

That seemed to amuse her. She turned and faced me.

"How'd you happen to be here just now?" she asked. "Looking for the john, or an autograph or…?"

I took out my cigarettes. Before I could ask if she minded, she helped herself to one. I shook mine loose and lit them both with Prince's matches.

"I'm an investigator working for Republic Pictures. I'm looking for David Prince. I'm talking to anybody who knows him, trying to get a line on where he might be. I understand you're acquainted." I tried not to put any meaning into the word.

She tried hard to look uninterested. "He's a regular around here. I didn't know he was missing though, so I guess I can't say I know him that well." She was so casual I might have believed her, except that I hadn't said he was missing. I sensed now wasn't a good time to press.

"Well, I'm sure you have things to do," I said, indicating the overturned furniture, torn sleeve, etc, "I won't keep you." I laid a business card on her table. "If you think of anything."

"I haven't really thanked you properly," she said, "for riding to my rescue. Could I buy you a drink before you go?"

I didn't get offers from girls like her every day. Or even every other day. I told her I'd find a table, and she said she'd meet me in twenty minutes.

+++

Duke had left when I got back to the floor. I found a far corner booth where it would be as quiet as it would ever get in a place like this. I thought about ordering a sidecar or something classy but ended up with another beer.

It was late, and the place was only half as full as before. There was a comedy act on stage—a sort of cowboy Mutt and Jeff team. The mug of the duo was a bandy-legged runt who looked a bit like Elmer Sneezeweed. He punctuated every corny joke with a sour toot on a harmonica. I didn't find them funny, but the crowd yukked it up. They'd had more to drink than I had.

Fifteen minutes later, I looked up to see Valerie coming my way. She'd ditched the cowgirl dress and was wearing a simple blue skirt and a silvery silk blouse that didn't do her any harm. She'd scrubbed off the stage makeup and wore only lipstick and a little something around the eyes. Her hair looked a shade darker without all the spangly attire. Drinks stopped midair and heads swung around as she passed by. She was that kind of girl.

"Enjoying the show?" she asked with a weary smile as she slid in across from me. She glanced at the stage and made a face. "Lefty and Earl. Ten weeks, and they've done the same dozen jokes every single night. But the boys love them." She indicated the laughing cowboys all around us.

Without being asked, the waiter came over and set a bottle of beer in front of her. She didn't ask for a glass and didn't look apologetic about it.

"So, you're a private eye. How does a man get into that line of work, Mr. Ross?"

"He fails at everything else," I said. "And please, call me Nate."

"Nate." She smiled as if she liked saying it. "I'm Val."

"Val." I smiled back. "I was a cop." I hoped it was explanation enough.

"And now you're not?"

"And now I'm not."

"It must be tough on family life, being a policeman. Tough on a marriage."

"It was."

"Is that why you gave it up?"

"The job, or the marriage?"

"Either, or both."

I laughed and took a drink. "I'm the detective," I said. "Shouldn't I be questioning you?" I meant it as a joke—and a change of subject—but she looked a little hurt.

"Is that why we're sitting here?" she asked. "Business, not pleasure?"

"Does it have to be one or the other?"

"I owe you," she said, "so I'll let that pass." She set her beer down. "Go ahead then, ask away."

"No need to get huffy," I said. "I was a cop and I had a wife. I ended up on the right side of some wrong business at work. She encouraged me to do the honest thing. I did, and she was proud, she said, even though it got me pushed out of a job. What she didn't count on was that most of our friends were cops, too, and when the boys turned their backs on me, their wives did the same to her. She stood that for as long as she could. When she couldn't stand it anymore, she left."

"I'm sorry," Val said. "I didn't mean to—"

"No, it's fine," I said. "I guess you're entitled to your questions, too."

We sat in awkward silence for a few seconds while Lefty bleated on his harmonica and the crowd roared.

"Where is she now?" she asked at last.

"Seattle. Married again. She's happy, I guess. I hope so, anyway."

"And you? Are you happy?"

"Me? I live alone in a rented bungalow, eat all my meals in diners, and poke my nose in other people's business for a living, which gets it broken now and then. Every cop in L.A. knows my name, and hates me for betraying the brotherhood. I don't think too highly of most of them either, so that part's a wash. On the other side, times are tough, and jobs are scarce, but a guy in my racket in a city like this can always keep the bills paid. Once in a while you even get a chance to help someone out. So I guess I'm as happy as I deserve to be. As happy as I'm likely to get."

"Are you half as cynical as you pretend to be?"

She was direct, I'd say that for her. I liked that.

"If you're going to assume I'm pretending, doesn't that answer itself?"

The comics on stage wrapped it up, to more applause than I thought they'd earned. Maybe I just wasn't feeling funny tonight. The next act was a quintet of guys whose attire ran more to checkered shirts and plain boots than sequins and rhinestones. For flash they each wore a rodeo buckle like a Packard hubcap. They lined up across the stage, and only the ones on either end played instruments—a string bass and a guitar. The three in the middle sang in low, sleepy voices. They did a couple of down-tempo numbers—slow, melancholy tunes that didn't liven up the place any, but made socializing easier.

We were near the end of our beers. Without asking, Val signaled for two more. I'd either given her enough to satisfy her feminine curiosity or convinced her that my life story wasn't the stuff of which great conversations are made. She spent the next half hour telling me hers. I listened attentively, partly out of professional habit, but also because I liked her slow, lazy drawl. She could stretch a vowel across the room.

She was born in Texas—which explained the accent—and grew up in a little town called Muleshoe. I laughed, and she assured me with mock indignation that it was not a joke. She and her singing partners weren't really sisters; I'd guessed that much. They'd partnered up a few months back, hoping to get some radio and movie work that would land them a recording contract. They'd set their sights on Republic because Gene Autry made his films there when he wasn't doing his radio show or making records. Herb Yates, minor mogul that he was, also helmed a record company or two, so the girls had high hopes for their latest gig singing onscreen in Yates' ambitious new project.

The mention of *Stardust Trail* brought us around to David Prince. Now that we'd gotten all the getting-to-know-you stuff out of the way, I figured it was safe to lob a few questions in that direction.

"He's the writer on the film," she said, "but I don't work with him. Most of our time's been spent in the recording studio. We've been on set a couple of times for publicity photos, but Wednesday's the first day we're actually doing any scenes. I've seen him here more than I've seen him at the studio."

"What kind of guy is he when he's here?"

"He drinks. You don't come to a place like this if you don't. Maybe he drinks more than most."

"Ever any problems in that line?"

She wiped condensation off the neck of her bottle with a fingertip, then absently dried her finger on the tablecloth. She fiddled with the little cowboy hat ashtray. "Oh, they've had to drive him home a time or two."

"Any rows with anyone?" In my experience, drunks were allergic to peace and quiet.

She smiled at that. "I guess I wouldn't be the only one to tell you. He's bumped horns with a couple of the boys here and there."

"Over what?"

"Girls, mainly. Cowboys tend to be a little old-fashioned where women are concerned. When they're fairly sober, anyway. David Prince is more…Hollywood, I guess you'd say."

"A lech?"

"I wouldn't go that far. He's not grabby, or a door peeper, anything like that. Mostly language, the kinds of things he says. Off-color jokes and such. He rankles the boys sometimes"

"Ever had his clock cleaned over it?"

"Not that I know of."

"Anyone in particular he's had trouble with?"

She thought a moment. "Ed Jarboe, I guess. But nobody gets along with him."

Speak the devil's name, they say, and he'll show his face. The backstage door opened and Jarboe came out onto the floor. He went to the bar, hooked a boot heel on the brass rail, and ran predatory eyes over the room. When they lit on us, they stopped, and his face went dark and wolfish.

Val noticed him and fidgeted. Her blue-green eyes had an uneasy look.

"What was that about, backstage with Jarboe?"

She gave me a tentative smile.

"If you tell me, you'll save me the trouble of finding out some other way."

"I suppose you could, couldn't you?"

"I'd be a poor sort of detective if I couldn't. "

She took a deep breath and picked at the label on her beer with a thumbnail. She watched her thumb work as though it fascinated her.

"I caught him going through my things," she said. "I walked in from our last set and there he was, pawing through my trunk and my dressing table."

I could see Jarboe as a sneak thief or worse. "He take anything?"

She shook her head.

"He give any kind of explanation?"

"He said he thought I might have something that belonged to him."

"What?"

"When I asked him, he got real nasty and said I knew damn well what, and I'd best give it up."

"Then what?"

"I just figured he was drunk. He usually is, though he's supposed to lay off it when he's working. I got mad, the way he was grinning at me and fingering my…" She turned a charming shade of pink. "…my undergarments. I keep a gun in my trunk, so I grabbed it and told him to get out. He made like he was leaving, but then he grabbed me and we tussled and the gun went off. That's when you came in."

I looked at Jarboe. He was leaning on the bar, talking to the kid behind it, but he kept sneaking glances in our direction. I noted with satisfaction that he was rolling his cold beer bottle against a swollen lip.

"Maybe I ought to have another word with Mr. Jarboe," I said.

"No!" A few heads turned our way, and Val turned a shade pinker. She lowered her voice. "No, don't do that. I'll speak to Mr. Gowdy about it, and he won't bother me anymore."

"Mr. Gowdy?"

"Joe Gowdy—the owner here. He's a gentleman. He'll see it doesn't happen again."

"You're sure?"

"I'm sure." She tilted her head to one side. "Aren't you sweet to offer, though?" The tone was milk and honey, but her eyes were still worried. "You'd make a fine cowboy yourself, Nate Ross."

As I pondered the ridiculousness of that notion, Val's two partners appeared at our table. Jean, the brunette, was flushed with excitement. Madeline, the brassy peroxide job, was half in the bag. She looked at me like a junkyard mutt looks at a pork chop. Without invitation, they crowded in next to Val.

"Good lord, girl," Jean panted, breathless as a mile sprinter, "we heard you shot at Ed Jarboe."

"I did not shoot at Ed Jarboe, nor anybody else," Val said, in a snappish, hush-your-mouth tone. "I dropped my gun and it went off."

"That's not how Ed tells it, darlin'," Madeline said. She had the same accent at Val's, but her rasping, mannish voice made it anything but charming. "I heard him telling Chet at the bar that you tried to put out his running lights." She fished a cigarette out of her purse and lit it with a turquoise-studded lighter as she fixed Val with a level stare. "He lay hands on you, did he?"

"He did not," Val said. "We had a little disagreement, that's all."

"Sure you did," Madeline said, blowing out a lungful. She looked at me. "Ain't you going to introduce us?"

"This is Nate Ross. Nate, meet my partners Maddie and Jean."

"Howdy," Jean said, turning bright button eyes on me. She wriggled in her seat like a frisky puppy. I hoped she was housebroken.

Maddie offered a masculine handshake. "Pleased to meet you," she said, her cigarette bobbing in the corner of her mouth.

"Ladies," I said, flashing them my best five-dollar smile. I kept on smiling as I compared the three of them, sitting side by side. All class, kindergarten class, and no class. I gave no real thought to Jean, but Madeline interested me. Not in the usual way. She was trash; I'd seen that from the stage. Up close I had better reasons. I'd smelled her perfume ten feet before she reached our table—the same stuff that hung in the air at David Prince's apartment. I took a good look at her big, over-painted mouth as it opened like the Broadway Tunnel and flapped in meaningless chit-chat with Val. It wore the same gaudy shade as the butts in Prince's ashtray. Maybe Val didn't know the guy well, but her big "sister" couldn't make the claim. Asking Maddie outright would get me nothing; I might as well brace a smoke shop Indian.

Our two drop-ins showed no signs of budging, so I figured I was done for the night. I thanked Val for the drinks and said polite goodbyes. I could feel Jarboe's eyes stabbing at the back of my skull all the way out the door.

Chapter Six

Late next morning Duke phoned me at the office. He hadn't wasted any time; he'd asked a couple of cowboy buddies and gotten directions to Prince's hideaway.

"While I have you on the horn," he said, "I told the wife about running into my old high school pal, and she's anxious to meet you."

"Really? She looking for embarrassing stories from back in the day? I can tell her a few."

"To tell the truth, I think Josie's just happy to hear I have any friends who aren't in the movie trade. Anyway, how about having dinner with us Thursday night? Sardi's? My ticket."

I wasn't really the dinner-and-cocktails type, and Sardi's was a little tony for my taste. On the other hand, I was curious to see what kind of girl had married Duke.

"Sure, Duke, you're on." As an afterthought I added, "All right if I bring a date?"

I could hear the grin in his voice. "Sure, bring anyone you want."

We settled on half past six and hung up.

+++

I gassed up my coupe and headed for Chatsworth. I had no trouble finding the way in to Prince's cabin. It was off the old stagecoach road that served as a main highway in these parts. Duke had said to look for a little bridge of railroad ties over a drainage ditch, and a double-sided gate of heavy timbers just beyond. From there the path—nothing that you could call a road—ran through a narrow, steep-walled canyon, and wound serpentine through heaps of red boulders and sparse clumps of trees.

The house was three or four miles up the canyon, tucked into a box-like clearing on the east side. It was bigger than I'd pictured. "Cabin" had conjured up images of an Abe Lincoln affair, but this was more what I'd call a lodge. It was a long rectangle, cedar-shingled all over, and sat on a high foundation of river rock. A wide porch ran along the front and down one side, with steps at either end. A stand-alone garage was at right angles to the back of the house, and next to that was a small, open-faced barn fronted by a pipe corral. A strong breeze blew down the canyon. That and the squeak of the open corral gate on its hinges were the only sounds.

I didn't bother knocking. The door was unlocked, so I went in. The place was mostly one large room, filled with rustic furniture upholstered in Indian blanket designs. One corner was a kitchen area with cabinets, a small table and chairs, and a big, wood-burning cook stove. Stairs along the wall in the opposite corner led to a wood-railed loft, apparently the sleeping quarters. A small bathroom underneath the loft was the only separate room.

Like the apartment, the place was neat and tidy, but someone had clearly been here, too. If it was the same party who'd searched the apartment they hadn't bothered to do as neat a job. It might have been done two hours ago or two weeks; there was nothing to say which.

I checked the loft first but found nothing much. A change of clothes in the closet, but no dirty laundry. If Prince was here in the last couple of weeks it wasn't for long. Whoever had searched had stripped the bed down to the mattress, so there was no telling whether it had been slept in.

The living room and bathroom told me nothing. Toiletries in the cabinet looked like stuff Prince would have kept here for his visits. The cabinet had been rifled, so whatever someone was looking for was something that could have been hidden just about anywhere.

They'd given the kitchen the same treatment. Cupboard doors stood open, the supplies in them scattered about. Canisters of flour, sugar and coffee had been dumped into the sink. A nail keg used for trash stood in the corner, its cover tossed to one side. The one item of interest in the trash was a half-eaten ham sandwich. It was green and fuzzy around the edges; it had been there a few days. Prince wasn't the sort to go away without dumping the garbage. A plate and cup next to the sink had been rinsed but not washed. A coffee pot on the stove was still half full. It appeared that Prince had been eating—lunch, probably—and something or somebody had interrupted him. Not an emergency, if he'd taken time to rinse his dishes. He'd been in something of a hurry but hadn't planned to be gone long.

The stove was cold, but the remains of a wood fire were inside it. As I was closing it back up, something on top of the ashes caught my eye. A ghostly image of what had been printing. I scooped out the ashes and saw that a thin stack of papers had been tossed on top of the burning wood. They were blackened ash, but the smooth surfaces and sharp edges were discernible. In the back of the firebox I found one fragment about the size of a calling card that had drifted loose from the pile. It was a newspaper clipping. Whether the fire or age had made it brittle and yellow I couldn't tell. One side was part of an advertisement for a clock shop in Dallas, Texas. It had been clipped through the middle of the ad, so whoever cut it out hadn't had clocks in mind. The other side was a news story, or part of one. The upper part had been burned away and the lower edge was neatly cut just below the words "continued on page four." What remained was a partial account of a train robbery, and a hunt for two men. That made it an old cutting; I couldn't recall news of a train robbery in Texas or anyplace else since I was a kid. Whatever it was I doubted it had much to do with the missing screenwriter. But just to be a good and thorough detective, I tucked it carefully inside my wallet.

I went out back to the garage. A Chevrolet coupe parked inside was shiny and clean under a thin layer of settled dust. I checked the notes Okel had given me. Prince's car. The engine was cold. The car had been tossed, too, along with the garage. There were no animals in the barn, but a one-horse trailer had been rolled into the corner. Piles of dry horse manure in the corral showed that it had been occupied, but not too recently. Water in the galvanized trough was scummy and floated a few leaves and dead flies.

I closed the corral gate behind me and started walking the grounds around the house, searching for I didn't know what. A sound like someone blowing a raspberry and a blur of movement off to my right startled me. About twenty yards west of the house, a horse was emerging from a break in a line of stumpy trees. It stopped to idly nibble at the grass, and if it saw me it gave no sign. It was a sort of khaki color with a dark brown mane and tail and black forelegs. It wore a saddle and bridle.

As I approached the horse it raised its head and eyed me. Its ears twitched, and it sidled a few steps away and continued nipping grass. When I got within fifteen feet it lifted its head and made the raspberry sound again. I didn't know how to interpret that.

I said "Hey there" softly and inched forward with both hands held out front. The horse gave me a sidelong look but stayed put. I hadn't been this near a horse since I was a boy. I wasn't sure what to fear more—being bitten or kicked. Since they sounded about equally unpleasant, I did my best to stay away from either end. I eased up beside the horse and laid a hand against its shoulder. The muscles quivered and the animal made a contented sound. That reassured me.

Up close I could see the reins dangling straight down from the horse's bridle. One dragged in the dirt and the other hung about a foot off the ground; it appeared to have been broken off. The horse wasn't injured, that I could see, and there was no sign that its rider, assuming there'd been one, had been hurt. A pair of cowboy saddlebags hung across the horse's rump, behind the saddle. I went through them as best I could with the big animal walking in slow circles around me. One contained what I dimly remembered as horse-grooming tools. There was a wide, flat brush, a hoof pick like a screwdriver with its blade bent to the side, and a thing that might have been a potato scrubber—a curry comb, I remembered it was called. The other held a wallet and a set of keys. Inside it I found Prince's driver's license, some other papers of no interest, and seventy-eight dollars cash.

The key ring held keys for the car, what looked like the keys to the cabin, to Prince's apartment, and two or three smaller keys—desks or padlocks maybe. One small brass key with "USPO 17" stamped on it looked like a post office box key. I pocketed these items.

I looked toward the gap in the trees where the horse had appeared. A winding dirt trail snaked through and disappeared over a little hill beyond. Horse tracks running both directions were sun-baked into the hard ground. The trail was wide enough for a car, but I saw no tire tracks.

"Stay," I told the horse, doubting it would do much good. I started down the riding path, looking all around me as I went. Tom Mix might have gleaned something from the horse tracks, but he wasn't here. To me they said nothing except that horses had passed through.

Nothing else along the way interested me until I saw the birds. As I crested the hill I looked out over a wide, flat expanse beyond. The trail through it ran straight as a bullet between clustered boulders and clumps of brush. Fifty or sixty yards out, alongside the trail, several huge black birds squatted. A couple others floated in lazy circles overhead. I'd been so intent on the ground I hadn't noticed them before. I'd driven through the desert enough to know turkey vultures when I saw them.

Those on the ground clustered around something I couldn't make out. When I got within a hundred feet, I caught the smell. Faint at this distance, but unmistakable. At fifty feet the stench was stronger, at twenty it was intense. I shook out a handkerchief and held it over my nose and mouth. It didn't help much; the air I sucked through it smelled like clean linen and death. As I drew closer the birds started flapping irritably and took off one by one. Now I could see what had held their interest. It was a man's body.

Between what Mother Nature and the birds had done to the face, Okel's photo wasn't much help. The hair seemed about right. He looked heavier than Okel had described him, but when a body's been out in the sun for a while you can't always go by descriptions. Whoever shot him had figured if one bullet was good, half a dozen were better. What had been a fancy green-and-white cowboy shirt sported several finger-sized holes, and the entire shirt front was brick red and stiff with long-dried blood.

I didn't give more than a cursory look around, then walked back up the trail. Prince's cabin had no telephone, but I'd passed a roadside bar and diner a couple of miles back down the highway. I'd call it in from there.

The horse had moved up near the house and was still eating grass. I thought about putting it in the corral but wasn't sure I could manage it. Just as I reached my car, a shot sounded in the distance and dirt kicked up near my feet. The report echoed off the canyon walls, making it impossible to tell where it had come from. A second shot followed and a bullet smacked my car, punching a neat hole in the fender. At least that gave me a general direction. I hunkered down on the opposite side of the car and sneaked a look through the windows.

The shots must have come from high up the north canyon wall. My .380 would be useless at that range, but holding it in my hand made me feel better. I raised my head as much as I dared to scan the entire canyon wall for any sign of the gunman. Nothing. Beside the house the horse continued to calmly clip grass.

After what seemed like ten minutes—more likely two—crawled by with no sign that the siege would continue, I heard a dull, drumming sound from the slope opposite me. Through the trees about halfway up the canyon side I caught a flash of movement. A mounted, cowboy-hatted man on a reddish horse, moving fast and heading east toward the highway. I yanked open the passenger door and clambered across into the driver's seat. I kicked the starter and took off down the long drive in a spray of gravel, keeping watch on the canyon wall as I drove. Now and then I saw, or thought I did, flashes of a horseman through the rocks and trees. I kept my head as far back as possible for what little protection the door post offered. If I could see him, he could see me, and the high ground was his. The highway was several miles away, and there were no roads in between other than the goat track I was on. Not that that would matter much to a man on horseback.

The road sloped up as the canyon narrowed, and the dark, threatening walls on either side of me grew lower and lower. I'd caught another glimpse or two of the rider, still bearing toward the highway. If he reached it first, he could ambush me as I passed through the gateway and turned on to the main roadway. Pulling ahead and letting him get behind me didn't sound any more appealing. As I weighed the options, I saw him, or his dust wake, not more than twenty feet above the road, and maybe thirty yards ahead of me. I was still maybe a mile from the highway.

The road now was an up-and-down series of ruts, ridges, and blind curves.

I might come over one of the crests to find my assailant waiting on the other side. I had to reach the highway first. The final stretch was a hundred yards of straight, level road across an open field, where there'd be no cover. At the far end of that was the heavy double gate, secured by an iron hasp in the middle. Good citizen that I was I'd closed and refastened it behind me. Beyond the gate the drive narrowed to the little bridge, which had no rail, the drainage ditch below it about eight feet wide and four deep. The only way onto the highway was through the gate and across the bridge. I'd have to ram the gate.

As it turned out, I didn't have to ram the gate. Topping the last of the little hills, I was startled to see a figure standing in the road ahead, looking out across the highway and beating clouds of dust from his clothes with his big tan cowboy hat. His horse lay on its side at the edge of the road, thrashing its legs feebly.

I ground to a stop and was out of the car, leaning over the hood with my gun on him before he even seemed to notice me.

"Fun's over, Tex," I said, hoping I didn't sound as shaky as I felt. "Let go the hat, and get your hands high where I can see them."

He gave me an incredulous look, snorted in derision, and slapped the hat onto his head. He was maybe in his fifties—wiry, not too tall, with a weathered face and hair like steel wool. I recognized him instantly. He was the cowboy who'd been snooping into my car outside Prince's apartment. He didn't raise his hands, but took care to keep them away from his body as he walked over to the downed horse.

"Aw, shit," he said softly. Over his shoulder he said, "You can stow your pistol, pard. I ain't the one shot at you." He said it matter-of-factly as though he were remarking on the weather.

I stepped out from behind the car but kept the .380 pointed in his general vicinity. It was going to take more than an aw-shucks Will Rogers act to convince me.

He turned to face me. "I'm guessing that there's a .30-30 bullet hole." He pointed at my fender, and I glanced at the damage. The hole was neat and perfectly round, about the diameter of a cigarette.

"Rifle bullet," he continued. "I got no rifle, nor boot for one on my saddle. Just a six-shooter in my bags and I'm going to need that. Unless you're willing to shoot this mare. That front leg's busted all to hell."

I looked at the horse. Its coat seemed darker than what I'd seen through the trees, but I couldn't be sure. It made wheezing sounds and moved its head restlessly, flashing the whites of its eyes. One foreleg was bent straight outward where there was no joint. The leg bled freely, and a dagger of white bone protruded. I'm not one to get all fluttery at the sight of blood, but the big animal's obvious suffering made me queasy.

I lowered the gun to my side but didn't holster it; every now and then I'm wrong about people. The cowboy took my movement for consent. He squatted down and worked the saddlebags loose, then fished out a big stag-handled single-action Colt.

"A damn shame," he said. With no more preamble, he stood, cocked the big piece, and shot the horse through the head. The snorting and thrashing stopped. He stuffed the big pistol back into the saddlebags and started unfastening his saddle and bridle.

"If you didn't shoot at me," I asked, "who did?"

He answered without looking up. "Tall fellow on a sorrel." Before I could ask what the hell a sorrel was, he continued. "I didn't get a good look. He was moving too fast, and had too much start. This old girl was a good trail mount, but no runner."

"I saw you yesterday," I said. "Over on Marmont, looking in my car."

He nodded his head.

"How come?"

"I'm a nosy fellow, I guess. I was just curious who was poking around in Dave Prince's rooms."

"Are you a friend of his?"

He stacked the saddle and bridle on the road and stood to face me. "Friend ain't really the word. I know him. I'm working on a picture he's doing at Republic."

"*Stardust Trail?*"

"Yeah." Without warning he stepped up to me, right hand extended. "I'm

Dusty Vanner."

This took me by surprise. I had to shift the .380 to my left hand to return the handshake. I felt foolish doing it, so I just holstered the damned thing.

"Nate Ross," I said. "Why so interested in the guy, if you're not friends?"

"He owes me fifty dollars from a poker game a couple of weeks back, but he hasn't been on the set. So I thought I'd pay him a call." He hooked a thumb at the saddle. "Seeing as I'm afoot now, you mind giving me and my gear a ride back to town?"

"Only if you're in no big hurry," I said. He may as well know; it would be all over the *Stardust Trail* set by tomorrow. "But forget about your fifty bucks. Prince is dead."

His eyebrows lifted just slightly; his face was otherwise unchanged. I described in no great detail what I'd found.

"I need to let the police know," I said. "There's a diner down the road a few miles. I can drop you there if there's someone you can call. I'll need to meet the cops back up at Prince's."

"If you've no objection," he said, "I'll tag along."

I wasn't keen on the idea. Then again, he was a witness—to the assault on me at least. It'd be saving the cops some shoe leather if they could talk to him now, and I needed all the police goodwill I could get.

We piled Vanner's gear in my trunk and drove to the diner. I got from him on the way that he'd been a cowboy in Oklahoma and had come out to California a couple of years back, when his part of the country went from farm and ranch land to desert overnight.

"So many others came," he said, "that jobs got scarce at the central coast ranches and up in the San Joaquin. But Hollywood had plenty of work for fellows who could rope and ride." He said he made a decent living as a horse wrangler and "henchie"—bit players usually cast as bad guys.

"Silly as hell," he said, "real cowboys taking good money to be pretend cowboys. But it lets me sleep indoors and keep three meals a day under my belt." He laughed. "I just hope the folks back home don't ever spot me in one of the damn things. I'd never live it down."

I phoned the police operator from the diner. Vanner and I had a quick cup of coffee, then drove back to Prince's cabin. The horse was still next to the house, lazing in the sun. Vanner took charge of it. He led it into the corral, stripped off the saddle, and brushed and combed its coat. He brought out hay from the barn and refilled the steel tub with fresh water.

I watched all this while I smoked a cigarette on the porch. When he'd finished, he joined me.

"I'm not sure what they'll do with his horse," I said.

"That there's a Fat Jones horse, same as I was riding."

I asked if Fat Jones was a type of horse. He smothered a laugh.

"Fat Jones is a fellow owns a stable in the Valley," he said. "Rents out horses and rigs to the movie companies. He'll be happy to get that one back, I imagine. Might make up for the one I lost him."

We sat and made small talk for a while. I told him Republic had hired me to find Prince. He didn't know, or didn't admit knowing, that there was anything amiss with Prince. After an hour or so, a big sedan crunched its way down the drive and two detectives got out.

If Republic had been shooting a cops-and-robbers film, they couldn't have cast two likelier-looking Joes. They were standard L.A.P.D. plainclothes types; one was large, 45ish, a little saggy around the middle but still plenty hard, and the other was maybe thirty, slender and athletic. Both wore nondescript suits and fedoras cocked at identical angles. The big man's jacket fit him like the wrapper on a ham; the kid had sprung for a tailor. The big cop had a cold cigar stabbed into the corner of his mouth.

We met them at the bottom of the steps. The big guy looked Vanner over without evident curiosity and then eyeballed me. His face was lumpy, shapeless, pockmarked; it looked like a wad of chewed gum. His small eyes were hard and shiny as thumbtacks. His reddish Errol Flynn mustache might have been a decoration on any other face.

"You the private dick that called this in?" he asked, in a voice like a foghorn. I said I was, and he thrust out a big, hairy mitt. "Gimme,"

I handed him my license. Without looking at it he passed it to the younger man.

"I'm Queenan," the big man said. "Lieutenant out of Homicide. This is

Sergeant Bernal."

The young detective gave us a polite nod. Nobody shook hands or offered to. Bernal read my license and gave me a meaningful look but said nothing.

"So," Queenan went on, "who got chilled, and what do you two have to do with it?"

"The dead man's a mile or so down that trail," I said, and pointed. "A guy named David Prince. This is his place. He's a screenwriter working for Republic Pictures. He went missing a while back, so they hired me to find him."

Queenan listened with an expressionless face. "So I guess you earned your fee." His thumbtack eyes drifted to Vanner.

"This is Dusty Vanner," I told him. "He's working on Prince's current film. He's a…" I looked at the cowboy. I wasn't sure what to call him.

"Stuntman and bit player," Dusty explained.

"Why'd you bring him along?" Queenan asked me.

"I didn't. I came looking for Prince because he was missing. Mr. Vanner showed up because Prince owed him money."

There was a flicker in Queenan's eyes. Say "money" to a homicide dick and he hears "motive."

"You found what when you got here?"

I walked him through the sequence of events since my arrival—the ransacked house, the rancid food, the wandering horse, the riding trail, Prince's body with a chest full of slugs. I gave him Prince's wallet but held on to the news clipping and the keys. Only when I described being shot at, the chase, and finding Vanner on the road did Queenan show much interest.

"So you didn't know this bird before today?"

"Right." I didn't mention seeing Vanner the previous day.

"But you believe him when he says it was another guy shot at you?"

"The bullet hole in the car's from a rifle," I said. "He's only carrying a handgun."

"Yeah?" Queenan said. "How about you show me this handgun?"

I gave Bernal my keys and he and Vanner walked over to my car. They came back, Bernal carrying Vanner's Colt by the barrel.

"One shot fired from it, Carl."

Queenan's eyebrows rose and he looked at me and Vanner in turn.

"I had to shoot my horse," Vanner said. "She smashed a leg."

"Which would explain the dead horse down near the gate," Bernal said.

Queenan gave him an irritated look. He took the big pistol and looked it over. "Jeez, I thought they only packed these pistolas in horse operas nowadays." He looked at Vanner. "You got a carry permit?"

"Do I need one?" Vanner asked without rancor. "I'm on private land."

"Blah," Queenan said, waving a hand like he was fanning away a bad odor. I'd learn that was his standard reply when he had no snappier comeback handy. He handed the piece back to Bernal without looking at him. "Hold on to that, Frank, until we've had a look at our stiff." He motioned me toward their car. "Let's go."

We all piled into their sedan. Bernal drove and I sat up front with him, while Queenan and Vanner got in the back. We started down the riding trail.

Queenan took out a little notebook. "What's your name, gummy?"

"Nate Ross."

There was an electric pause in the air. Queenan's tone had been none too friendly to begin with. Now it took on a nasty edge. "Nate Ross," he repeated as though tasting something he didn't like. "Nate Ross that used to be a county dep?"

"Yeah."

He slapped the back of Bernal's seat. "Well, we're a cinch to bust this case, Frankie. We got the D.A.'s star witness on our side. This guy loves to testify in court, if we can only pin this on a copper."

Bernal frowned at him in the mirror and gave me a sideways look that might have been sympathetic. He said nothing.

I didn't need to point out the spot; the birds were back. Most of them scattered as we got out. A couple optimistic ones perched fifty feet away and sat watching us.

We walked over to what was left of David Prince. Queenan winced at the odor. He took out a little tin of mentholated balm and rubbed some around his nostrils and in his mustache—an old cop's trick. Bernal and I used our handkerchiefs. Vanner pulled his bandana up over his nose, bandit style. For a civilian, he didn't appear to be any more bothered by the sight than we were. He seemed more interested in the hoof prints that pocked the ground around us.

Queenan silently counted the bullet holes. "Somebody wasn't jokin' around." He looked at Bernal. "A week at least, huh?" Bernal nodded. Queenan looked at me. "How long you say this guy's been missing, stoolie?"

"Two weeks. And you can blow stoolie out your ass."

He chuckled. "Hard guy. I wouldn't get too lippy, pal. You ain't quite in the clear here."

"Sure," I said. "I shot him a week ago. Got myself hired to find him two days ago, then called you out today to show off my work. I'm eccentric that way."

"I ain't had time to check out your story. Until I do, I'm keepin' an open mind. Anyway, could be your pal here done it. What caliber's that hogleg, Frankie?"

Bernal took Vanner's pistol from his waistband. ".44-40."

Queenan looked at the holes in Prince's shirt. "Maybe," he said.

Bernal, meanwhile, was circling the ground around the body, poking about in the clumps of brush. A few yards away he stooped and used his handkerchief to pull something out.

"Got shell casings, Carl," he said. ".45 auto." He looked side to side. "Half dozen or so."

Queenan looked annoyed. So much for Vanner's wheel gun. "Before we forget," he said to me, "what are you packing?" I showed him my .380. He ran his thumb over the ornate engraving, the pearl grips. He snorted. "Might have guessed you'd carry some kind of pimp's piece." He handed the gun back. He looked disappointed but satisfied. "Well, let's not stand around out here with all this damn stink."

He got back in the car and sat scribbling notes. Bernal got a canvas tarp from the trunk and draped it over the body, weighting the corners with rocks. The two diehard buzzards flapped away in disgust.

We started back to the house. Queenan was irritated to learn there was no phone. We drove on to the diner, where he called for the coroner and the crime scene boys, then we returned to the house. Queenan went inside to look around while Bernal stayed on the porch with Vanner and me and took precise notes of our statements.

I should've kept my mouth shut, but I had to ask when he gave my license back. Yes, he'd recognized the name. Yes, he'd heard the whole story—some version of it, anyway.

"You don't act like you hate my guts about it," I said. "Or do you just hide it better than your boss?"

"I wasn't there, pal," was all he said. "Anything?" he asked, looking up as Queenan came back out. Queenan shook his head.

"Nope. Rotten sandwich, like he said." He pointed his chin at me. "But he would notice that. He's got a nose for anything rotten, this boy does."

I'd had about enough of his gaff. I hated guys like him, who mistook big and loud for tough, and thought a badge in the pocket was an anointment from God. I'd have knocked him off the porch and enjoyed the trip to jail for it, but Bernal seemed like an okay guy and I didn't want to make him any more work.

"Anything else you need from us?" I made a point of directing this at Bernal and not his superior.

"I guess not for now," he said. He questioned Queenan with his eyes.

"Blah." Queenan fanned the air again. Bernal handed Vanner back his pistol. "You keep that thing in leather while you're in my town, cowboy," Queenan said. Vanner just nodded.

Bernal walked us to the car while Queenan glared at us from the porch.

"Don't let him get under your skin, Ross," Bernal said.

"He may get my fist under his jaw next time he pops off."

"Nah, don't talk like that. Look, I wouldn't piss on the guy's head if his hair caught fire, but we're partners. You understand."

I understood. "Sure," I said.

He smiled. "Okay then." Probably just to rankle Queenan, he shook hands with us. "We'll be in touch, boys. Thanks."

He walked back to the house. Vanner turned down a ride back to town, saying he'd ride Prince's horse back and return it to the stable. He unloaded his gear from my trunk, and we said goodbye. I'd been hoping to ask him a little more about his dealings with Prince on the drive back. Maybe he sensed that. I wasn't sure.

I tried ringing up Phil Okel when I got back, but he was long gone for the rest of the day. It would have to keep until morning.

Chapter Seven

After breakfast I took a drive to the public library. A half hour spent conferring with a couple of dry reference books and a curly-haired research librarian whose dimples had dimples, and I came away with my answer. Nobody had robbed a train in Texas since the Newton Gang in 1914. More recently than I'd have thought, but a long way from the day before yesterday.

While I was there, I used the phone directories to scout out a private investigator in Dallas, Texas. An ad caught my eye for "Everett Nesselroad, Specialist in Missing Persons." It claimed Mr. Nesselroad was a former federal agent with extensive experience and a world-wide intelligence network at his fingertips. None of which explained why he operated out of north Texas. Still, he looked like my best bet.

I dropped by the office to get my mail and check for messages. No mail of importance and no messages at all. I called Nesselroad. He wasn't what I'd expected; the voice was more Minnesotan than Texan. I didn't ask. I just gave him such details as I could glean from Prince's clipping. He assured me he'd take it from there and would, of course, extend the professional discount.

Then I figured I'd better fill Okel in before he read about Prince in the papers. His office said he was out at the Monogram Ranch in Newhall on the *Stardust Trail* set.

I was making for the door to head out there when the phone rang. It was Frank Bernal calling to say that they'd confirmed that the dead man was David Prince. They'd made him on fingerprints; his were on file from half a dozen drunk arrests. I didn't envy whoever had taken them from the stiff. Getting postmortem prints from a body as far gone as Prince's was a particularly nasty job. It involved rehydrating the dry, decaying flesh of the fingertips, and often required slicing the pads off with a razor blade to get readable impressions. Not a task for weak sisters.

Bernal also confirmed the murder weapon was a Colt semi-automatic. That was about all they had so far. That cinched it—I'd found Republic's errant scribe. Who put six or seven slugs in him wasn't my concern; that was for Queenan and Bernal to puzzle out.

+++

I filled my tank at the corner gas station and pointed my heap toward Newhall. An hour later I was bouncing down a winding dirt road through Placerita Canyon. A mile or so in, I saw a little village taking shape on the horizon. Closer, I could see plank and adobe buildings sprawled over several acres dotted here and there with black oaks and pepper trees. This ranch was used by half a dozen little studios, and its buildings and false fronts served as the town du jour for whatever oater happened to be filming. Today it was *Stardust Trail.*

A hundred yards before I reached the outskirts I found the road blocked by a big blue sedan with Republic's emblem on its side, and two tough-looking studio coppers loitering alongside it. One sat on the running board, eating a sandwich, and the other leaned cross-legged on the fender and smoked a chubby cigar—gingerly, like he had to make it last until New Year's. A 12-gauge pump lay on top of the front fender, and a Tommy gun leaned muzzle-up against the running board.

Smoker watched me approach and said something to Sandwich, who made an impatient gesture with his free hand. Smoker gave him an irritated look and sauntered over, hitching his Sam Browne belt as I pulled to a stop and got out.

"Can't go no farther, buddy," he mumbled around his cigar. "Filming going on. Nobody gets in but cast and crew. Sorry."

I gave him a business card. For all the impression it made I might as well have handed him a cancelled stamp. But he perked up when I mentioned

Okel, even took the cigar out of his puss.

"Wait a sec, Bud," he said. He ambled over to a pole-mounted telephone and jiggled the hook. Sandwich watched me with a mixture of suspicion and resentment, probably annoyed that I'd taken his attention off his lunch. He laid his ham on rye aside and rested his hand near the chopper.

Smoker finished his call and came back, all politeness. He showed me a clear patch off the road where I could park and told me in an apologetic tone that I'd have to walk in from there so as not to disrupt shooting. I parked the car and legged it for the bogus burg, wondering why it took such heavy artillery to guard a movie site.

At the far end of the field where I'd parked, a few cowboys were unloading horses from trailers. A couple others waited nearby on saddled mounts. One of the riders glanced my way then trotted his horse over and stopped in my path. I looked up into the grinning face of Ed Jarboe.

"Well, I'll be damned," he said. "It's ol' Wild Bill Hickok himself." His speech was wet and slurry owing to a huge wad of tobacco in his cheek. It helped camouflage his puffy lip.

"Wild Bill," I said. "Wasn't he the one who got shot playing cards?"

"That's right. Turned his back when he ought to have not."

"I'm more careful than that."

He spit a prodigious stream over his shoulder. He misjudged, and most of it ran down his shirt sleeve.

"You best be. I still got business to settle with you."

"I'll be here for a while."

"No, here ain't no better than the club. I can't afford to get sacked. I got me a line or two in this picture. Hell, you may be lookin' at the next Spencer Tracy."

With brown drool running down his arm. Sure, and I was the next J. Edgar Hoover.

"Maybe that's just the easy way out for you, Ed," I said. "Maybe you're only good for muscling dames around. Maybe you'd piss yourself in a real fight."

He stiffened in his saddle. "You talk an awful lot, mister."

"Stop me any time."

"When I'm good and ready."

"I'll be sure and keep my back to the wall."

He jerked his horse around and rode off, leaving me waving off a cloud of dust.

Another uniform met me at the arched gateway and handed me off to a skinny, harried-looking kid who led me at a half run along a twisting path behind and between buildings real and fake, and through a jungle of cables, dollies and light stands, to a little covered patio hemmed in by shoulder-high adobe walls. A couple of long tables held coffee urns and plates of nondescript sandwiches. Phil Okel came through a low doorway at the back of the patio.

"Hey, Nate," he called with a friendly wave. "Grab a cup and a sandwich if you want, and we can talk in here."

I passed on the food but took a cup of coffee. I was instantly sorry; it tasted like potting soil. Phil showed me into a dingy, dusty little room with garlands of cobwebs in every corner. The only furniture was a pair of vaguely Spanish-looking wooden chairs with a small, absurdly ornate table—studio props, clearly—and a little modern desk.

"Field office," Okel said with a wink. "Makes my rabbit hole at the studio look pretty snazzy, don't it?" He waved me to one of the prop chairs. It was as uncomfortable as it looked.

"I'm guessing you got news for me," Okel said. "Good news, I hope. I can always use some."

"Sorry, Phil," I said. No point pussyfooting. "Prince is dead. Shot to death at his little ranch out near Simi."

"Well, shit on a stick!" Okel said. "Dead don't surprise me, the damn rummy. But shot dead? What do you got on it?"

"Not much. Somebody fed him a chest full of .45 slugs—emptied their piece from the looks of it. They wanted him good and dead. Probably killed a week or so ago. Cops are on it now, of course."

"Any idea who or why?"

"Not for sure. But somebody took a couple of shots at me as I was heading out to call the police." Okel's eyes widened. "Maybe related, maybe not. All sorts of loonies up in the hills."

"You get a look at 'em?"

"Just a guy on a horse. Fast horse. You acquainted with a man named Dusty Vanner?"

"Vanner? A little, yeah. He's here today, I think. One of them Okie cowboys they use for color in the films. Stunt work, bit parts, horse wrangling. They're a dime a dozen. Farmers back home, half of 'em, though Vanner might be the real McCoy. What about him?"

I explained how I met Vanner, and that I was confident he wasn't the shooter. I left out that I thought his poker winnings story was bullshit.

"You know where he lives? I'd like to talk to him a little more about what he saw."

"Not offhand. Most of these cowpunchers don't live anywhere. They make camp out in the boonies. The ones that do live in town stay in rooming houses, usually four or five to a room, and move around when anything cheaper opens up."

As an afterthought, I added, "How about Ed Jarboe?"

"That turd mixed up in this?"

"Not that I know of. I had a run-in with him at the Hackamore. And we just had a nice little chat outside."

"Shady asshole, but directors keep hiring him 'cause he's good on a horse. Like I said, half these day-playing cowboys are just drifters. All they know about a horse is which end bites and which end shits. Can't sit a saddle any better than Shirley Temple, couldn't rig a halter if you paid 'em triple."

He caught my look. "Don't let this cheap suit fool you," he said. "I was a fair horseman in my youth. U.S. Cavalry—back when the cav had more horses than tanks. Anyways, then there's guys like Vanner—rodeo riders, ex-ranch hands, and so on. Last, you've got a few like Jarboe. Grew up with horses and know their stuff, but mostly bums and hoodlums. Dime-store desperados."

Leave it to Phil to never use one word when ten would do. When it dawned on him he hadn't answered me, he added, "You could likely find either Jarboe or Vanner any morning at the Gulch."

"The Gulch?"

"Gower Gulch." He grinned. "What the cowboys call the corner of Gower and Sunset, kitty-corner from Columbia Studios. They congregate there in droves every morning, use the drugstore's pay phone to call Central Casting and check on jobs. Your boy Vanner would be there most mornings. But why bother? You found Prince, so I guess that closes the book as far as you go."

"Sure," I said. "I'm happy to leave Prince to the L.A. coppers. But I take it personally when somebody tries to aerate me. I'd like to know who that was, and why."

"Yeah, I suppose you would. Well, anyhow, I'll get you paid off on our end of it p.d.q."

"Might as well wait until next week. They want me at the inquest."

"Sure, kid, sure. Mind staying put while I call the old man, in case he has any questions?" I told him that was fine. "Jesus, he's going to have puppies," he said as he dialed the phone.

I smoked a cigarette while he made his call. From the squawking I could hear through the receiver Okel was right. Puppies were being had—litters of them. He wedged in a word here and there as the hysterics on the other end allowed. No questions for the ex-employee, it turned out, though there was a brief wrangle when Okel mentioned paying for my time at the inquest. Yates seemed to think I should throw that in for free, as my civic duty. He didn't know much about civics in L.A.

Okel looked winded and spent when he hung up the phone. He pulled a bottle and two glasses out of his desk drawer. Without asking, he poured two shots and slid one over. He held up his glass.

"To Herb Yates. May the bastard have a stroke before he gives me one."

"Herb Yates," I said, and we drank. Decent stuff. Yates must have paid better than Phil let on.

"Well," he said, putting the bottle back to bed, "so long as you're here, you want to watch a little movie-making in action?"

I would have passed—I had things I wanted to do—but I happened to look through the window and saw Val Cady and her sisters. They were sitting in folding chairs under a wide canvas canopy at the far side of the plaza. They wore outfits even more colorful than their stage costumes. A makeup girl was hard at work on Maddie. Val had her nose in a script, and Jean just gaped like a newborn at everything around her.

I'd like to have strolled over and said hello, and invited Val to Sardi's on Thursday, but it looked like they had a scene coming up. I didn't want to distract her. With any luck I could catch up with her later.

"I can stick around," I told Okel. "Might improve my education."

+++

It amazed me how many people and how much time and futzing around it took to set up the simplest film shot. Electricians and lighting guys scuttled around, cameramen swore and moved their heavy equipment here and there—and here again, prop men flitted in and out, big reflectors were shifted around, and everybody seemed to have a say in the end result, or to think they did. But nothing was ever final until the director, from his perch on a long-legged stool, looked it over like God upon the newborn earth, and saw that it was good.

Okel introduced me to Perry Mills, the director, first waiting for Mills to bawl out a couple of extras who'd missed a cue. Mills didn't bother to dismount his throne to shake my hand but extended his like the royalty he evidently thought he was. There was no ring to kiss, so I just grabbed hold. Once when I was a kid, I'd picked up a dead squid on Venice Beach. It hadn't been half as cold or flabby as this guy's mitt. That told me all I needed or wanted to know about Perry Mills.

I didn't see Val during any of this hubbub. The crew shot two or three scenes, or maybe one scene from three different angles—I couldn't really be sure. We were on the far end of the phony town's main street, clustered around a little adobe shack that stood off by itself, that they shot from the proper angle to make it look like it was in the middle of nowhere. Afterward they repeated the whole rigmarole with lights, cameras, etc, moving it all further out and away from the shack. I picked up enough to understand that they were shooting a scene where a stagecoach comes rolling out of the distance and pulls up alongside the adobe. I also gathered that King Perry had decreed that they'd get it all in one take, or heads would roll.

"Quiet on the set...action!" Mills yelled. Everyone piped down at once. The only sound besides the cranking of the cameras was the drone of a few stray bees not subject to Perry's fiats. The only thing moving was the flunky kid who'd escorted me in. He stood on the bed of a truck behind where Mills sat. At the word "action," he whipped a small flag through the air to signal the stagecoach, which sat about a quarter mile out on the horizon. At the flag, the driver whipped his team and the big coach left a rooster tail of dust behind it as it clattered our way.

Mills watched through field glasses as the coach drew closer, nodding his approval. At a cue I didn't see, two horsemen appeared out of a little gully alongside the road and fired their pistols into the air. The driver whistled and cracked the reins and the four horses pulling the coach surged like thoroughbreds hitting the home stretch. The bright red-and-yellow rig under the brilliant blue sky, and against the red desert floor dotted with gray-green yuccas and Joshua trees, made a very pretty scene. It must have looked aces through a camera lens. Evidently, Mills was pleased; he wasn't screaming at anybody.

The coach continued toward the little adobe with the two horsemen trailing behind and popping off a shot now and then. When it got within thirty yards or so, close enough that I could see the sweat shine on the horses' backs, I could see that one of the "bandits" was Dusty Vanner. There was a sudden loud crack like a rifle shot, and the coach's right front wheel came loose and headed off in its own direction across the flat sand. The rig dipped down and tipped crazily to the right. If I'd been inclined to think this was all part of the show, I'd have known better when the whole thing tumbled onto its side then, striking a couple of stumpy Joshuas, leapt five feet off the ground. It somersaulted in midair and crashed down into the dust again, rolling over and over like a colorful tumbleweed.

The quiet scene around me became instant chaos. An agonized shout seemed to rise in unison from the company. People started running—some toward the crash, a few back among the false-fronted buildings, shouting for help. I fell in with the first group. We sprinted toward the wrecked vehicle. I ran past Perry Mills, who stood up and sat down again, still looking through his binoculars, his mouth agape.

The horsemen who'd been chasing the coach separated. One peeled off to chase down the terrified horse team, which still galloped in harness with the coach's tongue bouncing between them, dragged part of an axle and one wheel behind them off into the tules. Dusty Vanner dismounted near where the driver and the man riding shotgun had been thrown when the coach flipped. I ran to his side as he crouched by the driver. He hesitated just the slightest bit as he recognized me.

"Hey, Ross," he said as he whipped off his bandana. "Check on that fellow yonder, will you?" He gestured towards another figure lying half hidden in a clump of brush. He started bandaging a nasty cut on the driver's head, and I went to have a look at the other man. Ten feet from him, I could see that there was nothing I could do. He was lying on his back with his head at an angle that only a broken neck would allow. The blood coming from his ears and soaking the sand around his head had stopped flowing. I felt for a pulse just to be sure. Vanner looked up and over at me. I didn't need to tell him. His mouth formed a grim line; he only paused a moment, then went back to tending the driver.

There'd been nobody inside the coach—the long shot hadn't required it—so we had no one else to worry about. The cowboy who'd gone after the team rode up and dismounted before his horse stopped moving. He handed the reins to a hatless guy in shirt sleeves, who looked clueless as to what he should do with them, then he knelt down beside Vanner.

"One of the trailers got a cut on the flank, but otherwise the team's all right. What about Jack and the other old boy?" Vanner took the cowboy's proffered bandana and started fashioning an arm sling.

"Jack busted his head pretty good and his arm's broke in a couple of spots. His insides are all right so far as I can tell."

"Shit," Jack mumbled. "I got worse than this from trying out that snorty bronc up to old man Tanner's that time. You was there."

"That I was," Vanner said. "Now hush until we can have a doc look you over."

"Shit," the driver repeated. He laid his head back on Vanner's rolled-up jacket.

"What about shotgun?" the cowboy asked. Vanner gestured toward me with his chin and shook his head. The cowboy lowered his head and pulled off his hat.

A gaggle of grips showed up with a flatbed truck and unloaded two stretchers. They lifted Jack onto one of them and set him gently on the truck bed, then came over for the second man. One of the stretcher bearers turned a little greenish at the sight of the dead man, so I took over. We laid a blanket over the body and loaded it beside Jack, then the truck trundled them back through the little movie town. They passed Phil Okel, who was coming out at a brisk walk. The driver stopped and spoke briefly to him, then continued on. Okel panted his way up to us.

"I was checking on my two boys out on the road when they rang me," he said. "What the hell happened?"

"From where I was," Vanner said, "it looked like that front axle just buckled. Jack couldn't give me much. Said he just heard a snap, then all hell cut loose."

Okel looked at me. I shrugged. "I can't tell you much more, Phil. There was a loud crack and the right front wheel flew off. "

Okel shook his head and gnawed his mustache. He gazed back towards the adobe, where Perry Mills still sat rooted in his canvas chair. He'd lowered the binoculars.

"Look at him," Okel said, "still planted on his prissy ass. Probably figuring how to work the crash into the story, the shitheel. Jumping Jesus, but Yates is gonna go off his rocker over this. Especially if…" He shot me a look. "You looked over the wreckage yet?"

"No, why?"

He ignored the question and walked over to the smashed hulk of the stagecoach. It had come to rest on its left side and now sported only its rear wheels, the left front one having gone off behind the horses. I followed him over, and Vanner followed me. I didn't know what had become of his horse.

"Holy bucket of shit," Okel said under his breath as he looked at the broken axle. When I looked closely at it I understood why. Though the bottom half of the heavy oak rod was splintered, the top half had been cleanly sawed through. "I was afraid of that."

"You suspected already?" I asked him. "How come?"

He started to speak, then looked at Vanner.

"We'd better go check on the driver," he said. As we walked back to the building together, Okel got the driver's name and particulars from Vanner. Jack was an old rodeo rider, well known to most of the cowboys. The dead man was an extra named Art Kelly. Vanner didn't know much about him, just another day player sent over by Central Casting.

When we reached his office, Okel was told that Jack had been taken to a prop warehouse and made comfortable until an ambulance could be called out from the city. One of the "townie" extras had once been an army nurse, and she was tending to him for now. Okel asked Vanner to go ahead and check on the driver, saying he'd meet him there.

"I got some calls I need to make," he said. "Yates and the sheriffs—Yates ain't gonna like that. But I'd like to talk to you after. Can you stick around?"

"Sure, Phil, sure."

He left me out by the food tables. The sandwiches didn't look any better than before, and I knew three hours wouldn't have improved the coffee. I decided to see if maybe Val was free by now.

I didn't see her or the other two at the makeup tent, but they'd probably know where she'd gone. I walked over to the girl I'd seen painting them up and turned on the Nate Ross smile.

One thing I'd learned already about the movie crowd: they were a gossipy lot, and the gossip didn't have to be true, or even plausible. So long as it was titillating it would be passed dutifully along. Quickly, too; Western Union had nothing on the Hollywood grapevine. The moment I asked the girl where Val was, a ripple of excitement seemed to pass through her. Her eyes got large, her cheeks flushed, and she answered in a furtive, breathless way.

"Gosh, mister, you should have seen it. Sitting right here when she heard the news. She screeeamed,"—she shrieked the word in an ear-splitting imitation—"and passed out cold." This girl didn't know me from Adam, but sharing gossip made everyone pals. Her voice changed to a salacious whisper. "I guess they must have been friendly, y'know?"

The dead extra had been sixty at least. When I expressed my doubt she huffed with exasperation. "Not that news. Ain't you heard? Somebody killed Dave Prince. This show's out one writer."

I got from her that Maddie and Jean had taken Val home for the day. I waved down the nervous kid who had escorted me in and had him tell Okel I had to go, but I'd call him in an hour.

+++

Back home I took a quick shower and put on clean clothes, then rang Okel at the ranch.

"Sorry I had to leave," I told him. "Something came up."
"That's okay, kid," he said, "but can you come out to the studio tomorrow morning? The old man wants to see you."

"Yates? What for?"

There were a few seconds of dead air before he answered me.

"Between you, me, and the fencepost, that mess out there today wasn't the first trouble we've had on this set. Neither was the Prince deal. That's all I better tell you, and you didn't get it from me. Yates will fill you in. Can I tell him you'll be here?"

"I'll be there."

Chapter Eight

After I talked to Okel, I drove to Val's apartment. The dinner invitation would wait for another time, but I wanted to see that she was doing okay. I also wanted to find out why she'd gotten the screaming mimis from hearing about the death of a guy she claimed she knew little and liked less.

She lived in a place over near Franklin, not new, but respectable. Such places could still be found in Hollywood if you knew where to look or knew someone who knew. It was hers alone; she didn't bunk with either of her phony sisters. With any luck I'd be spared their charms on this visit.

Maddie answered my knock. So much for luck. She didn't look any more pleased to see me than I was her, but we each made half an effort not to show it.

"Val's sleeping," she said as she closed the door behind me. "But stick around if you want. She's a light sleeper." She fired up a cigarette and offered me one. I passed. "Jean just ducked out to the drugstore. Val don't keep a drop of anything in the place, and my nerves are about frayed out. I don't suppose you're packing a flask?"

"Spoils the drape. My tailor would never forgive me." Her fishy stare said she didn't like my sense of humor. I tried not to get a lump in my throat. "How's she doing?"

"Aw, she'll be fine. If that ditz hadn't dropped the news on her, so sudden-like…"

"What gives there? Why did she get swoony because Prince is dead?"

"You're the detective. Why would you think?" She looked me over for a long moment, and a malicious little smile crept into her eyes. She shrugged. "Us girls don't tell all our secrets. You want to know, she can tell you. Or not."

The front door opened and Jean came in, a bagged bottle under her arm. She plopped her purse in a chair and slid a pint of Old Crow out of the paper sack.

"Do you know the clerk at the drugstore asked me if I needed a date for the party? Then he winked at me, like that." She demonstrated. "Old coot's fifty, if he's a day, and fat to boot. Ain't there a gentleman in this whole damn town?"

Only then did she seem to notice I was there. "Hey, Nate." She smiled and started to unpin her hat, but Maddie stayed her hand.

"Listen, sugar," she said, picking Jean's purse up and handing it to her, "why don't we go and see if we can find us a party? Val's in good hands." She looked at me with her best version of a sweet smile.

"All right, I guess," Jean said with uncertainty. Maddie took the bottle from her and plunked it on the table.

"Plenty of this where we're goin'," she said, and they went out.

I lit a cigarette, and to kill time thumbed through yesterday's newspaper. I was trying to decide whether the crossword puzzle was worth the effort when the bedroom door softly opened. Val came out, blinking a little in the afternoon light. She wore deep green silk pajamas and matching kid slippers. She, or someone, had scrubbed the thick makeup off her face, but none too carefully. Traces of it showed around her jaw. Her eyes were tired and swollen.

She looked at me in confusion for a second. Her lips tried to form a question, but she frowned as if she couldn't quite figure out what it was.

"Hello," I said. I'm slick with the patter when I want to be.

"Where—where are the girls?"

"You just missed them. I think they wanted to let you get some rest."

She nodded sleepily. She padded over to the kitchen and ran a glass of water from the tap. She came back, curled up on one end of the sofa, and silently sipped her water.

"The girls fetched a bottle," I said, "if you feel like something stronger."

"Ugh." She made a disgusted face without looking my way.

"Coffee, maybe?"

It took her a moment to register. She nodded. "Coffee would be good."

I went into the kitchen, rooted around until I found all I needed, and put the pot on to boil. When I returned she was still sipping water, staring at nothing. I sat in a wing chair at right angles to her—close, but not too close.

Two or three minutes rolled by before she spoke. She still didn't look at me.

"I guess you want an explanation."

"I don't need it right now. That's not why I came."

"I knew he was in trouble," she went on. "I didn't know what kind—I still don't. I only knew it was bad. When you showed up looking for him, I didn't know whether you were…" She turned to face me. "I'm sorry."

"How long had you known him?"

"We met in Texas. In Muleshoe," she added with a mirthless laugh. "A little over a year and a half ago. He was on one of his research trips, digging up stories of the old days. Ma had lived on the plains, and she knew some wild characters in her youth. She was sick, so I was doing what I could. I had a job waitressing in a little roadhouse, doing a song or two on weekends. Sang for a weekly show on a little radio station that broadcast all over Bailey County. Then one day David Prince walked in, talking nothing but Hollywood and throwing money around like a bootlegger. Pretty exciting stuff for a girl from Muleshoe. He started coming by the house, first to see Ma and listen to her stories, then after a while to see me. When Ma died last year, I came out here to try my luck. Dave helped me get jobs, and I met the girls through him.

"What about your father?"

She paused, turning her water glass in her hand then setting it aside. "Is the coffee ready?"

I went over and poked my head through the doorway to check on it. "Not quite yet," I said, taking my chair again. "A couple of minutes."

She sat silent for a moment. "I never knew my father," she said at last. "He died when I was three or four. In prison." She looked at me for a reaction. I guess she thought I'd be shocked. "I'd appreciate it if you kept that to yourself. Not the kind of thing I care to advertise."

"Sure, kid, sure."

"I never knew any details—why he was locked up or anything. Ma wouldn't ever talk about it."

She was staring into space again, her cheeks burning with shame. I went to get our coffee; I thought maybe she needed a minute. I came back and set the tray on the table in front of her. I sat on the sofa.

"So now you know what kind of girl I am," she said. "A jailbird's daughter. For all I know, a murderer's daughter." She stirred a lump of sugar into her coffee.

"Don't tell me you buy into all that Old Testament 'sins of the father' stuff."

"Don't you?"

"I'd be in pretty sad shape if I did."

"What does that mean?"

"I told you why I'm not a cop anymore. It was the truth, but not the whole truth. My father was on the sheriff's department before me. I thought he was some kind of hero when I was a kid. Couldn't wait to follow in his footsteps. Proudest day of my life, and his, was when the sheriff handed me my badge. It didn't last long. I found out my dad, the man I'd always pictured battling crooks like the guys on the radio shows, was on the payroll of every rum runner and gambling joint in the county. It was no secret; everyone on the department knew. Talk about sins of the father—they all just assumed I was the same. The straight guys mostly avoided me, and the crooked ones expected me to play along. The old man was retired by then, but it didn't matter. You can guess what his advice was. 'Don't make waves, kid.' 'Get the gravy while you can.' 'Never turn on a brother.' When I talked to the grand jury, he gave me pure hell about it. Called me every kind of dirty traitor, turncoat, spy, coward. Said he was ashamed to call me his son. It was our last conversation."

"You haven't spoken at all since?"

I shook my head. "We went our separate ways. I tried calling a couple of times, but he'd hang up. I wrote, but he never answered. We lived ten miles apart, but it might as well have been a thousand. He started drinking full time, I heard from my uncle. Then one morning about six months ago he got his old duty revolver out of mothballs. He cleaned it, oiled it, loaded it, and shot himself. Didn't leave a note. Most of the family blamed me, so I wasn't even welcome at the funeral."

"Good Lord, Nate. I'm so sorry." She laid her hand on mine.

"I didn't tell you this because I was looking for sympathy. We're none of us to blame for what our fathers are, or were. They made their choices and we make ours. Good or bad, those are the only ones we have to own up to."

"I'm not so sure that helps me." She gave me a rueful smile. "My choice was Dave Prince."

"It's not a bad choice to care about somebody."

"Even if he's a louse?" She'd tried to keep it reined in so far but was starting to slip. A couple of tears slid down her cheeks. "I knew what kind of fellow he was. After a while I knew. But he got me out of that dusty little town, and he brought me here where I had half a chance at a real life."

She was crying pretty freely now. Her words started coming in breathless little bursts.

"I knew there were other girls. I knew there always would be. But I loved him anyway. I really did."

That did it. She fell against me and buried her face in my shirtfront. I held her tight as her shoulders heaved and sagged, and her breath came in moist, ragged gasps. Her tears made a complete wreck of my best silk tie. Between the bouts of snuffling and wailing, she managed to get out a few more words.

"You must—you must think I'm the—biggest fool in the world."

I stroked her hair and said, "No." More smooth patter. I might have thought so. But here I was with my arm around a beautiful doll, about to spend the night in her apartment holding her while she cried herself out over another guy. The world, hell—she wasn't even the biggest fool in the room.

Chapter Nine

I wasn't in the best of moods for my meeting with Herb Yates, but I'd promised Okel I'd be there and hear the "old man" out. I disliked the Republic head even before he opened his mouth. I'm normally an admirer of the self-made man—the type, that is, who's a little surprised, and humble, and grateful over his success, because he knows he's caught plenty of lucky breaks along the way. Yates struck me right off as the other kind—the kind who deluded himself that he got where he was alone, through his own smarts and sheer force of brains and will, and that achieving that made him some sort of superior creature. It was plain in his eyes, the angle of his bald head, the thrust of his jaw, in the way he looked down his eagle beak at me like I was the first scuff in his new Florsheims. When he uncorked his hole and spoke in grating Brooklynese, he only confirmed it.

"Mr. Ross, have a seat." It wasn't an invitation—it was a curt order, from a man clearly used to being obeyed without question. He didn't offer to shake hands. I guess he couldn't be sure I'd washed. I took the seat; I was willing to see him that far. We sat on opposite sides of a desk that took up most of the fairly large room. I thought we might need megaphones to hear each other across it.

"Phil Okel informed me about Mr. Prince's unfortunate death. Nasty affair. I assume the police have matters well in hand."

"They have them in hand, anyway," I said.

"I see." He stared at a spot in the air about a foot above my head. Whatever was there must have fascinated him; his eyes didn't leave it for most of the conversation.

"With that in mind," he went on, "it seems we may consider this—case, I assume you would call it—closed."

"I guess that depends."

"On what?"

"Well," I said, "if I may be permitted an assumption, I assumed you'd want to know who killed your writer." I didn't care, particularly, but if Yates was willing to pay me to find out, it was okay by me. I was in this far.

"Isn't that within the purview of the police? I have faith they'll bring the murderer to justice."

"Oh, they'll arrest one, you can count on that. Might even turn out to be the guilty party. Law of averages and all that."

He almost forgot himself and looked me in the eye. His eyes retreated to their spot in the air.

"You were a policeman yourself, weren't you? Why's it you have so little regard for their methods?"

"I'm too familiar with their methods, and their reasons. Pressure's always on to make a pinch in a case like this. It doesn't have to be the right one as long as it sticks. Justice has less to do with it than numbers. And good press."

"Perhaps if I called the police chief personally and explained the gravity of the matter."

"That might work if your name was Louis B. Mayer."

That struck a nerve. His face turned the shade of a pomegranate, and his eyes bored holes in me. "I don't care for your insolent manner."

"And I don't care for the word 'insolent.' It implies I owe you some sort of deference."

"Don't you? I'm paying you."

"I haven't seen any money from you yet, Yates. I don't count the two yards I got for returning your toy cowboy—that's a done deal. When I'm hired to do a job for someone, I do that job, and they give me money in exchange. It's a straight business transaction, and as far as I'm concerned it makes us equals. If you want deference, you'll have to shop elsewhere—I've got none to sell." I snatched my hat off my knee and got up.

"Sit down, Mr. Ross," he said. "Please." The "please" braked me. I sat, but kept my hat on, just in case.

Yates smiled. "I'm not entirely the hard-assed bastard most people make me out to be. I'm in a tough racket and you either put up a tough front or you get bulldozed. But I respect a man who won't be pushed around. I don't see much of that in my position."

He lifted the lid on a humidor that could have held King Tut and took out a long, black cigar. A motion of his head said I should do the same. I hadn't had lunch yet, and was still a little sore, but what the hell. I don't get to smoke a rich man's cigars every day.

Smooth, very smooth. Probably cost more than my suit. We blew cigar smoke over each other's heads for a good three minutes before he spoke again.

"I'm going to be frank with you, Nate. May I call you Nate?"

"As long as you don't call me insolent," I said around my cigar.

"I need your help on another matter," he went on. "I imagine Phil Okel's told you we're trying to keep things quiet around here. As quiet as you can keep anything in this gabbling town."

I nodded.

"It's not just the Prince matter. That's bad enough—worse, now that there's a murder and police involved. What Phil didn't tell you—on my orders—is that this isn't the first problem we've had on the *Stardust Trail* shoot."

I frowned and nodded and put on my best "news to me" face.

"Before the first day of filming," Yates said, "there was a fire on a sound stage, and some railroad car sets built for the film were destroyed. A week in, some developed footage disappeared from the lab and had to be reshot. Other things have happened along the way: essential props have inexplicably vanished, an entire shooting crew and cast lost a day due to stomach distress. Broken lights, electrical shorts, all of suspicious origin. Recent incidents have been more serious, and clearly intentional. A few days back two stuntmen's saddle girths were cut and the riders injured—not seriously, thank God. But now two deaths: David Prince and this day player..." He consulted a notepad on his desk. "Arthur Kelly."

"Looks as if someone doesn't want your movie made."

"Exactly."

Chapter Ten

I learned from a call to the Hollywood branch that the closest post office to David Prince's ranch was in a little country store about five miles north of it, along the old stagecoach road. I took a drive out that way and found the spot with no trouble. It was the first building I came to and appeared to be the only one for miles in either direction.

It was a quaint, rustic little place—one of those one-stop shops that manages in its 600 square feet to carry every possible necessary for life in the sticks. At the rear of the store, just to the right of a cold case stocked with cured meats and dairy goods of questionable vintage, was a little barred bank teller's window. A placard next to it displayed the current postage rates. This was the post office. On the other side of the window a triple row of brass-fronted postal boxes ran floor to ceiling, thirty-six in all. Assuming I was in the right place, Prince's was box number 17.

The key fit. Inside the box I found a couple of circulars of no particular interest, addressed to "box holder" and a hand-written note to Prince from the postmaster—no doubt the old gent currently measuring out pipe tobacco for a customer in filthy overalls—reminding him that his box rental fee was past due. Beneath these items was a stiff envelope with no return address. It has been in the box for some time; the Hollywood postmark was several months old. It was addressed to "Kit Rawls" in handwriting that, from the samples I'd come across, I was sure was Prince's.

I knew the law frowned on taking another man's mail, but I was hazy on how it applied to a dead man's, especially if addressed to one who technically didn't exist. I wasn't going to stand here and wring my hands over it. The old jasper at the counter wasn't likely to pinch me, postmaster or not. I stuck the envelope in my pocket and put the other stuff back in the box.

As an afterthought, I kept out the past due notice before I locked the box. I could picture a few situations where it might be handy for a guy in my trade to have a P.O. box in a dead man's name, at an out-of-the-way post office. I folded the note around a two-dollar bill, slid it between the bars of the teller's cage and walked out.

In my car I slit open the envelope and pulled out the contents. No letter, only a photograph. An old photograph—the cabinet card style popular in my parents' time and before. Imprinted in scrolled gold lettering at the bottom of the card was "J. Deane, Photographer," and below that, "Waco, Tex." There was no other printing or any writing front or back to identify the photo. It was a studio portrait of two men—one standing and one seated in a fancy, carved chair. They were stiffly posed in front of a painted backdrop of a forest scene. Judging from their clothing, the photo dated to around the turn of the century. Both men wore suitcoats, stiff-collared white shirts, neckties, and gold watch chains stretched across lapelled vests. They also wore grim expressions, which meant nothing—people in these early photos seldom looked anything but grim. They were nondescript men, both of ordinary build. The standing man must have been significantly shorter; he stood only a head above the seated man. Both had very close-cropped hair, and the short man had a dark, full beard, while the seated man was clean shaven.

There was nothing in the photo to distinguish it from those that could be found propped up on just about every mantel in America. I had no idea what it was or what it meant, or if it meant anything at all. Prince was an inveterate collector of old West stories and paraphernalia; it might have been that the picture was just something he'd picked up in his travels, something that caught his interest. But if that were the case, why take the trouble of mailing it to himself? And why under his pen name? Why leave it unopened inside his postal box? It obviously had some value and was a thing he wanted to keep safe and hidden. But why, and whether it had any connection with his death, I couldn't say. Not yet.

+++

I checked in at the office before driving to Sardi's. Nothing new—slow news day. I locked the photo safely away. Private eyes in stories always have safes for their valuables. Me, I have a desk drawer that locks. A ten-year-old could jimmy it, but it did have a cleverly designed false bottom it would probably take a twelve-year-old to find. I stashed the photo away there, confident I could handle any twelve-year-old hoodlums who might come around.

+++

The dinner with Duke and his wife was pleasant enough. Duke was his usual, gregarious self. He told most of the school days stories himself, leaving me not much of anything to talk about. I was a little preoccupied, anyway. Josie was a sweet, pretty, quiet girl. She seemed a little refined for a meat-and-potatoes guy like Duke, but it was clear they were crazy about each other. I wasn't sure if she disliked me, or my trade, or was just a little put off that I'd come stag and there was no girl talk. Maybe I just wasn't good company tonight. Whatever it was, when the wine and talk ran out, I got the sense she was as glad as I was to say goodnight.

Chapter Eleven

Next morning I rolled out of bed extra early, had a quick breakfast, and went straight to the office for a strategy meeting with myself. I had told Yates I'd take on his case. Since I was already hip deep in it, I might as well be paid for my trouble. He was content to let the L.A. cops quietly deal with Prince's murder and for the sheriff's department to handle Kelly's death, and for me to stick to finding out who was sabotaging his project. I wasn't so sure. It seemed pretty likely the two deaths were related, but that didn't mean they'd be investigated that way. L.A.P.D. and the sheriffs weren't famous for playing nicely together; each department considered itself the big fish in a huge pond. I figured I'd best keep my options open as far as the two homicide cases went. I still didn't especially care who had killed Prince, but I did have a personal stake in the case; somebody had shot at me, a thing I didn't like to encourage. As for the sabotage angle, I was content to handle that any way Yates wanted, so long as it was my way.

Something about the whole set-up scratched at the back of my brain. Some piece was a bad fit, like brown shoes at a white-tie dinner. I scribbled notes and played around with them. Somewhere about my third cigarette and fourth cup of coffee—or maybe the other way around—I got it. It was Prince's murder itself. The sudden leap from petty vandalism to cold-blooded murder. Then there was the sequence. The movie cowboys' saddles had been monkeyed with after Prince was cold. If someone was going to escalate to murder, why would he drop back down again to pulling glorified kid pranks? It made no sense that I could see.

It seemed my best bet—my only bet—was to start with the big kazoo—the murder. That took me back to where I didn't really care to be; I needed to know who killed Prince but, more importantly, why. I'd have to be pretty discreet—after all I wasn't supposed to be dipping my fingers into an official police case. I also needed—wanted, at least—to find out who had taken pot shots at me, which may or may not have been Prince's killer. Lucky for me I had a witness for that, who coincidentally or not was also a witness to the stagecoach wreck.

+++

Okel had told me all the cowboys congregated most mornings at the corner of Sunset and Gower. He didn't exaggerate. Before I was within a block of the corner, stylish Hollywood had become a sea of plaid shirts, turned-up blue jeans and ten-gallon hats. I'd hoped to find Dusty Vanner discreetly, but that wasn't going to be easy when the street as far as I could see was filled with lookalikes.

I parked and worked my way down the sidewalk. Clusters of cowboys gathered on either side, smoking, joking, telling tales of horses ridden, stunts performed, and sundry other bits of real and movie derring-do. No sign of Vanner among them. Okel said that the Columbia Drugstore was the hub of activity here, where the day players loitered around the store's pay phone and took turns calling Central Casting to line up jobs for the day.

I asked two or three of the men, who looked like they might carry some weight with the others, if they knew or had seen Dusty Vanner. Each query got me a version of the same reply: a stony look, a pause, and a curt answer along the lines of "Don't know him, friend." I could always try Central Casting, but I figured they'd have no better idea where to find Vanner. Movie cowboys apparently weren't known for keeping fixed addresses.

I'd just gotten my fourth freeze-out and had decided to sap the next yokel who claimed not to know Vanner when I heard a familiar voice calling my name. I turned to see Max Terhune shouldering his way through the cowboy throng. It was slow going; every cowboy he passed hailed him with friendly words and, good-natured guy that he was, he returned greetings, slapped shoulders, and shook hands every step of the way. I decided it would be easier to work my way to him since I didn't have to run the goodwill gauntlet.

I made my way to where Max was trapped in a knot of good old boys, politely listening to a recitation of films they'd done together. He managed to break loose with some vague words about needing to "have a word or two with this fellow"—meaning me. The cold, suspicious stares I'd gotten thawed a degree or two. They were probably deciding I was some sort of studio suit.

"I wouldn't expect to find you out here," I told him. "You're working steady."

"Yep," he said. "I'm a lucky fellow that way. I just come down to get some boots repaired at the shop 'round the corner. How 'bout you—out here on detective business?"

"Sort of. I'm looking for a cowboy named Dusty Vanner. You know him?"

"Dusty? Sure. We've done a picture or two together." He peered up and down the boulevard. "Haven't seen him around today, though."

"Nobody has, or will say. These boys are more tight-lipped than a bunch of Folsom yardbirds."

Max's grin returned. "I don't doubt a few of them are just that. Most of 'em, it's just their way. For them, if you don't know a man, you don't ask many questions. He minds his business and expects you'll do the same. They don't mean to offend."

He said he had to get out to Republic, but first he waved over a couple of the cowboys. "Boys," he said, "I'd appreciate it if you'd help my friend Mr. Ross here out. He's all right. He's the fellow got Elmer back from them hooligans. He's looking to talk to Dusty Vanner."

"Sure, Max. You bet," said the shorter of the two, a cheerful, bow-legged little guy called Reese.

"Thanks. See you, Mr. Ross." Max ambled off and I followed Reese towards the next corner. He peppered me with questions the whole way—how did I know Max? Was I in the movies? Did I work at Republic? Did I know Gene Autry? Did I think this new kid, Roy Rogers, was really going to take Autry's place? They were pointless questions, since he didn't give me the chance to answer one before he lobbed the next at me. Max's vouching seemed to have put the kibosh on the close-mouthed cowboy business, at least where this guy was concerned. By the time we reached the corner, I hadn't answered any of Reese's questions and he didn't seem to notice. He pointed out a

Mexican café a few doors down.

"You should find Dusty yonder," he said. "He's partial to old Felipe's menudo. He ain't in there, come find me and we'll run him down." I thanked the gabby little cowboy. He shook my hand with a mitt no bigger than a ten-year-old's, but a grip of iron.

I found Vanner perched on a stool at the café counter, spooning up the last of a mixture that smelled like it would melt brass.

"Hey, Ross," he said. "Stand you to a bowl of menudo?" I said thanks anyway. Though I'd weathered my share of hangovers, I'd never acquired the taste for the local remedy. A guy had to have some regard for his insides.

"I was hoping we could talk a little," I said, taking the next stool. "We didn't get to finish discussing David Prince the other day."

"I don't know I could tell you much more about him," he said. He looked around and lowered his voice. "If it helps though, I got a pretty good idea now who it was we were chasing."

"How's that?"

"When I dropped that horse off at Fat Jones' place it was pretty late. Old Waldrop, the cranky old cuss that works the horses, give me hell about the one I lost. 'You damned cowboys is hard on the stock today,' he says to me. I asked him what he meant, and he said that he'd had another horse returned a few hours earlier, damn near ridden to death. He showed him to me, and it was that big sorrel your bushwhacker was riding."

"Did he give you a name?"

Vanner nodded and took another look to be sure we weren't overheard. "Ed Jarboe."

"He's sure of this?"

Vanner nodded again. "Said Jarboe came in like old Dan Scratch was on his tail, with some cock-and-bull story about trying to outrun a freight train. Told him he'd best keep the whole business under his hat, or else." He chuckled. "He don't know Ike Waldrop too well."

"This Waldrop was sure it was Jarboe?"

Vanner shrugged. "He ought to know. Jarboe's one of the regular boys who picks up horses and tack for the shoots. I don't see Ike would have cause to lie about it. I don't know what reason Jarboe would have to shoot Dave Prince, but if he didn't, why take a shot at you?"

I told him about my clash with Jarboe at the Hackamore Club.

"Could be, I guess. Bushwhacking a man would be Jarboe's kind of play. Still, it sure looks awful funny him being out there. I'm not a big believer in coincidence."

"Neither am I."

Chapter Twelve

Clarence "Fat" Jones lived up to his name. He looked like a beach ball in bib overalls and a straw hat. I'd have pegged him as just another relic of L.A.'s horse-and-buggy days, one of the legion of stubborn holdouts clinging to their rural lifestyle in a landscape rapidly paving itself over. But Jones had shrewdly found a way to have the best of both worlds. His North Hollywood stables, a 19th century operation smack in the midst of 20th century urban sprawl, was a main supplier of horses, wagons and tack to Hollywood's movie makers. By helping others simulate the old West, Fat was doing his part to keep it alive.

Dusty Vanner introduced us at the stables as we stood in the hazy sunshine of an L.A. morning. Fat was a genial type with a crooked grin made more lopsided by the plug of tobacco perpetually tucked into his cheek. If he'd worked in front of the camera instead of far, far behind it, he might have been a comic sidekick of the Smiley Burnette or Andy Devine type.

Fat gave me an enthusiastic, unsolicited tour of the stables, the rolling stock, and showed off with particular pride his cadre of especially trained movie horses—some trained for jumps, others to fall on cue, some to buck, some to rear, some just to pose and preen and make their riders look larger than life. He rattled off by memory which horses had appeared in what films under the rumps of which famous actors. Although I found it all interesting and instructive, it was only a sidelight to my real reason for coming here: I wanted to talk to Ike Waldrop, the stable hand, about Ed Jarboe and his run-down horse.

After half an hour of the guided tour, Fat had to excuse himself to deal with some wranglers who'd come to pick up wagons and oxen for a shoot in Arrowhead.

"Sorry about that," Dusty said as Fat wobbled off. "That old boy's like a proud papa—likes nothin' better than showing off his family." I didn't really mind much. Anything I could learn about this business of shooting Westerns might come in handy.

Dusty asked one of the grooms and found out Waldrop was in the "big barn" overseeing the re-shoeing of a dozen or so horses slated to go out on location the next day. Dusty led me to a big corral behind the barn where a couple of farriers were busily prying off old horseshoes. The horses were being led out from the barn, one by one, by a man of indeterminate age, who might have been fifty or a hundred. He had an oddly bird-like build; he couldn't have been more than five-foot-six, but more than half of that was legs. His trunk was almost a perfect oval and his balding, overlarge head was perched on a scrawny chicken neck. The bird illusion was enhanced by a nervous, flitting manner and by long, skinny arms. Arm, rather; his right sleeve was pinned up above the elbow. His left arm made up for the missing right by doing three times the work. Whether lifting, pushing, pulling or just flapping and waving as he talked, it was in perpetual motion. Dusty caught the bird man's eye and waved him over.

"Nate, this here's Ike Waldrop." The man looked at me without any pretense of friendliness and gave a noncommittal grunt. There was nothing birdlike in his expression. His eyes were shrewd and watchful, and I had the sense that nothing around him went unnoticed. An ideal quality in a witness.

"I can't spare a whole lot of time," he said. The voice was deep for a man of his size and build, with a distinct Oklahoma twang. "Ever' damn outfit in town's shootin' outdoors this week." He motioned to a small outbuilding off one end of the corral. "We can talk in the office."

The "office" was no more than a tool shed, about sixteen by twenty feet and filled with wooden wheels and axles in various states of disrepair and littered with the assorted tools of the blacksmith's and wheelwright's trades. We navigated through an Amazon jungle of leather harness and tack hanging from beams and rafters, to a back corner where an ancient roll top desk stood.

Its pigeonholes overflowed with bills, receipts, cancelled checks, contracts, and assorted other ephemera. Waldrop lighted on a sprung swivel chair and waved us to a couple of tall milk cans with folded grain sacks on top. We sat on the makeshift stools while the old man plopped down on the rickety desk chair.

"I told Dusty here," he said, jabbing a finger in my companion's direction, "all there was to tell. Now I reckon you expect me to tell it all over again." He snatched a greasy old cob pipe off the desktop and stuck it in his mouth without lighting it

"If you don't mind," I said.

He gave an indignant snort and mumbled around the pipe. "I only mentioned it the first time 'cause I don't like that skulking sumbitch, him or his pack of shitbird friends." He glared at me and yanked the pipe back out. "And I don't like nobody ill using my horses." He waved his lone arm wildly in the air. "If it was up to me, I'd hang the bastard by his…"

"Mr. Waldrop," I said, hoping to head him off before he worked himself up to an aneurism, "I can see you're a busy man. If you could just answer a couple of quick questions, I'll be on my way."

He shoved the unlit pipe back in his mouth. "Suits me. Fire away, then."

I asked him about that night. He told me more or less what Dusty already had. Jarboe had come in near dark riding Jim Dandy, one of the stable's younger, faster horses. He claimed to have taken the horse with Jones' permission, but Waldrop had checked and found out that that was "pure horseshit." The horse was wearing the stable's saddle and bridle, but Jarboe was carrying a rifle and a leather scabbard of his own. He told Waldrop he'd been hunting coyotes. The horse was winded and sweat-soaked; Jarboe claimed he'd raced a freight train as a lark on his way back.

"More horseshit," Waldrop said. "Wasn't no freights passed through since the day before. I told that lyin' peckerwood if he ever brung a horse in looking like that again, he was gonna need that rifle. By God, I meant it, too."

"What about the horse Dusty brought back that evening?" I asked.

"You mean after he broke old Susie's leg?" He gave Dusty a malevolent look. "That was Pepper. Dave Prince liked to play cowboy, go hole up in his place up there in the pass. He wasn't up to that much riding, though, so Fat let him take an old single trailer. He'd had Pepper for a couple weeks or so."

"Was he supposed to keep the horse out that long? Wasn't anybody concerned?"

Waldrop shook his head. "You never knew with Dave. Might be up there a day, might be a month or two. One of them bullshit ar-teests. What's the word? Erratic. That's it—he was erratic. And a drunkard, of course. Still, a damn shame what happened. Not a bad fellow."

In our ten minutes together his mood had switched gears from belligerent to businesslike to mournful, almost tearful. And he claimed Dave Prince was erratic. I could see that I'd gotten about all I could. I dropped a card among the debris on the desk and thanked him for his time.

"My pleasure," he said with a look and a tone that said it had been anything but. He dropped the pipe next to my card and went away, leaving Dusty and me to find our own way back out through the labyrinth of leather.

Chapter Thirteen

My reception at Gower Gulch was different when I returned. Reese and his pal must have spread the word that I was Max's friend; I was greeted and treated almost like one of the gang. Faces darkened a bit when I said I was looking for Ed Jarboe. Although he was technically a brother in this little fraternity, he was clearly a black sheep. Nobody had seen him for a couple of days, and this time around I was sure I wasn't being stonewalled. A couple of the cowboys helpfully pointed out friends of Jarboe's—who were few—among the crowd, and warned me that those men wouldn't take kindly to my asking questions about him. When I walked back to my car, I saw those same three or four cowboys skulking in doorways, glaring at me. I guess it was supposed to make me weak in the knees.

None of the Gower Gulch crowd knew for certain where Jarboe lived. One said he'd heard Jarboe bunked at the Hackamore, and another had heard that he sometimes worked on Joe Gowdy's ranch in Placerita Canyon, not far from the movie town where *Stardust Trail* was shooting. I wasn't interested in driving that far today, so I figured I'd try my luck at the Hackamore Club first.

+++

The club was nearly empty when I got there. I ordered a beer at the bar and looked around the place. A couple of vaguely familiar faces from my first trip here, or Gower Gulch, or both. But no Jarboe. The bartender told me he hadn't seen him. He picked up the house phone and made a brief inquiry, then came back over and topped off my beer without being asked.

"Stick around," he said.

A couple of minutes later I was joined at the bar by two of the cowboys who'd tried to spook me at Gower Gulch. Both were youngish, medium-sized guys, solid built. One was a slouchy fellow with a much-abused nose that made mine look like John Barrymore's, and three days' growth of stubble smeared across his face. He wore a mock friendly grin that never quite reached his eyes. The other stood still as a lamp post, and appeared to have about as much personality and sense of humor.

They moved in close on either side of me. The sloucher leaned an elbow on the bar. His partner stood like he'd been spiked into the floor. Sloucher spoke up.

"Name's Deke; this here's Ray. You're Nate Ross, ain't you?"

I didn't bother shaking hands. Boys like this weren't big on the social graces. I just nodded and sipped my beer.

"Why you lookin' for Ed?" Deke asked.

"Personal business."

"What sort of personal business?"

"The personal sort." I sipped more beer. I could do this all day.

"Uh-huh," Deke said. "Well, Mr. Joe Gowdy wants to make your personal business his business." His grin widened. Ray nodded in solemn agreement. I guess that made it official.

"Let's all go see the man," Deke said. "Nice and friendly like." He pulled up a shirt tail to show me a gun tucked into his waistband. Ray cocked his head toward the back room. I followed them toward the backstage door with Deke at my back. We filed down the corridor for what seemed half a mile until we reached a door covered with fancy tooled leather. Ray turned and reached under my coat in one smooth motion. I batted his hand away and felt a cold muzzle pressed to the nape of my neck.

"Easy, partner," Deke drawled. "No irons allowed in the boss man's office. You'll get it back when you leave." Ray pocketed my .380 and banged a horseshoe knocker on the doorframe. I heard no answer, but Ray opened the door and we followed him in.

If I'd thought the cowboy décor was overdone in the club, it was because

I hadn't seen the owner's office. The walls were covered with split logs for a cabin effect, and hung with branding irons, horse blankets, bear and wolf pelts, and artwork of the Remington and Russell type. The chairs and sofa were built of buffalo horns fitted together in wildly intricate patterns and were upholstered with brass-studded leather in bright whorehouse red. Centered along the rear wall was a huge tiger oak desk trimmed in the same tooled leather as the door.

Behind the desk stood a character right out of the horse operas I'd watched as a kid. About my height, but his wiry frame made him seem even taller. Thick, longish hair hung in silver waves behind his ears and over his collar. His Buffalo Bill goatee and outlandish handlebar mustache were forty years out of date, but somehow suited him. He wore a brown tweed suit cut and trimmed with western flair, and a silk tie with a hand-painted stagecoach scene on it. A massive gold watch chain with an Indian head fob stretched across his red brocade vest. A huge white ten-gallon Stetson lying on the desktop completed the ensemble. He stepped around the end of the desk and stretched a long arm toward me.

"Mr. Ross," he said in a honey-dipped Texas drawl, "I'm Joe Gowdy. Come on in." The crescent of a smile showed under the big mustache as we shook hands. His handshake was sturdy and businesslike. "Sit yourself, please."

He waved me to one of the bizarre bull horn chairs facing his desk. I sat down and hung my hat on my knee. He dropped into the chair's mate beside me and turned it to face me. "I appreciate your agreeing to meet with me."

"I didn't get the idea it was voluntary."

"My apologies if the boys cut up a little rough. I'm afraid they may have played the heavy in one too many Westerns." He looked at Deke and Ray with mock reproach. "You can leave us now, fellows. I'll holler if I need you."

Ray laid my .380 on the desk corner nearest Gowdy and he and Deke walked out. Gowdy paid the gun no attention.

"What can I do for you, Mr. Gowdy?" I figured I might as well take the bull by the horns, so to speak.

He smiled. "Joe, please. I must say, I admire a man who gets right to business. I'm a fairly straight shooter myself, so I'll come directly to the point. I was curious what your interest is in Ed Jarboe."

"As I told your men, it's a personal matter. No offense meant."

"Oh, none taken, I'm sure. I respect a fellow's right to keep his affairs his own. But my concern is this: I run a peaceful, respectable place—not always an easy task given the crowd my establishment draws. Your dealings with Ed have already brought one ruckus under my roof, including a bit of gunplay. Fortunately, no one was harmed, but I'm sure you can understand that I'm not anxious to have such doings repeated."

"I see you stay pretty well informed. So you must already know I had nothing to do with the gunshot, and that what happened afterward was nothing Jarboe didn't ask for."

"Certainly. His conduct was most ungentlemanly, and not the sort of thing I tolerate in my employees. I've spoken with him about it, and I'm more than confident it won't happen again. However, if you don't feel the matter's settled to your liking..."

"It was settled then as far as I was concerned. But it may be that your boy doesn't feel that way. He took a couple of shots at me the next day."

The smile froze for an instant. This was clearly news to him. I gave him the basic facts without mentioning why I was prowling around a lonely canyon in Chatsworth. He didn't ask.

"You're certain it was Ed?'

"I have a reliable witness who says so. Two, actually."

He chewed on that for a moment. "If it helps at all," he said at last, "old Ed's a pretty fair hand with a gun. If he'd meant you any real harm, I doubt we'd be having this talk."

"I don't know if that does help."

"Well, I have to say this news disturbs me, and I assure you I will take it up with Ed. But it does bring us back around to my original concern. I can't have you looking to even up any scores here."

I laughed. "If that's all that's worrying you, Joe, rest easy. I'm not here to square things up with Jarboe. I just want to ask him a question or two about why he shot at me."

"Surely, that's obvious."

"Maybe." I thought it over for a moment. There was probably no harm in mentioning Prince's murder now. If Gowdy hadn't heard about it yet, that wouldn't be the case for long. So I filled him in. That Prince was dead, he seemed to know. That Jarboe had been out to Prince's cabin, he didn't.

"Do you feel that Ed is implicated in this business?" Gowdy asked.

"I wouldn't go that far. Yet. Let's just say his presence there raises questions—questions I'd like to have answered."

"Do the police consider him a suspect?"

I shook my head. "They know I was shot at. I haven't talked to them since I learned who did it."

That interested him. "Why not, may I ask?"

"If he only did it because of our run-in, I'd prefer to keep that just between us. If it did have some connection to Prince's death, I'd like to know more about that before I pass it on." I stood up. "Now," I said, "I've answered your questions. How about you answer just one for me. Where can I find Ed Jarboe?"

He held up a palm. "I haven't the faintest notion, Nate, and that's God's own truth. He lives in a small apartment just upstairs, but he hasn't been there—or here in the club—in several days. I'm as interested in his whereabouts as you are. For different reasons, of course." He took out a wallet and slid out a crisp C-note. He laid on the desk between us. "Would this buy a couple days of your time to locate him?"

"Keep your money, Joe." I put on my hat. "No point paying me for a job I'm already doing for myself." The truth was I didn't trust this guy and didn't care to go on his payroll.

"All right. Could I ask, at least, that you let me know when you do find him?"

"I'll do what I can." I reached across him to pick up my gun. He made no move to stop me but stood and offered his hand.

"Best of luck, Nate."

Deke and Ray were holding up the corridor wall outside the office. They looked a little disappointed as I passed by and tipped my hat. They tailed me out to my car, just to feel they'd earned their day's pay, I guess.

+++

I took a midday break to pay a sort of debt. I was feeling a little guilty. Here my old pal Duke was an up-and-coming movie star, and I had never seen a single one of his films. If nothing else, it would give us something more to talk about next time we had dinner. A few of the older movie houses downtown had weekday matinees, and a couple of those showed nothing but Westerns. The films they ran were all a few years old, but I figured it wouldn't hurt to see Duke's early stuff.

The audience was light; mostly kids skipping school and old codgers who'd been around when real cowboys still rode the range. I had never seen a Western with sound. The stories didn't seem to have changed much since the silent days, but hearing the horses and the gunshots made them a little more exciting, I guess.

The first film was *Riders of Destiny.* Duke played a bird named Singin' Sandy, because the gimmick was that any time he was about to throw lead, he'd break into song. The first scene showed him riding through the Joshuas in Lancaster, from the look of it, strumming a guitar and warbling a funereal little number about "guns a-blazin'" and "blood a-runnin.'" It was obvious that it wasn't him singing, and they filmed him from such an angle that you couldn't see he wasn't really playing the guitar either. The result was so comical I must have sprayed popcorn thirty feet. I don't know who I made madder, the old buzzards or the truant kids.

After that, though, it settled down to be a pretty good picture. Duke was in a black hat, because the other characters weren't supposed to know whose side he was on. But the audience wasn't fooled; the old men cheered as loud as the boys every time Duke went into action. I got so caught up in the story myself that I almost forgot it was my old pal up there.

I could see why people like Yates thought Duke was lead material. He definitely had what Hollywood calls "presence." I knew some of that had to do with the way they lit him and photographed him, and it didn't hurt that he was a head taller than everyone else in the film. But most of it was just Duke. The guy owned any room he walked into. He always had.

Chapter Fourteen

There's a sixth sense that develops when you deal with crooks long enough. It goes by all sorts of names, but every cop has it. Every PI worth his fee and expenses has it. I had it, and it kicked in as I stopped by the office after my day at the movies. As I walked down the empty corridor there was no visible reason—there never is—but I knew something was out of whack. I just didn't know what.

I stepped up to my outer door and listened. Nothing. I slid my keys out with one hand and my .380 with the other. Quietly as I could, I unlocked the door and, standing to one side of it, pushed it open.

No squad of tough boys with blackjacks and burp guns waylaid me, but there was an almost palpable charge in the air. It made my hair bristle. As I stepped in, I noticed my desk chair was pushed back against the wall under the window. It had been under the desk when I'd left yesterday; I was sure of that. Somebody had been in here.

If they were looking for a big money score, they'd picked the wrong boy. A roll of postage stamps and half a bottle of middle-grade bourbon were the only things of even marginal value in the place. And I ruled them out on the first pass. It hadn't been the cops; the job was too neat for that—no busted furniture. I took a quick inventory, which is an easy task when you don't have much to begin with. Assuming someone didn't break in just to use my phone for a long-distance call to Kenosha or Keokuk, I knew there'd be something missing.

After a few minutes' search I found it, or rather, I didn't. My locked desk drawer had been jimmied. A sweet job, too; the lock wasn't broken and the wood wasn't scarred. I moved the filler—fingerprint school catalogs, overdue bills, and so on—and I pulled up the false bottom. The drawer was empty. Whoever was here had been looking for Prince's old photo, and they'd taken it.

I went through the place thoroughly, twice. Nothing missing but the photo. There was no point calling the cops in. Maybe there were prints to be had, but I'd get the horse laugh for reporting a burglary where the only thing taken was a photograph that didn't even belong to me. A photo that, for all I knew, was nothing more than a picture of Dave Prince's great uncles. I locked up again and headed downstairs to Gus's place.

+++

Gus's nephew, Benjy, was working the counter. He was a smart, watchful, sharp-eyed kid. Living through three armed robberies teaches a guy to stay on his toes.

"Morning, Mr. Ross," Benjy said as he slid a cup of coffee at me across the scuffed wood counter. He'd filled it only to about an inch from the rim.

"Hiya, Benjy. Go ahead and top me off, kid. I left my flask in my other jacket."

He filled my cup. "What's the word on all this city hall business, huh?" Benjy said, planting his elbows on the counter. Our fine metropolis was in the midst of recalling its crooked mayor. It was a political first—the recall, not the crooked mayor. "You think the Shaw crowd's really out?"

"I don't know," I said, uninterested. I could think of no bigger waste of time than debating L.A. politics. The faces changed, but the game never did. "I think the boys who drummed up the recall better consider a lengthy vacation when the dust settles. That gang's got a long reach."

"Maybe time to take the wife to Tahiti, huh?"

"Maybe to the moon." I took a quick look around. Nobody else in the place but a couple of rusty old geezers rattling their racing forms in the far corner booth. They were regulars.

"Say, Benjy, you see anybody strange around this morning or last night?"

"Strange? Like how?"

"You know, strange looking—doesn't fit the neighborhood. Strange acting—like maybe someone who'd stick a gat in your ribs and demand the till. Strange."

"Strange." He nodded, thinking. "There was a guy yesterday evening, but I didn't think too much of it." He looked sheepish. "You get all sorts, so…"

"I get?"

"Well, he came out of the stairwell," he said, pointing. "Five thirty or so. He didn't look like a guy was getting teeth drilled or buying insurance, so I figured he was one of yours."

"What sort of guy?"

"Cowboy," he said. "Big tan hat, checkered shirt." I pressed for details and he gave me a photographic description of Dusty Vanner.

"You see him go up? Or where he came from?"

Benjy shook his head. "I looked up and seen the stairway door close, maybe a half an hour earlier. But I didn't see who it was."

Half an hour. More than enough time to toss my office. I drank the last of my coffee and dropped a half-dollar on the counter. "Thanks, pal. Be good."

+++

Vanner had given me his address at the café. His hotel wasn't as seedy as I'd imagined. It wasn't the Biltmore, but for a seven fifty a day bit-playing cowboy, likely no stranger to a blanket roll in the sagebrush, he was doing all right.

His room was on the ground floor—good and bad news for me. Good because I had no stairs or elevators to navigate, so less chance of meeting anyone there who'd remember me. Good also because it was easier to beat a quick retreat if necessary. Bad because I was more exposed to nosy neighbors and passersby, and less likely to hear anyone approaching. It's like that in my line of work—any advantage is usually cancelled out by an equal disadvantage. If you're lucky you break even.

He wasn't home, or I'd have taken the direct approach. But one more plus to a place like this is cheap locks; I had no trouble getting in. The room wasn't much, but a guy like him wouldn't need much. Murphy bed, small dresser with bottle and glasses on top, shaving stand in the corner, a couple of chairs and a card table by the window. Shared bathroom—I'd passed that in the hallway. The rugs were clean, and the wood floor was glossy and smelled of oil soap.

I started with the bed. I pulled it down, went through the pillowcases, checked under the sheet and under the mattress, felt the quilt all over. Nothing. Likewise the dresser. Nothing taped under the card table or the chairs. The shaving stand was clean. Vanner didn't have much in the way of personal effects; a couple of extra shirts, a worn pair of jeans, a corduroy coat. His horse tack he probably kept at the stables; I'd have to check that next. One promising item, and about the only thing left to examine, stood on end in the corner. It was a canvas-rolled bundle, about three feet high and a foot thick, fastened around the middle by two leather straps with roller buckles. I undid the dingus and rolled it out on the floor. It was a kind of cowboy travelling kit; inside was a heavy blanket, another shirt, extra socks, and a little canvas bag with shaving stuff. But no photograph.

I never heard the door open. I had my back to it and was engrossed in going through the bedroll. Nate Ross, the street-savvy shamus, sneaked up on by a cowboy wearing boots with clunky two-inch heels. Not the way to win trophies from the Cloak-and-Dagger Guild.

I came up off the floor as the bundle sailed over my head and plopped down in front of me. It was about a foot square, wrapped in faro table green oilcloth, and bound with a leather thong. I spun around, reaching for my .380. Dusty Vanner stood in the doorway, his big Colt held loose at his side. His weathered face wore a wry grin.

"I bet that there's got what you're after," he said, laying the big Colt on the dresser. "Go ahead, open 'er up." He closed the door behind him and leaned on it, his arms crossed.

I carried the bundle over to the table, undid it, and folded back the oilcloth. Inside was a thick stack of papers. The missing photograph was on top. I looked at Vanner. He shrugged and said, "Go on and look through the rest of it."

I flipped through the sheaf of papers. It was a mixed bag. There were letters—both typed and handwritten—a few old photos, miscellaneous copies of official documents, and scribbled notes. Most of it was newspaper clippings. Those were about evenly divided between yellowed, tattered cuttings dating back thirty years or more—mostly from Texas and Oklahoma newspapers—and more recent ones from newspapers all over the Western states. The older ones mainly dealt with a Texas train robbery in 1902. Prince's burned clipping came to mind. Some described the trial and conviction of the two robbers, and their murder of two officers who were transporting them to prison. The more recent articles all seemed to be about rodeos.

When I'd read enough to get the idea, I looked up at Vanner for an explanation. I picked up the photo from Prince's mailbox.

"Let's start with this," I said. "Why'd you take it from my office? Who are these guys?"

"That's two different questions," he answered. "I took it because I've been looking for it for a while now. I had a notion you had it, but I wasn't sure why. I didn't know what your game was, or if I could trust you."

"What changed your mind?"

"Duke Wayne. I ran into him earlier today at the Hackamore. We got to talkin' about this and that, and your name come up." He went to the dresser, uncorked the bottle, and poured two drinks. He brought them over to the table, and we pulled out chairs and sat.

He took a sip of his whiskey and gave me a lopsided grin. "Guess I ought to have talked to him before I busted into your office. He gave me your bona fides, so to speak."

"Did he?" I sipped my own whiskey.

"Yes, sir. So I guess it's time to give you mine." He dug into an inside vest pocket and laid something on the table in front of me. It was a badge. An old-time hand-engraved job, a silver circle with a cut-out star in the center. Around the circle was engraved *Deputy United States Marshal*. Across the star it said *Western District, Tex*.

"You're a federal deputy?"

"Was," he said. He nodded towards the stack of papers. "A good many years ago."

"Well, I'll be damned." I picked up the circular badge, hefted it, ran my thumb around its milled edge. "I thought all you old West law dogs wore stars."

He smiled. "That there's easier for the doc to pull out when you get it shoved up your ass." Funny, I'd heard L.A. coppers make the same joke about their shields. I picked up the photograph.

"So this is why you came out to Prince's that day?"

Dusty shrugged. "I guess my poker winnings story was a little weak."

"It stunk. But what made you think that he had this? If it was just something he'd picked up in his research…"

"*Stardust Trail* made me think so."

"I don't follow."

"Have you read Prince's script for the picture?"

"No."

He pointed to the faded clippings. "Well, you'll find most of it in there."

"You mean Prince based it on a true story?"

He nodded. "Yep. Oh, he changed things around some, gave people different names, gussied it up quite a bit. But the meat of it he took from this old case here. I don't know when or how Dave Prince got on to it. I thought everybody'd pretty much forgot it, except for me."

I took Prince's clipping out and read it again. It made sense now. Everything in it matched up with what was in Dusty's file. It looked like I didn't need the Nesselroad agency after all. I took some more whiskey and lit a pill.

"Ok, so, fill me in here." I waved my cigarette over the pile of papers. "How did you come into the case?"

"I had a friend, a fellow deputy name of Clyde Goss. The marshal wanted to personally escort these two train bandits—Abe Shandy and Del Maynard—up to Leavenworth. The Federal pen—the train they'd robbed was hauling U.S. mail. Marshal Brickman wanted one deputy to go along, so me and Clyde cut cards to see who'd go and who'd stay behind. Clyde was always lucky at cards. So the two of them boarded the train at Austin." He leaned forward, rested his forearms on the table. "Brickman was a good man, but he was a presidential appointee, not a lawman. He let Maynard's wife and Shandy's mother ride along in the car, since the boys was going away for ninety-five years each. Somehow or other—we never did figure exactly how—the women handed off pistols to their men when they was a couple hours out. They shot old Brickman dead, and Clyde put up one helluva fight, but it was two on one. Still, he shot both them boys up pretty good before he went down. They jumped off the train, handcuffed together and all, and lit out in the dark. The engineer pulled the train in at the next stop and they brought a doctor on board, but there wasn't nothing he could do for Clyde."

Vanner knocked back his whiskey and went over to the window. He stood quiet a moment, looking out at the night.

"I got the wire at Austin," he said. "First thing next morning I lit out with a party of rangers and local law. We found Del Maynard out on the prairie, gut-shot and half out of his head. The cuffs was still dangling from his wrist. We backtracked toward where they'd jumped the train, looking for Shandy. All we found was his right hand. Ol' Maynard had used a sharp rock to…dissolve the partnership, you might say. He wouldn't say nothin' about what happened. A couple of our party took him back to the lock-up in Austin, and the rest of us stayed out there to look for his partner. No luck. But we found him a couple weeks later. He'd made it twenty-some miles to a little old line shack left over from the cattle driving days. Been there a while from the looks of things. He'd knocked over a kerosene lamp and burned the whole place down around him. Three of Clyde's bullets in him, his right hand missing, and his head stove in. There's honor amongst thieves for you."

"What happened to Maynard?"

"They patched him up, and when he was fit to travel, I took the murdering sumbitch to Leavenworth myself. He never stood trial for killing the marshals or his partner. Federal lawyers figured ninety-five years was enough, I guess. Maybe it would've been, I don't know."

"It must be hell to lose a friend that way," I said. I'd been lucky enough in my time as a deputy to escape that particular pain. It was one benefit of having few friends on the job.

Vanner nodded and refilled his whiskey. "The hell wasn't over, neither. Three years into his stretch, Maynard and another con escaped." He laughed bitterly. "You won't find nothing about that in them news clippings. It was an embarrassment to the government, and they managed to keep it out of the papers. The other fellow was caught a few weeks after. But Maynard had the devil's own luck—he was never found. Neither was the $60,000 him and Shandy took in the train holdup. If he got his hands on that he had a damned good stake to go wherever he wanted, start over."

"So you're still looking for him, is that it?"

He nodded. He sorted through the stack of documents and pulled out a yellowed old half sheet.

"Prison records was burned up in a fire not too many years after. This here's about all I had to go on." He slid the paper over to me. It was a wanted flyer from the time of the train robbery. Along with the names and descriptions of Maynard and Shandy it had two small head-and-shoulders photos. They were badly reproduced, but clear enough that I recognized them as the images in Prince's photograph.

I picked up the photo and studied it. According to the flyer the man standing was Abe Shandy and the other was Del Maynard.

"Wasn't much trail to follow," Vanner said. "Shandy's only kin was his mother, and she died not six months later."

"How about Maynard's wife?"

"Never could get boo out of her. Probably afraid of being tried herself for helping them escape. She moved away not long after, dropped out of sight. He didn't have no other family, and a fellow like him don't make many friends."

He picked up the newer stack of clippings.

"I'd hear bits and pieces over the years," he said. "Maynard seen here or there, by boys who'd known him back in the day. Supposed to be riding in rodeos—he was always a damn fine horseman. I followed that circuit for some time, but it always come to nothing. Then along come the moving picture business, and Westerns being turned out by the bucket load, and a lot of those old-time rodeo boys figured that was an easier way to turn a dollar. So I headed out here to try my luck."

He tossed the clippings aside. "Fool's errand, I suppose. It's going on forty years. Half the old-timers are dead now. Hell, I doubt I'd know Del Maynard if he come walking through that door."

"How'd you get onto Prince?"

"I heard talk goin' around about this new Republic picture, *Stardust Trail*. When I heard what the story was, I figured it couldn't be no coincidence. Made me wonder where Prince had heard about the case, who he'd talked to. What else he knew."

"What tipped you that he had the photograph?"

He dragged the cabinet card toward him, studied it. "I seen a copy once. Years ago. The boys had it done one summer while they was skylarkin' in Waco. Shandy's ma and Maynard's wife each had a copy. So did half the whores in Texas, probably. Used to be one in the Rangers' files, but things have a way of disappearin' over the years."

He held up the flier. "Far as I knew, this was all that was left of it. Then Dave Prince got rip-roarin' drunk at the club a few weeks back and let on to a couple of the boys that he was 'sittin' on a goldmine' as he put it. Said he had proof against someone. Some old, buried secret they were payin' him to keep under his hat. Mumbled somethin' about a photograph. Well, when I heard that, I fastened onto Dave Prince like a tick. Then he up and decided to leave town, hole up at this place in the hills. I kept tabs as best I could, but I couldn't set up camp there. I was comin' out to check on him again when you come along."

"So what were you thinking then? That I killed Prince to get the photo?"

"No, I knew you were searchin' for somethin' at his place in town. I watched you at the cabin from the time you drove in, so I had a pretty good idea it wasn't you. But I knew you was holdin' back with the police; I saw you pocket them keys. So I figured maybe they weren't all you'd kept back."

I ran the whole story down for him—the burned clipping in the stove, the keys, the photo in the post office box.

"So," I said when I'd caught him up, "if you didn't kill Prince and I didn't kill Prince, who did? Maybe his golden goose got tired of dropping eggs."

"You're rulin' out Ed Jarboe?"

"Well, he's too young to be your fugitive. And we know how he does business. I doubt he's got the stones to shoot a man face-to-face. Anyway, he'd be a damned fool to go back out there if he had."

"Well, he strikes me as a damn fool. But I still think you're right. I saw those tracks out there where Prince was layin'. Jarboe didn't make 'em—him nor his horse. Somebody smaller, lighter."

That was worth knowing. But it didn't help explain what Jarboe was doing out there in the first place. It was a long ride just to take a couple of pot shots at me, and he couldn't have known he'd find me out there. Something was screwy where he was concerned. And now he'd made himself scarce. Or somebody else had.

"So now that all our cards are on the table," Dusty said as he refilled our glasses, "what do we do next?"

"We? Look, Dusty, your story is interesting and all. It'll probably make for a hell of a movie. But I can't spare time just now to help you track down a guy who broke jail thirty-odd years ago."

"Even if he killed David Prince?"

"You said yourself the tracks out there were left by someone smaller than Jarboe. Doesn't sound like your Del Maynard."

"Don't mean he didn't hire it done."

"Okay, say you're right. As curious as I am, I'm not getting paid to look for Prince's killer. That case is in the capable hands of the L.A.P.D."

"So's Ed Jarboe shooting at you. But you're spendin' plenty of time on that."

"That's different. That's personal."

"Well, this is pretty damned personal to me."

"I understand. It would be to me, too. But I'm a little tied up on another case at the moment."

"A sabotage case, for instance?"

"Who told you that?"

"I got eyes. I saw that coach axle. And I been on *Stardust Trail* since the start, remember. There's been plenty of other funny business."

"Who else knows about it?"

He laughed. "Who don't? Hell, it's all the boys have been talkin' about."

So much for Yates's cloak of secrecy. "All right, so it's no secret. But you can see why I'm not looking for any jobs on the side."

"Fair enough, but don't you think we might just be followin' the same trail?"

"How's that?"

"If Prince was killed to keep Del Maynard's secret, maybe somebody's tryin' to stop *Stardust Trail* for the same reason."

"Why would Maynard be worried because they based a movie on his case? Who'd even remember, at this point? And, forgive me, but who besides you would care?"

"Right there's the point. He'd have no way of knowin' whether somebody like me was still interested, still doggin' his trail. It's a long time back, but we're not all dead yet. Anyway money's a mighty powerful draw."

"Money?"

"The railroad put up a $20,000 reward for Maynard when he busted out. Quietly, so as not to shame Washington. They was set on gettin' their $60,000 back. That reward still stands."

"After all these years? Is that optimism, or sloppy bookkeeping?"

"Couldn't say. But it'd be one big reason Maynard wouldn't want no attention on his past life. Twenty grand ain't what it was in '02, but there's plenty around would sell out their own mamas for less."

"So what's your plan—we find this guy and split the reward?"

He fixed a cold eye on me and stood up. "I don't give a red shit for the railroad's money. I'm after a bastard that murdered two good men. But if that's what gets you to help me, hell, you're welcome to the whole shebang."

"Oh, sit back down. Let's not start going for our six-guns over this. Maybe I'm not quite as slummy as you think."

He sat. "Well, what's your idea, then?" His temper was still bubbling under the surface.

"There's something in what you say. I'm not saying I'm convinced the murder's connected, but if that's why Prince was killed, I guess it makes sense someone might also want to put the quietus on *Stardust Trail*."

"All right," Dusty said, taking a satisfied sip of his drink. His normal unruffled demeanor was slowly coming back.

"But it could also be," I said, "that Prince's murder is part of the scheme to shut down the film, and that that's being done for some other purpose altogether."

"I'd say that's unlikely."

"So would I. I don't think murder was ever in that plan. I think Kelly's death was unintentional. Of course there is a third option: That Prince was killed for some different reason altogether. Seedy types like him get on the wrong side of all sorts of people."

"Yeah," Dusty said. "But I don't see that. He's working on *Stardust Trail*, blackmailin' somebody because of it, and ends up dead. Hard to believe there's no connection."

"Agreed. But if we're going with the first theory, we need to find that link."

"As I see it, that brings us back to Ed Jarboe. Jarboe's skulking around, and shooting at you, right after you found Prince dead? Can't be coincidence, can it? I say we start where you already were. We look for Jarboe."

Chapter Fifteen

One thing's certain about the Ed Jarboe type; they don't sock a lot of money away for rainy days. Unless somebody was hiding him out and supplying food, board, and necessaries—and I didn't see him having that kind of friend—he was going to have to pop up from his hidey-hole before long and go to work. Whether at the Hackamore, on a film set, or as odd-job man on Gowdy's ranch, he'd need cash soon.

Stardust Trail wasn't shooting today. It was too hot for a drive to Newhall, and I wasn't sure how welcome I'd be nosing around Gowdy's place. The club was the most likely choice, anyway. I wasn't convinced we'd find Jarboe there, but there were other points in its favor. One, Val should be there. I hadn't had a chance to talk to her since the other night. Two, Gowdy had told me Jarboe had an apartment above the club. Being the thorough and conscientious detective I was, I figured it was high time I searched it.

It was Friday, and the place was packed with day-player cowboys itching to fling their week's pay away on a little mild debauchery. Empty tables were few and infrequent and the horseshoe bar was garlanded with a daisy chain of exuberant cowpokes, linked at the elbows.

No sign of Jarboe, but Deke and Ray dutiful patrolled the floor and tried in vain to keep the aisles passable. It wasn't easy in an undulating sea of cowboy hats, but I spotted Dusty among the group at the bar. We'd agreed to go in separately so nobody would get wise to our newfound partnership. We could be sure that the likes of Deke and Ray would be watching my every move, so we'd use that to our advantage.

Dusty knew how to jimmy a lock; he'd proved that in my office. He would go backstage when the time was right, slip up the back stairway located conveniently near the men's room, and let himself into Jarboe's place. Meanwhile I'd just wet my beak on the club floor, making sure I stayed plenty visible and keeping an eye out for any sign of trouble.

Our plan's main flaw, from my end, was that I had to avoid the backstage area. If Val was around, I'd have to talk to her out here—not quite the cozy and intimate setting I'd have preferred.

I didn't see Duke tonight. I got polite nods from three or four of the cowboys I'd seen at Gower Gulch, or on the set, but none of them approached or spoke to me. Deke and Ray spotted me right off. Deke made his way over to where I stood waiting to pounce on the first open table.

"Ed still ain't here," he said. His permanent grin irritated me. I was sorely tempted to wipe it off his face, using the floor to do it, but I tried not to give him the satisfaction of knowing it.

"I'm just meeting a guy here," I said. "He's maybe going to sell me a horse."

He looked me up and down and the grin widened. "What the hell would you do with a horse, city boy?"

"I'd ask you the same question, Deke, but I'm worried the answer might give me bad dreams."

It took a second, but the grin melted away. "You start any trouble in here, you're liable to need that fancy-ass bean shooter of yours."

I gave him my most innocent eyes, and he drifted. He and Ray and a couple other hayseed hoodlums held a confab near the backstage door, then fanned out to the four corners, the better to keep tabs on me. I snared my table just then. It was a small one, barely enough for me and my drink, but it was all mine.

Dusty took advantage of the spreading out of Deke's crew and went to the backstage door. Nobody paid any attention. Just another thirsty cowpoke with three beers in him, ready to make room for three more.

I'd been so busy swapping urbane chit-chat with Deke, I hadn't noticed the music. The current act was a guy in a white hat with a silver band, and a shirt embroidered all over with colorful sunsets and cactuses. He picked guitar like he might know what he was doing and belted out a couple of Jimmie

Rogers' tunes. Not much of a singer, but he could yodel all day long. The crowd ate it up.

When he finished, the little guy in the giant hat trotted out and announced the Cady Sisters. The house lights went down, and the girls came out in their spangled get-ups. I didn't recognize the song they played, but I caught myself humming it for days after.

When the lights came back up for their next tune, "Cowboy Moon," I caught Val's eye right away. She looked better than I'd expected, considering. Her stage smile was bright, and she looked in high spirits. Hard to say for sure—I knew performers had their tricks. When they'd finished their last song, I thought I saw just a hint of uneasiness in her eyes before she bowed and slid behind the curtain.

Five minutes later, the shrimp in the ten-gallon lid came up to my table. He looked thirty years older close up. He tipped his hat like a Kentucky colonel and wheezed, "Miss Cady asked me to give you this, sir." He laid a small, pale green envelope on the table and disappeared. Inside was a note on matching paper, written in a feminine but precise hand. It said *Nate, Sorry I can't sit with you tonight. Another time soon.—Val.* Looked like this evening was going to be all work and no play for this dull boy.

A smart guy would have taken the hint and dusted off. But smart guys had daytime jobs. Anyway, Dusty was still upstairs. The place had thinned out enough that I could get a spot at the bar. I went around to the back leg of the horseshoe. From there I could watch most of the floor without being obvious about it. Deke and his boys only gave me cursory glances as I moved. I guess they were getting bored with me too.

For the next forty minutes or so I nursed a beer and killed time by stacking my change. Small change on large, then large on small. Lefty and Earl were doing their shtick on the stage, but I was far enough away that all I could hear was the drunken laughter.

It was nearing midnight when Dusty came back through the backstage door. He stopped along the way to speak to a cowboy or two, then went straight outside. None of the house men paid any attention. I made my beer last another ten minutes then left my little coin ziggurat on the bar and walked out. Ray made a show of giving me a nod, just so I'd know he noticed.

+++

Two blocks down the street, Dusty pretended to be thumbing a ride. I pulled over and picked him up.

"How was the hunt?" I asked him as we drove back toward his rooming house. "I hope your night was more productive than mine."

"Well," he said, "I didn't find squat tying Jarboe to Del Maynard. But I came across a couple of interesting items. There's a .30-30 Winchester under the bed. Dollars to donuts it's the one put that hole in your fender."

"Okay, I like the sound of that. What else?"

He took a folded sheet of paper from his shirt pocket. He unfolded it and held it toward me on the flat of his hand. "Looky there," he said.

I squinted in the dim, intermittent streetlamp light. "Coffee grounds?"

"Sawdust."

"Sawdust?" I didn't connect it right away. "The stagecoach axle? Come on, there's no way to prove –"

"In his pants leg," Dusty said. He was wearin' black dungarees on the set the other day. One belt loop torn loose—that's why I recall. Had cuffs turned up high like all the boys wear 'em. The same britches are hanging over a chair in his room. When I moved it, this spilled out of the cuff."

It wasn't much, but it wasn't nothing.

Chapter Sixteen

I awoke to rapping at my front door. My table clock said it wasn't quite four a.m. As my fog lifted, I figured the brush salesman next door must have come home blotto and mistaken my house for his. He'd done it more than once. The pickle-puss nag he was married to, I was lucky it didn't happen every night. I threw on my robe and dropped my gun in the pocket, because you never knew. I shuffled to the front door, cursing the guy who invented brass knockers and his whole bloodline back to Adam.

I swung the door open, set to propel the brush man toward his own crib and his screeching harpy. Duke Morrison stood there in full cowboy regalia, minus the hat. For a second, I thought I'd come home blotto myself. He breezed in like it was midday and I'd invited him to tea. Which it wasn't, and I hadn't.

"Come on, Nate," he said in a bright and cheery voice. "Pin your diapers on. We're going on a little adventure."

"Duke, what the hell? It's Saturday. And do you know what time it is?"

"I wear a watch. Now get your ass cleaned up and dressed. We've just got time to make it."

"Make it? Make it where?"

"Iverson Ranch, out Chatsworth way. I've been thinking. If you're trying to get to the bottom of this *Stardust Trail* business, the cowboys—the stunt guys and henchies—could be a help. They know what's going on, if anybody does. If they don't, they can find out."

"Okay." He was making sense so far—as much as anybody makes at four in the morning.

"Problem is," he said, "like I told you, they're a tight group, not too talky with outsiders. And no offense, but you're not the world's most personable guy."

"The point being?"

"The point being, I'll introduce you around, good and proper. Once they see you're a good egg, they'll be glad to help."

"I've got things to do here, Duke."

"What do you have that won't keep?"

"I need to find Ed Jarboe—ask him a few things."

"All the more reason to come along. He's usually part of the crew that brings horses and tack."

That was a point. Anyway, I could see there was no arguing. "Fine, fine," I said. "Make yourself comfortable while I have a shower and shave."

"Skip the shave," he said. "And no coat and tie, either. We're going to a movie ranch, not a courthouse. Put on some blue jeans."

"I don't own any."

"Got a pair of chinos? Wear those. And a work shirt. Boots if you have 'em." He grinned. "We just might get you on a horse today."

"Like hell you will. I don't ride."

"You used to do all right."

"We were kids. I haven't been on a horse in twenty years, at least."

"Aw, it's like riding a bicycle," he said. "A big, sweaty, stinking bicycle. Where's your kitchen?" I pointed him to it. "You get ready," he said. "I'll make coffee."

Usually I make it to the office before I know if I'm going to have a good day or a bad day. I had this one pegged already. Suddenly, I missed my drunken neighbor.

By the time I'd showered and dressed myself up like the old geezers who play checkers in the park, Duke was setting coffee on the table, whistling a tune. God, how I hate people who are cheerful in the morning.

"We can grab a bite to eat on the way," Duke said. "Drink up—daylight's comin'."

+++

"Is this your John Ford picture we're going out on?" I asked Duke as he steered his coupe toward the Valley.

"No, we don't start shooting that until the fall. This one's for your pal, Herb Yates."

"Tell me about the other one. What's it called?"

"*Stagecoach.*"

"Catchy title."

"Laugh it up, wise ass. It's going to be a damned good picture—better than anything I've done yet."

"Well, I hope it works out for you, Duke. I mean that. Tell you what, I'll even go see this one—scout's honor."

"You haven't seen any of my films? Not one?"

"Funny you should ask. I went yesterday afternoon. One of those little movie houses downtown. I caught you on a double bill."

"Which two?"

"Let's see—one was called *Ride Him, Cowboy*. You were running around on a big white horse called Duke. Cute gimmick."

His face lit up. "I kind of liked that one. The picture, not the horse."

"The other one was called *Riders of Destiny*."

"Oh, shit." The pleasurable look faded. Even in the half-light I could see his ears turning cherry red.

"Gene Autry must be relieved you gave up the singing cowboy business."

"Tell you what. How about I drop you off here and you walk the rest? It's only thirty miles or so."

"Don't get your Irish up. I'm just ragging you. I actually thought you were pretty good once you put the guitar down."

He gave me a murderous look. "Thanks."

I decided I'd better leave off there. Thirty miles was a long hike.

"So what's this one you're shooting today?"

"This is a Mesquiteers picture."

"The same one you were working on at Republic the other day?"

"No, that one's in the can already. We shoot 'em in a hurry. Republic tries to put one out a month."

"Jeez, that's quick."

Duke laughed. "If you'd see 'em, you'd understand. The one we're doing today's called *Santa Fe Stampede*, though I don't recall that there's a stampede in the whole damn picture."

He went on to explain that the Three Mesquiteers films were a Republic staple—they'd made over a dozen before he acted in his first one. The three leads tended to rotate. This would be Duke's third, and he was contracted to do several more. He'd taken over the part of Stony Brooke from an actor named Bob Livingston. The films were lightweight, formula Westerns, but very popular.

The talk drifted to *Stardust Trail*. Duke was interested in the film, and of course he'd heard the rumors of sabotage. I knew he could keep it buttoned, so I told him about the whole Maynard/Shandy connection. I also told him about Ed Jarboe's shooting at me, and the sawdust. I didn't tell him about Dusty's past—that was Dusty's secret to tell. I didn't mention Val, and he didn't ask.

+++

We reached the Iverson Ranch just as the first hints of the sun were creeping over the hilltops. This place was as much like the Monogram Ranch as it was different. It had its own Western town with boardwalks and false-front buildings, plus scattered outbuildings of various descriptions. There were barns, cabins, adobes, a big, three-sided ranch house. The main difference was the terrain. Where Monogram's surroundings were a mixture of low, green hills and desert, here the brushy foothills were higher and interspersed with scattered formations of red rock that gave it a more rugged, primitive look.

A dozen or so cowboys and crew members were gathered around a bonfire. They hadn't lit the fire to keep themselves cozy, I soon learned, but to warm up the cameras so they would work properly.

Duke exchanged greetings and said simply, "This is Nate Ross." A few cowboys gave me curious looks from under their wide brims, but nobody asked. I was with Duke and that was enough.

I'd flatly refused to wear the cowboy hat Duke had offered. My fedora would do; a sun-burned neck was a small price to pay for not feeling foolish all day. He'd insisted I don a pair of hiking boots left over from my days of outdoor treks with my father. When I balked, he simply said, "Snakes." I wore the damn boots.

By this time the other cast and crew started arriving in small bunches, saying perfunctory hellos, and going off to make their individual preparations for the day's filming. It was interesting to watch Duke on the set. Although he was one of the film's stars, and treated everyone with friendliness, he tended to spend what down time there was socializing with the stuntmen and cowboy players rather than his fellow actors.

I got a warm greeting from Max Terhune, who insisted on telling anyone who'd listen about my rescue of Elmer. Via Max, I also got a friendly hello from Elmer himself. The little woolly-headed dummy had already given me the willies. Having him roll his eyes and speak to me made my neck hairs stand up and dance. Max introduced me to Ray Corrigan, the third Mesquiteer. He'd done more of the films than either of his cohorts. He was also a shrewd businessman, who'd built his own Western movie ranch just across the Ventura County line. The money he made renting that out to Republic and other studios was fast making him the richest of the Poverty Row crowd, next to Gene Autry. I'd never have guessed it; he struck me as a down-to-earth Joe and toted his weight like everyone else here.

Duke made sure I met all of the cowboy crew, starting with Yakima Canutt. He was a tall, leathery ex-rodeo champ, and Duke's number one pal on the set. He was running the stunt crew and served as Duke's double; they were about the same size and build. Duke admitted that most of what he knew about cowboying he had learned from "Yak," who was a genuine specimen.

Two other real-life cowboys on the crew were Dunk Carroll and Joe Lopez. Carroll was a little bulldog of a guy, sixty if he was a day. He'd ridden in Pawnee Bill's Wild West Show in his youth. Joe was a younger man, medium-sized and rail-thin, with a huge, black handlebar mustache. According to Canutt, Joe came from a line of horsemen that stretched back to Cortez, and his family had inhabited New Mexico since it was old Mexico.

George Sherman was the director on this shoot. He was a different kind of bird altogether than Perry Mills. Sherman was a stumpy little New Yorker who'd directed three times as many films as Perry had, or ever would, and had no grandiose notions that he was an artiste. He worked on films that were written quickly, shot quickly, and went in and out of theaters quickly. If they lacked the subtlety and artsy flourishes that graced the sort of stuff Mills made—or aspired to—they made up for it in one important respect. They sold tickets.

This was a much more relaxed set than *Stardust Trail*. Whether that was due to Sherman's easy-going style, the familiarity of the cast and crew, or the fact that this film wasn't trying—or expected to—compete with big-budget stuff from the majors, I couldn't say. But the difference stood out. The people making this picture were having fun.

I was annoyed when I found out Jarboe wasn't coming. Two of his buddies brought out the horses. But the trip wasn't completely wasted; I got a crash course in Western moviemaking and stunt work.

The cowboys accepted my presence pretty readily once Duke gave me the nod. He'd warned me not to ask any "detective" questions right off, but to give them a chance to warm up to me. So I spent most of my time with them listening to their yarns—they were all natural storytellers—and learning some of the finer points of film stunts, particularly horse work. Before today, I'd have thought that "Running W" was a ranch; I was surprised to learn it was a trip-wire gimmick to make a galloping horse fall on cue. It wasn't a "gag"—as the stunt men called the various tricks of their trade—that horse-loving cowboys were fond of. They preferred training horses to do the stunts required of them safely, and without the aid of mechanical doohickeys. Joe took special pride in Nero, an ink-black pony he'd culled from the Fat Jones stock to train as a "falling horse." He had taught Nero to fall from a stand-still, to simulate being shot. To prove the horse's smarts, he offered me a personal demonstration. I declined his offer to sit "on the hurricane deck," so Joe climbed aboard Nero himself.

"Now," he said when he'd settled into the saddle, "just watch what this old booger can do." He gave a sudden, sharp whistle and the horse's legs gave way. They folded under him, and his chest and belly thumped down into the dust. Joe gave a soft whistle, then expertly stepped clear as the pony rolled over on his side, gave a kick and a snort, and lay still.

"There you go, Nero. Thata-boy," Joe said. He slapped Nero lightly on the rump and the horse sprang upright and took the apple he offered. The other cowboys who'd gathered to watch clapped and hooted their approval.

I didn't get to spend the whole day hobnobbing with cowboys or admiring horse tricks. The crew had come out here, after all, to shoot a movie. They soon got down to it, and it was a more orderly process than what I'd seen thus far. Sherman and his company worked together like parts of a well-timed engine. There was little of the grousing I'd seen with Perry Mills at the tiller, and what little there was seemed to be in jest. The cowboys were a rambunctious lot, but when the cameras were rolling they were all business.

Duke, somewhat to my surprise, was an excellent horseman, and did quite a few of his own stunts. He'd always been a pretty good athlete, so I guess it was a point of pride with him. It seemed to be one of the reasons the cowboys accepted him as one of their own.

The trappings of this shoot highlighted the budget gulf between "B" quickies like this and a film like *Stardust Trail*. Smaller crew, fewer lights and cameras, bag lunches instead of a full spread, everything here was done on the cheap, and on the fly. Multiple takes were out. What was it that Okel had said? A take-a-minute, and a minute-a-take. It was no exaggeration.

By the time the day ended—and it didn't until well after dark—I'd have bet Sherman had shot enough film to make half a dozen Mesquiteer pictures.

+++

I was pretty well worn out by the time we headed back to the city. I'd thought my job called for long, irregular hours, but I couldn't see how these movie people kept up this kind of pace as a regular thing. No surprise that so many of them were snowbirds.

I slept while Duke drove. I was having a dream—something about being chased by a herd of horses—when I felt the car stop. I woke up and forgot most of the dream instantly.

"Here we are," Duke said. We were parked in front of my bungalow. I rubbed my face and took off my hat, because it felt funny. The side had gotten bunged in from the door post. I did my best to knock the dent out, but it was too dark to judge the result.

"Thanks for the field trip, Duke."

"The boys ought to be a little more help now," he said. "You need a hand, I'm bettin' they'll do whatever they can."

"Good. Thanks," I said. I opened the door. "Want a drink before you go?"

"No thanks, I gotta get home."

I was glad he turned me down. I was anxious to hit the rack and planned on getting up in time for a very late Sunday lunch. I said good night and shuffled up the walk, carrying my mangled hat.

Chapter Seventeen

Since Sunday was supposed to be a day of rest, I made a strong effort not to think about Ed Jarboe, or David Prince, or Del Maynard, or *Stardust Trail*. The result, of course, was that I thought about nothing else. No rest for the wicked.

Still, I woke up Monday morning in a better than usual mood. It lasted almost an hour. As I put the finishing touches on my necktie—full Windsor today, because I felt particularly dashing—the phone rang. I scooped it up with a flourish.

"Hey, Ross—Frank Bernal here. Listen, Queenan wants to see you down here tout suite. Can do?"

"I suppose. What about?"

"I wouldn't want to spoil any surprises. Half an hour?"

I hadn't eaten yet. I said I'd be there in an hour and hung up. I doubted they'd made an arrest in the Prince murder yet. Even if they had, they could have given me that over the wire.

+++

I got to Homicide about half past nine. Queenan was parked behind his desk. Bernal half-sat, half-leaned against a low bookcase along the side wall. In the corner stood a massive plainclothes cop—six-seven, at least, with shoulders like the fenders on a dump truck. The guy made Queenan look like a circus midget. He puffed on a cigar Lou Gehrig could have used for batting practice. It smelled like a burning sock.

Bernal greeted me and shook my hand, then returned to his bookcase. His cohorts stayed put. Queenan turned to the big cop with a smirk. "This guy and Frankie are real pals, Pat. My partner don't care who he's cozy with."

"And a good morning to you, Lieutenant," I said. Nobody offered me a seat, so I helped myself. I left my hat on; I was hoping for a short visit. Queenan jerked his chin at Paul Bunyan. "This is Sergeant Downs, with the sheriffs. He's working that wagon crash on the movie ranch."

Downs blew smoke at me in acknowledgement. In contrast to his size, he had a weak, almost nonexistent chin, and watery pale blue eyes that made him look like he was perpetually on the brink of tears. He regarded me with the same disdainful expression I got from all cops, especially members of his particular agency. I'd grown used to it.

"So, Lieutenant," I said. "Is this a business call, or…" I looked at the big guy "Wait. You're a cop, and your name is Pat Downs?"

"A scream, ain't it?" Downs said. His voice was high-pitched for a man his size, but it fit the weepy mug.

Queenan broke in. "Y'know, back when I worked uniforms at Central, we ran a beat car, guys' names were Smith and Wesson. Now if we're all done with hilarious handles, how about we talk a little homicide?"

"Fine with me. Who are we killing?"

He ignored me. "Let's talk about David Prince."

"I thought he was already dead."

Queenan slapped his thigh in mock amusement and said to Downs, "You can see why we're so fond of this guy. Who needs a radio when you can catch the Nate Ross show live?"

"Every day and twice on Sunday." I noticed Queenan getting a little pink above his collar, and I knew I could push him only so far. "Okay," I said. "Show's over for now. But what can I tell you about David Prince that you don't already know?"

"Well, see, you and your cowboy pal ain't much," he said, "but you're all the witnesses we got so far. You got any new dope on your end?"

"You told me to keep my beak out of it, remember?"

"Yeah, I do. But I know you peepers can't help nosing around. Just like a junkie's gotta have his needle, or else he gets the jimjams."

I wasn't ready to tell him about the photo, or about Dusty Vanner's dusty old case. I wasn't sure yet they were connected to Prince's murder, anyway. I ran down what I had on the *Stardust Trail* sabotage, most of which Downs probably already knew.

Queenan listened with genuine interest. "So you're thinkin' that's why someone bumped Prince? To put the kibosh on this movie?"

I didn't really think that, but it was fine with me if he did. I shrugged. "So far it's as good an explanation as any."

"Which would make our cases related," Queenan said, waggling a thumb at Downs. "I dunno, rings a little queer to me. What do you boys think?"

He looked from Downs to Bernal. Downs just screwed up his face and shrugged his massive shoulders.

Bernal fiddled with an unlit cigarette. "What's the motive?" he asked. "What's anyone gain from trying to scotch the film?" All eyes in the room swiveled my way.

"Don't look at me," I said. "If I knew that, I'd be on the phone to the Herald. You could read all about it in an Aggie Underwood exclusive, and I'd be moving to an office on Wilshire."

Queenan looked skeptical. Bernal studied his cigarette. Downs just stood there and tried not to cry.

"Yeah," Queenan said, giving me the fisheye. "You just be sure you keep us informed. A fancy office won't do you no good if you got no license."

Downs yawned, and said he had another appointment to keep. Queenan assured him they'd take down my full statement and send him a copy. The big cop just managed to clear the doorway on his way out. I started to follow in his shadow, but Queenan checked me. "Rest the dogs, pal. We ain't quite through here."

"Can't I give you a statement later?" I asked. I was anxious to start shaking the trees for Ed Jarboe.

"Now," Queenan said. "Anyway, we got more than that to discuss. Plant it." I sat back down.

Queenan started twisting a paper clip into painful contortions as he glared at me from under his shaggy brows. Finally, he spoke. "You play peek-a-boo with the police in this town, smart boy, your license is the least of your worries."

"Sorry, I don't follow."

"The truth, the whole truth, and nothing but the truth. Sound familiar?"

"It's an ad slogan for soap flakes, isn't it?"

"Can it. I'm not in a mood for any more of your comedy. Seems you sort of forgot that middle part."

"Did I?"

"You and me had a conversation not long ago. About a guy took a shot at you." He continued to torture the paper clip. "Ring a bell? Or do you get shot at so much it don't make an impression?" He didn't wait for an answer. It was probably just as well. "You was there, Frankie," he went on. "You remember."

Bernal nodded without looking up.

"Thing is," Queenan said, "you forgot to mention you knew who did it. Party named Ed Jarboe."

"Where did you hear that?"

"City of the Angels, pal. A little cherub told me." He didn't look like a guy who knew many angels. "Here's what I don't get. You got no problem burning coppers. Why cover for some shitkicker punk who took a shot at you?"

"I wasn't covering for anybody," I said. "I didn't find out it was Jarboe until later. And even then, I didn't have any hard evidence to back it. I still don't."

"Evidence is our business. You ain't a public badge anymore. Private citizens got a duty to cooperate with the police. It's what makes our fine system work."

"Last time I looked, it wasn't working any too well."

"You stonewall a murder investigation, pal, you're gonna find out how well it works. And how fast."

"So you're thinking Jarboe killed David Prince. Is that it?"

"I'm thinkin' this," he said. "You stumble on a guy who's been murdered, and another guy who's layin' in the weeds out there tries to clip you, I wanna have words with that other guy. That strike you as unreasonable?"

"No. But I don't think him shooting at me had anything to do with Prince."

"You got a better reason?"

I took a deep breath. I felt very tired all of a sudden. My head hurt. I told him about Val and Jarboe at the Hackamore.

He gave me a stony look. "You didn't mention no fight with this guy when we was at Prince's."

"I didn't have a reason to connect it. Like I said, I didn't know he was the shooter then."

"Shit," he said. "Well that sends our murder case right down the crapper. We could pull the clown in for sniping at you, maybe even book him for suspicion on Prince. But we'd never get the D.A. to file murder. Paper-thin, pal."

"Why not bring him in and sweat him anyway?"

"What for? Sounds like you don't think he shot Prince."

"No, but he didn't follow me out there to take a whack at me, either. Not on a horse. Anyway, he couldn't have known I'd be there. Which means he was already there."

He could see I had a point. It annoyed him. "And he was there doing what?"

I grinned. "You boys are the public badges. That's the first question you should ask him."

Queenan came out of his chair. "Look, Ross," he said. "Normally I admire a guy with cojones." He flung the mangled paper clip aside, put his palms flat on the desktop, and shoved his big face at me. "But I don't like you."

"Cojones," Bernal said, in beautifully accented Spanish. I'd almost forgotten he was there.

Queenan looked at him, irritated. "What'd I just say?"

"You said 'ca-ho-neeze'. Makes it sound like an Irish pub. The word is cojones."

Queenan went brick red from his necktie to the roots of his hair. "Excuse me to hell and back. I forget you're Mex, or I might, if you kept your mouth shut. I'm going out for a piss and a sandwich. When I get back, I want your boyfriend's statement on my desk, from Noah's flood to date. Can you manage that, Don Francisco?" He ripped his hat from the rack and jammed it on his head.

My Spanish is only so-so, but I understood the few words Bernal muttered as Queenan stomped to the door. They weren't nice words.

With a parting "Blah," Queenan walked out. Bernal grinned to himself and lit the cigarette at last. He dropped into Queenan's vacant seat.

"He doesn't speak Spanish, I take it." I lit my own cigarette.

"You've heard him," Bernal said. "He barely gets by in English. Don't sweat that stuff about your license. That's just gas. If he doesn't chew somebody's ass every day or two, he gets the shakes." He fished a tablet from the desk drawer and uncapped a pen. "You talk, I'll write, okay? You can look it over when I'm done."

I gave him the story on Jarboe, from our clash at the Hackamore to my talk with Waldrop at the stables. I left out our search of Jarboe's rooms and the whole Del Maynard angle. Likewise with *Stardust Trail*; I told him what'd I'd seen of the crash, and what I'd been told about the earlier incidents, but no more than that.

Jarboe was the link, and he'd faded into the wallpaper. Maybe L.A.P.D. could run him to ground, but I was still hoping to find him first. I doubted he'd talk to me, but once the cops had their hooks on him, he wasn't likely to do much talking. Not to me, anyway.

Chapter Eighteen

When I got back to the office, I called the pay phone at the Columbia Drug Store. Dusty had no telephone at his place, so it was my only way of reaching him. After a ten-minute wait, during which half a dozen voices came and went on the line, somebody managed to locate Dusty, and I heard his "Yep," in my ear. I was sure the voice was his because it was the first that didn't ask "Is this about a job?"

I told him about my meeting with the cops. He was no happier to hear they were onto Jarboe than I was. He didn't want to risk the ire of his fellow cowboys by tying up the phone, so he agreed to come right over to my office and talk.

The cars must have been running slow today. Half an hour went by and no Dusty. I was getting pretty hungry, so I locked up the place, tacked a note next to the door that read, *Meet me in the diner*, and went down to Gus's place.

+++

I was sitting in a corner booth, halfway through a corned beef on rye, when Dusty showed up.

Benjy stiffened when Dusty came in. He moved down near the cash register and nonchalantly rested his right hand near the .38 he kept on the shelf below the counter. He gave me a sideways look and I waved him off. He had to be curious why the guy he'd seen sneaking out of my building a couple of days ago was now sharing my table. But Benjy was a bright kid and used to seeing me in strange company. If I wasn't worried, neither was he. He came over and took Dusty's order without turning a hair.

"Sorry it took me a bit," Dusty said when Benjy had gone. "A call came in just as I was fixin' to go. Got some good news."

I never get tired of good news. I said I was all ears.

"The *Stardust Trail* crew's on the way up to Vasquez Rocks," he said. "Gonna haul in the gear and the stock this evening and make camp, so they can start shooting at sunup."

I didn't see the good news in that and said so. Dusty said he'd overheard a chance remark and confirmed it with a call to a friend at Republic. Jarboe was scheduled to be on the shoot. He was due to come up with the horses and wagons tonight, and was on the cast list for tomorrow. Mills was shooting a posse scene and needed top riders for the tricky terrain.

"When's he supposed to arrive?" I asked.

"They'll be headin' up any time now. They're gonna want to get up there, off-load everything, and get the horses corralled and settled before dark."

"We should get a move on, then. If we leave now, we might even be waiting by the time he gets there."

"I've been thinkin' on that," Dusty said. "That's a lonely spot, nothin' much around for miles. No telephones. Yates ain't gonna pay his studio cops extra time to go all the way up there and babysit. Be a perfect opportunity for somebody with mischief in mind. Wouldn't it be better if we could catch ol' Ed in the act?"

I had to agree with him. Our sawdust evidence wasn't exactly legit. Queenan would bust my chops if he knew about our search, and even if they got a warrant for Jarboe's place there was no guarantee it hadn't been cleaned up by now. If we could catch Jarboe dirty, Downs could arrest him for the stagecoach death—manslaughter, at the least—and Queenan and Bernal could squeeze him about Prince. Even better, I'd get first crack at him before they could make it up there to take custody.

Vasquez Rocks was in the desert fifty miles or so north of the city. It was off Highway 6, about midway to Mojave. The name came from a Mexican bandit from the wild old days who'd used it more than once to elude the posses that rode up from L.A. looking to burn powder and spill blood. He'd used it for good reason. Flat, scrubby desert surrounded hundreds of acres of gigantic, craggy rock formations jutting helter-skelter out of the earth. The jagged peaks and hogback ridges made for treacherous going on horseback, and provided countless crannies and crevices where an outlaw might lie concealed and wait in ambush.

Still, I was a long way from thrilled with the plan Dusty pitched. He knew Vasquez Rocks, and thought if we arrived before most of the crew, we could find a spot of concealment overlooking the company's campsite. Then we'd set up our own camp and make like old Tiburcio Vasquez himself. If Jarboe made another attempt, we'd be in an ideal spot to ride down on him—so to speak—and make the pinch.

It was a dandy scheme, except for a couple of points. Camping was never my idea of a good time, even as a kid. My old man had taken me several times, and tried his best to convince me it was a healthy and enjoyable experience. All I'd ever come away with was the dead certainty I wasn't cut out for life as a hobo. A soft bed, a door that locked, and a toilet that flushed for this boy.

Likewise, I'd always hated stakeout work. It involved long, monotonous hours of watching nothing happen, and nine times out of ten you got no payoff. The rigged slots in the casino ships off Santa Monica gave better odds. Plus, no matter how well rested and alert you were to start with, after a few hours the quiet and inactivity went to work on you. Your eyelids grew lead weights. Your brain drifted in its own fog. You felt like you hadn't slept in a week. Your senses started playing jokes on you out of boredom. You'd see movement where there was none, hear sounds where there was only silence. This was the danger zone, because if and when something did happen, you'd waste a second or two deciding whether it was real. And a second could make all the difference.

I reluctantly consented to go along with Dusty's idea. Maybe there were worse things than spending a night in the barren desert, freezing my ass off and sleeping among snakes and scorpions, all for what might turn out to be one giant boondoggle. And there were. Only after I'd agreed did Dusty mention, making no effort to hide his amusement, that Mills planned to shoot in the rocks for two days, maybe three.

+++

I was in a pretty foul temper on the drive up. We didn't talk much. Dusty napped most of the way, which didn't improve my mood. I saw few signs of life after we got clear of the city, other than the occasional roadrunner. Now and then one would fall in beside us along the highway and pace us for a hundred yards or so before veering off to scour the desert for lizards or whatever the hell else roadrunners eat.

Early on, we'd spotted one of the trucks carrying cameras and other gear out to the shoot. I made sure to stay well back from it. It was still a mile or so ahead of us when I came in sight of the distinctive triangular peaks rising like icebergs from the sea of dirt and scrub. As if an alarm clock had rung, Dusty opened his eyes.

I deliberately fell further back from the truck. About five miles on, the truck turned off the road and we saw the plume of dust following it as it made its way out toward the towering rocks. When we passed the spot where it had left the road I looked out toward the crags. I could see several trucks and horse trailers sitting in a flat clearing near their base and could just make out the movement of a dozen or so people scurrying around them.

Dusty directed me up the highway several more miles until we encountered a small billboard with a little side road just beyond it. The brutal desert sun had dried and cracked the billboard's lattice until most of it had crumbled. The sign on it sported a large arrow in what had once been bright red paint. In faded, barely discernible letters above it, was the word "Gas."

"Here we are," Dusty said, pointing to a tumble-down little gas station next to a rusty corrugated metal garage a quarter mile up the side road. I'd have guessed we were here without his help; as I looked around us in all directions, they were the only visible signs of man's presence on earth.

The station was a squatty, flat-roofed building of bleached stucco, faced with sun-purpled glass blocks. As I drove up closer, I thought we'd flubbed our clandestine entrance. A battered pickup truck with a two-horse trailer hitched behind it sat parked in the shade, such as it was, of the garage. Two cowboys lounged against it. I recognized one as Reese, the garrulous little cowpoke I'd met at Gower Gulch. The other was a beefy, pugnacious-looking type with a face like a boxing glove. I was sure I'd seen him working on the set at Monogram Ranch the day of the stagecoach wreck.

Before I could suggest to Dusty that we might need to fall back and regroup, he bailed out while the car was still rolling, strode over, and exchanged friendly greetings with the pair. By now they'd both had a good look at me, and Reese, at least, was sure to recognize me. So I pulled up near the pump and set the brake. A gangly, bare-headed kid in oily overalls trotted out from the office. I gave him two bucks and asked him to top off the tank. He nodded without a word and went to it. I walked over to join Dusty.

"You boys made dang good time," Reese said. "We didn't figure to see you for another hour at least."

Dusty cocked his head in my direction. "California driver," he said with a wink. "Nate Ross, this here is Billy Reese and Mac McLemore."

"We've already met," Reese said, pumping my hand with vigor. "Howdy, Nate."

Mac pulled off a tattered work glove and offered a massive bear paw. My knuckles crackled in his grip like firecrackers in a Chinatown parade.

Dusty explained that Mac and Billy were his close friends. He'd thought we might need a little help, so he'd sent them on ahead. I wasn't pleased that he hadn't clued me in before. But standing out here in the late afternoon sun with no shade but the hats on our heads, I didn't see any point in griping about it now.

Dusty outlined the plan he had in mind. From here, he and I would make our way up through the rocks to a spot he knew that would give us a good overlook of the movie crew's camp. Once I was situated, he'd come back here. He and Mac would drive the truck to the campsite, just two more crew members rolling in for the shoot. Reese would drive my car down there. One green Ford coupe looked about like any other, and with the coat of dust mine now wore—and a glob of mud to patch the telltale bullet hole—it wasn't likely to arouse any suspicion.

I studied the looming rocks in the distance. "How do we drive in there?" I asked Dusty.

"Hell, we can't from here."

Thanks to my outing with Duke the other day I'd seen the wisdom of dressing for the conditions, lace-up boots and all. Still, I didn't relish the idea of a six-mile hike, let alone a climb up those jagged slopes. I said so to Dusty.

"I planned for that," he said. "Bring 'em out, boys." Reese swung open the trailer's gates and he and Mac started leading out two huge, scruffy, iron-gray beasts.

"Horses?" I said. Mack and Reese grinned at each other. "You don't expect me—"

"Mules," Dusty said. "Better for pickin' our way through them rocks."

"Dusty," I said, "can we have a pow-wow over by the car?" With as much civility as I could muster, I said to his friends, "Excuse us a minute." The monkey grins on their faces weren't improving my disposition.

"All right," Dusty said. To his pals he said, "Saddle us up, would you, boys?"

We walked back over to the car. The kid had already filled the tank and checked under the hood and was now wiping the windshield with a rag that had more bugs and grime on it than the windshield did. He finished, popped the rag in the air, and stuffed it into his back pocket. He tried to hand me a quarter change.

"Keep it, chief," I said. "By yourself a Panama hat." He pocketed the coin with another nod, but still no language, and disappeared back behind the glass blocks.

"Look, Dusty," I said. "I agreed to this little hunt because I thought you had a point, and you know the turf, and because you have a stake in this business. I'm no stranger to hardship. My racket's full of it. I walk out the door every day expecting to be cheated, lied to, lied about, spit on, stolen from, shot at, sapped, and arrested. I seldom go home disappointed. I'm willing to put up with quite a bit to see a job through. I drove you out here to the middle of God's wasteland. I didn't blow my stack that you brought your two pals into this without consulting me. I'll spend a night or two squatting up in those rocks like a horned toad. I'll eat beans out of a can and sleep on the ground like a skid-row bum. That I'll do. What I won't do is go riding horseback across the desert like a—"

"They're mules," Dusty said again. Every muscle in my body tensed up at once. My hat felt three sizes too small. "If you have a better idea, I'll gladly hear it."

"I have one idea. But they still hang you for it in this state."

"So, we're agreed then?" he said with a maddening grin that made me wonder whether the noose was really such a bad way to go.

I started to speak, but my uppers and lowers had clamped themselves together like a bear trap. "I'll say this one more time, plain as I can," I managed to get out from between my locked jaws. "If you think there's the smallest chance, in the darkest, remotest corner of hell, that I'm climbing aboard one of those stinking, slobbering, shitting, four-legged flea circuses of yours, you haven't known me long enough."

+++

If you're not riding the lead mule, the scenery doesn't change much. Dusty had said we'd make better time if we rode single file, so that my mule only had to follow where his went. As if the view and the ride itself weren't monotonous enough, Dusty insisted on whistling the same random, discordant series of notes over and over again. I stood it for as long as I could.

"Can you whistle something else?" I called ahead to him. "Maybe something with a tune? Better yet, stop whistling at all."

"Just trying to pass the time," he answered over his shoulder.

"Time will pass whether you're making that damned racket or not."

"It's mostly for the mules. You got to keep a mule's mind occupied so's they don't get bored. Mules are a whole lot smarter than horses."

"Isn't that like saying a brick is smarter than a pipe wrench?"

I never should have asked. The inharmonious whistling gave way to a lengthy and detailed discourse on the merits of mules versus horses. It didn't make the time go any faster, and it did nothing at all to better my mood.

I'd agreed to this nonsense in the end because spending a day or two reeking of equine sweat and being gnawed half to death by horseflies was slightly less repugnant than the idea of turning around and driving another fifty miles home, and missing a chance to put the arm on Ed Jarboe. It was a close race, but Dusty and his filthy mules had won.

Chapter Nineteen

I was miserable before we'd made it half a mile. I hadn't sat in a saddle in two decades and even then, though I'd been an adequate rider, I'd never been fond of it. Anyway, a horse's sleek physique, with its tapering rib cage and gently curved-in back at least seemed designed for carrying a rider. Dusty's mules, on the other hand, were like something put together on a government grant. Whatever they were built for, riding wasn't it.

The thin twill of my khaki pants wasn't adapted to riding, and my round-toed boots wouldn't quite fit in the stirrups. With the bouncing and jostling on the trail, and my legs forked over the mule's massive, beer keg middle, I felt like the wishbone at Thanksgiving dinner. The saddle tended to slide back and forth, and the blanket roll the boys had fixed for me—they'd had a good laugh over my leather suitcase—kept smacking me in the base of my spine.

The trail out to the rocks was mostly flat and level. Small blessing. My ass was chapped in more ways than one, so I wasn't feeling inclined to let Dusty off the hook any time soon.

"You could have told me about the mules," I groused. "Maybe I'd have come a little better prepared."

"Would you have come at all if I'd told you?"

"Hell, no."

"Then you didn't leave me no choice, did you?"

The journey out to the huge rock formations took well over an hour—the longest week of my life. I spent the remainder of the ride turning over various revenge scenarios in my mind. Maybe I'd take Dusty out for a huge breakfast, liquor him up a little, then invite him out for a fishing trip on one of the little charter boats off Malibu. It'd give me pure joy to watch him run along the deck, face green as a five-spot, and lean out over the rail to chum the waters. With any luck, he'd fall overboard.

I was just picturing myself reluctantly fishing Dusty out of the bay when we rode into shadow. The angular rocks loomed high above us, like the jagged molars of some giant prehistoric canine.

Dusty halted. "Let's get down and take a stretch," he said. "It's a little rougher going from here."

Rougher going. I mentally chucked him back into the water as I climbed down and flexed my aching nether muscles. I dug a hip flask out of the pocket of a leather car coat tied to my bedroll.

"That ain't the healthiest thing just now," Dusty said. "You'd do better with water."

"Trust me, I'm drinking it for your health, not mine." Some petty part of me was glad he disapproved. It meant I wouldn't have to share. I took a quick nip and stowed the flask away again.

Five minutes later, we were winding our way through a narrow canyon lined with huge clumps of underbrush and sporadic clusters of trees, with striated terraces of rock on both sides. We snaked among the trees and brush, picking our way over ground that alternated between level, sandy areas and irregular slopes of solid rock. Soon there was nothing around us but high, craggy walls, ledges, and disorderly piles of reddish sandstone. I could see why old Vasquez and his gang had forted up here. Once we were full inside, I could only see the sky by looking straight up, and completely lost any sense of direction. I had to admit that now I was glad to have Dusty along. This was his sort of manhunt. He was as at home up here as I was navigating the asphalt trails and concrete canyons of Los Angeles.

The mules proved to be as sure-footed as Dusty claimed—a bonus when our path narrowed through loose rock or took us over little goat trails high against the rocky walls.

Overall, the trip through the rocks was less perilous than I'd pictured. Still, it was a relief to both my nerves and my keister when Dusty held a hand up, signaling a halt. We were in a flat clearing at the bottom of a sort of basin, still completely walled in. The rocky ridge ahead of us sloped gently up, rising maybe thirty feet from its base to its snaggle-toothed top.

Dusty shaded his eyes and looked up the slope. "The crew's just beyond this ridge. We'll make our camp down here. We can climb right up there easy enough," he said, waggling his finger in the air to follow the natural path up the rock face. "It's a shallow enough grade we can dang near walk upright. Keep our heads low and we can look right over, see everything that's goin' on in the camp."

"How do we get down there if something does happen?"

Dusty smiled. "Easy." He gestured toward a deep defile between sheer rock faces about fifty feet to our right. It was wide enough to pass through on a mule, with maybe four or five feet to spare. From here it looked like a dead end. "That little pass winds through," he said, moving his hand in a serpentine motion. "You go thirty yards or so, then you come out the other side. Hook around to your left from there, and the campsite's in sight, maybe another forty, fifty yards out."

"That close? We'll need to be pretty quiet in here."

"We got a hundred feet of solid rock between us and them. We'll want to be careful, sure, but as long as we don't blow no bugles or fire off no guns in here, we should be all right."

I had my doubts but figured Dusty must have done this sort of thing before. I was inclined to trust him on it.

"Let's get these mules picketed for now," he said. "Then we can make camp."

I had no idea how to picket a mule, nor even what that meant. Dusty took out two long spikes he had strapped to his saddle. Using a rock, and a leather glove to muffle the noise, he drove them into the ground about ten feet apart. He showed me how to tie a lead rope from the mule to the stake to keep the animal from wandering off. He took out a sack of grain and unslung a canteen. Using his hat as a dish, he fed and watered both mules.

"One more reason a mule's smarter than a horse," he said. "Mules won't eat or drink more than they need. A damn horse will drink till he about pops if you let him." The feeding, and the lesson, concluded, Dusty shook the excess water and mule slobber out of his hat and clapped it back on his head. I was glad he hadn't asked me to use my hat that way. I'd have had one hungry and thirsty animal on my hands.

With the mules seen to, we unloaded our gear and started setting up for ourselves. As we worked, Dusty laid out his plans for the remaining festivities. While I stayed here, he would take the mules and ride back to Mac and Reese, then they'd go on into the movie camp as planned. Only the cowboys and a handful of crew members would be spending the night out here. Most of the cast and crew—what Dusty called the civilians, would drive to Palmdale and stay in a motel. The cameras and other equipment would stay on site, along with the horses and wagons being trucked in for the shoot.

The few crew members remaining here would sleep in tents. The cowboys would set up off to one end by themselves and sleep under the stars. Apparently, this was their idea of a lark, almost a fringe benefit. Once it was dark, Dusty would sneak away and join me here. We'd take turns from then on; one watching the camp from atop the ridge, one sleeping down here.

It seemed pretty simple. Cold and monotonous, but simple. One bright spot—Dusty said we could risk a small fire to keep warm once it was dark.

"Sounds peachy," I told him. "One question: What if, you know, nature calls?"

"You're in the wide outdoors," he said. "So long as it ain't nowhere near my bedroll, take a leak anywhere you please."

"Sure. But suppose it's more than that?"

"I come prepared." He reached into his saddle bags and tossed me a copy of yesterday's *Herald*. He pointed back the way we'd ridden in. "Kick a hole in the dirt. Fifty feet, minimum."

I stashed the newspaper away, hoping it wouldn't come to that. If it did, I'd have preferred a copy of the *Times*. But I was in no position to be choosy.

We laid out our bedrolls in a concave area along the rock base, where we'd be more or less shielded from wind and weather. I doubted we'd see any rain. Looking at the dry desolation surrounding us, I doubted it had ever rained.

Dusty had a long coil of horsehair rope hanging from his saddle. I asked if

I could use it.

"What for?"

"To lay out around my bedroll," I said. "In case of rattlesnakes."

"You know that's an old wives' tale, don't you?"

"Maybe the snakes don't know it."

"God almighty." He fetched the rope and tossed it over. He took a Winchester carbine from a scabbard on his saddle and propped it against the wall. "I'll leave you this here, too. Know how to use a lever gun?"

"I'm not a complete tyro."

"Well, that's good to know, Nate."

"Anyway, I have a pistol."

"You might need something more. Coyotes don't come out much till after dark, and you can scare them off easy enough. But there's a few bears roamin' these parts. And the occasional big cat."

Exactly why I hated leaving the city. The wildlife there walked on two legs. I knew how to handle them.

Dusty pulled up the picket pins, tied my mule's rope to his saddle, and mounted up. "I'll see you after sundown," he said. "Try not to kill anything until I get back."

Before I could think of a snappy comeback, he was riding off. I had to settle for kicking a few sharp rocks underneath his bedroll.

+++

I soon got bored sitting around, with nothing to do but wait. I started up the rocky slope to see just how good a view we'd have from the top. Dusty had advised against going up there while the sun was still up, to avoid any risk of being spotted. But Dusty wasn't here now.

The going was easier than it looked, but I was thankful now that I'd worn the boots. I zig-zagged my way up without much more difficulty than climbing a couple flights of stairs, if you climbed them on hands and knees. When I got to the summit I stretched out on my belly in a shallow crevice, pulled off my hat, and peeked out through the "v" of a little sawtooth area.

As much as I hated to admit it, Dusty was right. Our ridge projected out over the flatland below, so that I had a literal birds-eye view of the camp.

The little patch of nowhere was bustling with activity. Thirty or so cowboys and other crew members were busy offloading trucks and trailers, setting up a row of tents and canvas awnings, and transferring lights, cameras and other movie-making paraphernalia into several horse-drawn freight wagons. Those would serve to haul the gear into the filming location tomorrow. Mills wouldn't have a motor vehicle near his set; he wasn't going to risk any tire tracks showing up in the footage.

Mills himself was down there, decked out like Captain Spaulding in a pith helmet and jodhpurs. He flitted around the camp, flailing his arms and shouting orders at anyone who'd listen. Which, from what I could see, was nobody. The crew was quickly and expertly putting together a working camp in spite of all Perry's determined efforts to help it along.

At one end of the camp the cowboys had erected a rough timber corral. They were bringing in horses and other livestock from several large trailers. The freight wagons were lined up alongside the corral, ready to be hitched up and rolled out at first light.

I was pleased to see Ed Jarboe among the cowboys. Maybe our little adventure would pay off. I also spotted my old pals Ray and Deke; I wondered who was keeping the lid on the Hackamore tonight. Those three, and a couple of others who looked to be about their class, worked together as a group. The rest of the cowboys seemed to work around them, rather than with them.

On the opposite side of the corral, the cowboys had staked out their own rude camp. It was nothing more than bedrolls laid out here and there—probably wherever the ground was least rocky—and a large canvas fly set up for shade.

At the end of the row of crew tents, the civilians had set up a big marquee tent. Perry Mills was supervising the furnishing of the tent with a small truckload of rugs, tables, chairs, a cot and washstand, and sundry other trappings of civilized life. Every king needs his castle, I guess.

After watching for half an hour or so, I climbed back down. I ate a quick meal—I'd had Benjy make up a couple of sandwiches—then I reread Dusty's copy of the *Herald* just to kill time. Even though I knew he'd mostly been ragging me—or I hoped he had—I kept careful watch on the rocks above me to make sure I didn't get jumped by something with teeth and claws.

+++

A couple hours later I was going stir crazy, so I crawled back up to the top of the ridge for another look. I took along a pair of field glasses I'd packed with me. The sun was low enough now that I wasn't worried about reflection giving me away.

Dusty and his two friends had arrived in the camp. I could see my car parked among the other vehicles at the far end of the campsite, closest to the road. Things looked more or less relaxed now that everything was in order and ready to begin the real work in the morning.

The group had thinned out. Some of them must have gone on to Palmdale already. Perry Mills was still around. I saw him come out of the big tent briefly, then go back inside. I didn't know if he'd be staying here. Maybe the cot was just something to rest on while he did whatever directors do when they're not directing.

One of rigs Mills had brought along was a genuine old West chuckwagon. The cowboys were already putting it to good use. Dusty and his boys, and several others, were grouped near the wagon and sat around a big cook fire they'd started going next to it. A couple were managing several large Dutch ovens that either hung over the fire or sat among the coals with more coals piled on top. I couldn't see what they were cooking, but once in a while the evening breeze shifted my way and the aroma made me wish I'd fed Benjy's sandwiches to the mules.

Jarboe and his little clique lounged in a far corner of the cowboy camp, passing a bottle. In work or leisure, the two cowboy groups didn't appear to want much to do with each other.

As the sun was lowering over the distant hills, one of the men at the chuckwagon gave a whistle and a shout. Cowboys and civilians alike lined up behind the wagon to be served up what looked like beans and cornbread, and hot coffee. A crew member carried a plate and cup into the marquee tent. Maybe Perry thought getting that close to the campfire would take the natural curl out of his hair. Jarboe and his party came over, got their food, and retreated to their own quarter. Dusty was one of the last in line. I hoped he would give some thought to his poor, hungry pal up in the rocks. It was getting pretty windy and chilly up on top, so I climbed back down to the warmer low ground.

+++

Night in the desert falls all at once. Where I was sitting, with tall rocks all around me, it fell even faster. I put on my car coat against the chill in the air, and sacrificed half a sheet of my *Herald* to start a fire with the few sticks of wood Dusty had carried in. He'd promised to sneak in a few more from the crew camp.

The moon was too low yet to be much help, and the fire only threw out light for about ten feet around. Everything else was blackness. I sat on a filthy horse blanket next to the fire with Dusty's rifle close at hand. After about forty minutes, I heard a light, scuffling sound from the direction of the passageway Dusty had pointed out. Rhythmic, like footsteps, but too faint for me to tell if they were human.

I grabbed the carbine and moved far enough away from the fire that its glare neither blinded nor exposed me. I watched the passage closely. Enough moonlight now spilled in that parts of one wall of the defile were dimly visible, the red rock dyed a deep indigo. All the rest was shadow. My instinct was to lever a round, but I didn't want to risk the noise. Half a second shouldn't matter, if it came to that.

In the stillness I heard a hissing sound. Faintly at first, it repeated a couple of times, growing louder by degrees. The third or fourth time I caught it. It was a voice, whispering, calling my name.

"Nate?" Silence. "It's Dusty. Hold your fire."

I saw movement along the half-lit wall and made out the familiar contours of Dusty's tall hat. I moved back to the fire and lowered the Winchester. "Over here."

Dusty joined me at the fire. He had a sheepish grin on his face. "Guess we ought to have worked out some kind of signal."

"I don't know. 'Nate, it's Dusty' seemed to do the trick. Here's your rifle—unfired."

Dusty laid the Winchester aside and displayed a gunny sack he was toting. "Brought some supplies."

The sack held several pieces of firewood, a thermal jug full of coffee, a tin pail full of beans and beef, and a couple of slabs of cornbread wrapped in wax paper.

We settled down by the fire to eat our meal. The chuckwagon food was tasty. It made me feel a little guilty about the rocks in Dusty's bed. Not enough to move them, but guilty.

Dusty ate quickly, then got up and wrapped the thermal jug in a horse blanket. "I got a nap on the drive," he said, "so I'll take first watch. Trade off every two hours?"

"Sounds good."

"If you still got anything in that flask, I wouldn't mind a taste of it now."

I handed him the flask and my binoculars.

"Get some sleep," he said. He tucked his bundle under his arm and started up the slope. With the darkness, it was slower going than I'd had earlier, but I soon saw him silhouetted against the moonlight at the top.

+++

I couldn't have been asleep more than ten minutes when he shook me awake. I was alert at once.

"Something up?" I shook off my blanket. I'd gone to sleep in my clothes, boots and all.

"No," he said. "Nothin's moving. It's your turn on guard."

I squinted at my watch. 2:30. I'd been out for four hours. Dusty was supposed to wake me two hours earlier.

"You look tuckered out," he explained. "With the ride and all. I don't usually need much sleep." He handed back my flask and I pocketed it. "Smoke now if you need to. Once you're up top a body could see a cigarette glow five miles off." I passed. I didn't want to leave the camp unwatched that long.

"See you in two hours," I said. I started up the rocks, empty-handed; Dusty had left the coffee and other stuff at the top. The moon was high now, so I had a pretty easy climb. I settled in as comfortably as I could at the ridge. The morning air was still, but a little damp. I stretched out on the blanket, poured myself a cup, and pulled my coat close around me.

Chapter Twenty

I peered through the binoculars and swept the camp below. Sound carried up here; I could plainly hear the occasional pawing and nickering of the horses, and the cowboys' snoring. The moon was full and bright and bathed everything in its hard, cold light. That was an advantage in that it made things easier to see, but a disadvantage in that it might make Jarboe leery of trying anything. Still, he'd been pretty brazen thus far. My gut said that he wouldn't let a little moonlight put him off.

The remaining coffee in Dusty's jug was lukewarm, which didn't make it taste any better or any worse. I drank it to have something to do. Dusty was already asleep. I envied him; I'd never been one who could drift off right away. Sore conscience, my old man would have said. But he'd been a quick sleeper himself, so scratch that theory.

Just over an hour later, as I lay trying without much luck to keep my body warm and my mind focused, I saw a flicker of motion near the corral. It wasn't the horses; it was a smaller, stealthier movement. By the time I'd decided it wasn't a night mirage and hoisted the binoculars, it was gone. Everything looked just as it had. As I silently cursed myself and was about to lower the glasses, I saw it again. A light-colored something was creeping along the backside of the corral, just beyond the fence. As it rounded the corner and moved along the side nearest me, I saw it was a man. When he reached the other corner and stepped from the shadows into the pale light, I could see it was Jarboe. That blew the cobwebs off my brain.

He soft-footed it silently across the little clearing between the corral and the wagons and disappeared from view between two of the big freight rigs. A moment later I heard a faint, steady, splashing sound and I smiled to myself. Couldn't fault a guy for relieving himself, even though one with any class would have done it at the corral, where the ground was already plenty fouled.

The noise stopped and Jarboe reappeared, carrying a large metal can with a bail handle. As he walked all around the wagon tipping the can, I heard the same splashing sound. A second later the breeze carried the odor my way. Kerosene.

I scrambled down the hill quietly as I could and woke Dusty. He was a light sleeper; he was out of the blankets and tugging his boots on before I finished telling him what I'd seen. He slid his big Colt out of the bedroll and stuck it in his waistband.

We hustled our way through the narrow pass and around the base of the hill. We sprinted, heads down, toward the cowboys' camp. I couldn't see Jarboe from there. We moved quickly and quietly as possible around the main camp, keeping the corral between us and where I'd seen Jarboe. With luck, any movement or noise he caught he'd think was the horses milling around.

Dusty motioned for me to go ahead, while he detoured into the cowboy camp. Rounding up a posse, I supposed. I made my way along the corral on the side closest to the tents. Keeping my head low I slunk along the neat row of tents, doing my best to keep an eye on the wagons, about fifty feet beyond. I caught one brief glimpse of Jarboe, still dumping kerosene. I'd have preferred to have Dusty with me when I braced him, but if I didn't get to Jarboe in time, my immediate problem was going to be a whole lot bigger. And hotter.

I crept around the end of the tent rows and took cover behind the chuckwagon. As I made my way around behind it, I had a clear view of Jarboe backing toward me, pouring kerosene alongside the last of the gear wagons. He stopped about fifteen feet from me, screwed the cap back on the can, and lifted it carefully into the wagon. I flattened myself against the chuckwagon as he moved a few feet to the side and pulled a cigarette lighter from his pocket.

There was no sign of Dusty, but I wasn't going to get another chance. I stepped out of the wagon's shadow with my .380 held low and said, "Don't do it."

He was quick; I'll give him that. He spun toward me and thrust a hand under his jacket. I leveled my gun.

"Don't do that, either," I said. He held his hands out at his sides, his back to the wagon. We stood staring at each other for a few seconds, or an hour—time tended to go sideways in situations like this. Nobody moved. Jarboe's left hand still clutched the lighter. He started to smile—that greasy smirk that always made me want to take a ball bat to him.

"Guess you got me red-handed, amigo. So I don't have much to lose, do I?" He held up the lighter and flicked back the lid. "You can shoot me, but I doubt you can stop me." His thumb touched the wheel.

I was deciding whether I believed that or not when a blur of movement at the wagon behind him caught my eye. The canvas cover flipped back, and Jarboe yelped as he was doused with something cold and wet. Dusty jumped from the wagon bed and tossed the kerosene can at Jarboe's feet. He moved a couple of yards to one side and held his big six-gun down at his waist.

"Go on and light 'er up," Dusty said. "I'm game for a fireworks show."

If Jarboe suspected a bluff, the strong smell quickly told him otherwise. For an instant I thought he'd make a sucker play for his gun. Just then, Dusty's two cowboy pals stepped out of the shadows, each cradling a shotgun. The cocky glitter faded from Jarboe's eyes; they became sullen and defeated. Snapping the lighter shut, he flung it to the ground and let out a string of barnyard curses under his breath.

"Now, Ed," Dusty said, winking at me. "What would your mama say?" Jarboe countered with a crack about Dusty's mother. Before he'd finished it, Dusty laid the barrel of his Colt across Jarboe's skull and dropped him.

Dusty picked up the lighter and tossed it to me. I patted Jarboe down and relieved him of the .38 under his jacket. I'd brought along a pair of handcuffs for luck. Mac and Reese stood Jarboe on his feet and I cuffed his hands behind him.

Perry Mills regaled me with some salty language of his own when I woke him, but he calmed down in a jiffy when I explained why I'd disturbed his dreams. The shenanigans on his sets had had him plenty worried. Not that he gave a damn about the damage, or the injuries, or the death of a day player whose name he'd no doubt already forgotten. Perry was counting on *Stardust Trail* to move him from Poverty Row to the ranks of the A-list directors, so bringing an end to the sabotage made me his new best friend. Lucky me.

We stowed Jarboe in Perry's tent while he roused his crew. I had Dusty drive my car back to the gas station, to call in the law. He'd wait for them there, and they could follow him back here.

+++

I kept Jarboe company while Dusty's saddle pals and their shotguns guarded the tent. A good thing, for as soon as word got around, Jarboe's cronies—Deke and Ray leading the pack—showed up, intent on freeing him. Dusty's boys held their ground, and Mills—plenty brave with well-armed cowboys at his back—fired the troublemakers on the spot and sent them back to L.A. forthwith. After they cleared out and the sun came up, things settled down to the routine, if you could call it that, of shooting the scenes the company had come out here to shoot.

Jarboe's spirits had rallied when his friends showed up, but now that they were out of the way he turned morose again. I'd loosened one of his cuffs and clamped it to the frame of Perry's cot so he could eat the breakfast the cooks had brought in. We were likely to have a long wait.

Jarboe sat on the cot, smoking a cigarette with his free hand—we'd doused him with water to be sure he wouldn't combust—and staring at his feet. I sat in a folding chair by the tent flaps, smoking my own cigarette and making a few notes. I'd have to tell this story several times over and I wanted to make sure I had the details down.

"They can't hang me for this," Jarboe said abruptly. There wasn't much conviction in it.

"I wouldn't bank on that, Ed. You killed a man."

"That was not my intention," he said. "I was just supposed to…I only wanted that coach to bust its axle so they'd have to call the shoot. Wasn't nobody supposed to die."

"Maybe. If so, all that means is it's not first-degree murder. You're still

139

likely to get slapped with second degree. Twenty-five to life, if you're lucky."

"The hell you say."

"Don't take it from me. The cops will be here soon enough. They'll be glad to explain it."

"I ain't never done more than six months, county jail. No hard time."

"Then you'd be wise to take any deal they offer you. If they offer."

"Shit." He dropped his cigarette and ground it out.

"You've got bigger worries than that, anyway. Dave Prince, for instance."

His head snapped up. "I had no part in that. You can't lay that off on me."

"I'm just saying it looks bad for you. You're out at Prince's when I find him dead. You take a couple of shots at me, run like hell, lie low ever since. It doesn't take a sharp copper to connect those dots."

"If I'd killed him, why the hell would I be hangin' about days later?"

"People have done crazier things. It's a mad world. You'll need something with more meat than that to keep your head out of the noose."

"Such as what?"

"Such as, for starters, what the hell were you doing there?"

"Maybe I was just following you, to get square."

"Following me on a horse? Don't insult me, Ed. I may be the only friend you have in this thing."

He snorted. "How's that?"

"As far as I can see, I'm the only one who doesn't think you killed Dave Prince."

He stared at me for a long time. I let him chew on it and went back to my notes. It took him a full five minutes to decide.

"I had business with the man," he said at last. "That's as much as I'm telling you. I went out there looking for Prince, but he wasn't at home. I was having a look about when I seen a car coming down the way. So I went up to the hills to keep a lookout, see if it was him, or somebody else was poking around. When I seen it was you, I guess I just lost my head." He shook his head. "I was only trying to put a scare in you. Hell, if I'd shot you dead, maybe I wouldn't be in this fix now."

"That's no way to talk to your friends, Ed."

Just then, Mac, poked his huge head in. "Dusty's back. Got the police with him."

Ten more minutes and I might have gotten the truth out of Jarboe. Some version of it anyway.

I heard Dusty's voice outside. "Right in here, gents." He came in, followed by Queenan and Bernal, and Downs, the sheriff's detective. Jarboe stiffened. He was done talking, or saying anything useful, at least.

Queenan looked in a worse temper than usual. The long drive hadn't done either of us any favors. Bernal looked like he always looked, cool and unhurried. In the city or out in the wilds—it was all just a job to him. Downs, his head nearly lost in the tent's peak, just stood there, talkative as ever.

Queenan's pig eyes mapped the whole scene: Jarboe cuffed to the bed, the empty kerosene can, Jarboe's lighter and pistol on the table.

"Well," he said, his cigar bobbing in time to his words, "here's L.A.'s ace crime solver doing an honest day's work for once. Pretty proud of yourself, ain't you, Ross? Well, I guess you got a right to be for a change."

I couldn't blame him for being sore. Cops always resented a guy like me doing their work for them. It might make the citizens wonder what their tax dollars were buying them.

"Watch this bird a minute, Frankie," he said, waving his cigar toward Jarboe. He looked at me. "You. Let's walk and talk."

He and Downs followed me outside. Squeezing his bulky body out through the tent flaps, Downs looked like the miracle of birth.

"So, give us the scoop," Queenan said, "and don't leave nothin' out, pal." He gave me the hard eye. "I mean nothin'."

I gave them a summary of what had happened, from arriving there to catching Jarboe with the kerosene. Queenan didn't look at me or ask any questions while I talked. He just nodded and puffed his cigar, dropping in an occasional "Uh huh" so I'd know he was listening.

When I finished, he nodded to himself, took out a notebook, and scratched a line or two in it. "How'd you know Jarboe would be out here?"

"Vanner told me. Jarboe's name was on the crew list."

"And you never thought to call us with that?"

"I wasn't sure he'd be here until I got here."

"Uh huh. You question him about that coach wreck, all these other goings on?"

"Not much. I figured I should leave that to you boys."

"But you did ask some questions. What did you get?"

"He pretty much admits tampering with the stagecoach. Claims he wasn't trying to hurt or kill anyone, just shut down the filming."

"Why?" Downs asked. I hoped it didn't mean he was planning to monopolize the conversation.

"We didn't get that far."

"What's he say about Prince?" Queenan saw my hesitation. "Don't even try telling me you didn't talk to him about that."

"He flat denies killing Prince. Says he was out there that day because the two of them had 'business.'"

"What kind of business?"

"He wouldn't tell me."

Queenan grinned. "That's okay. I guarantee he'll tell us. What else?"

"Says he shot at me because of our trouble at the Hackamore. Claims he missed me on purpose."

"Bullshit. If he'd killed you, he wouldn't be sitting in there now."

"He said that, too."

He scribbled a couple more notes, then gave me a long look. "So, what's your gut read on all this?"

"You really want to know, or are you just looking to give me the razoo?"

"You've had dealings with the guy. I haven't. So what's your take?"

"All right. I think he's working for somebody who doesn't want this picture made. Why, I have no idea. I don't think he killed Prince, but I don't buy his story about why he was there, either. It's not the whole truth, anyway. I'd like to know just what dealings Prince would have with a guy like him. I also think he's all show—you lean on him a little and he'll fold like a road map."

"So maybe I'll lean on him a lot. Okay, if that's it, we'll run this mug back to town and get to work."

I looked at Downs, then back at Queenan. "You're taking lead on this?

Aren't we in sheriff's territory?"

Queenan nodded. "That we are. But Bernal and me ain't been sittin' around playing tiddlywinks. Based on credible information obtained…" He pretended to consult his notebook. "…from one Nathaniel Ross, private investigator, we got a judge to sign a search warrant for your boy's flop yesterday. You wanna guess what we found?"

"The rifle that put a hole in my fender?"

"As a matter of a fact, I'm guessing we did. But that ain't the cherry. Looks like we also got the .45 auto that punched seven holes in David Prince." He paused to enjoy the effect. "You stayin' on here?"

"Not long. I've got some calls I need to make."

"Clear time in your busy schedule to drop by the clubhouse first thing tomorrow morning. We'll have your statement on this caper ready to sign. And unless your pal in there's harder than he looks, we'll have some answers, too."

Chapter Twenty-One

I dropped by Homicide a little after nine. Bernal was out. Queenan was unshaven and rumpled, but in a better mood than I'd seen yet. Almost jovial. He handed me a couple of typed sheets.

"There's your statement. Give it the once-over before you sign. Make sure we didn't skip nothin'." I glanced over the papers. It was nearly word-for-word what I'd told Queenan the day before. I had to admire the guy's memory.

"You're in high spirits today, Lieutenant. Did a rich uncle die and leave you a boodle, or did your horse come in at five to one?"

"A guy can't just be in a cheery mood? Jeez, there's no fooling you detective types. All right, I'll tell you—it's buy-one-get-one-free day here at the old Homicide Division."

"How's that?" I signed the statement and handed it back.

"Your boy, Jarboe. Not only do we have him dead-bang on the sheriffs' sabotage caper," he flourished the papers I'd given him, "I just finished an all-night chat with him, and he's confessed to shootin' David Prince. Two for the price of one." He snapped his fingers. "Like that." He held up another sheaf of papers in triumph.

"Did he actually do it?" I asked, "or did you just thump a confession out of him?"

He grinned. "One don't rule out the other. You know that. Anyway, there's the .45 Colt Frank found when we searched Jarboe's digs. Lab says the gun looks like a solid match. Frank's over there right now pickin' up the final report."

"What reason did Jarboe give?" Gun or not, I still wasn't buying him as Prince's killer.

"What is it always? Money or a dame. The dame, in this case. They both had the itch for some little hotsy-totsy singer at that hayseed nightclub Jarboe moonlights at."

If that meant Val, I wasn't buying it either. She wouldn't let Ed Jarboe carry her schoolbooks.

"What reason does he give for the *Stardust Trail* business?"

"He don't. And I don't care why—you caught him about to torch the whole works out there. Plenty good enough."

Just then, Bernal came in, whistling. He gave me a friendly nod.

"Morning, Ross." He dropped a file folder on the desk and turned to Queenan. "It's official. The slugs in Prince and the brass at the scene definitely came from Jarboe's gun."

This was making less and less sense. I wished I'd pressed Jarboe a little more when I had the chance. I wished I could talk to him now.

Every now and then wishes come true, even for me. The phone rang. Queenan snatched it up. "Lieutenant Queenan. Yeah. His bright mood seemed to darken a shade or two. "He does, does he? All right, thanks." He hung up. "Jail calling about Jarboe."

"Let me guess," Bernal said. "Screaming for a lawyer?"

"No." Queenan aimed a thumb at me. "He wants to see him."

Bernal's shine dimmed a little too. "What the hell for?"

+++

Nobody would ever mistake the Lincoln Heights jail for the public library. The Art Deco entrance gave the place an illusion of dignity, but on its quietest day the pandemonium behind those double doors would have sent a legion of librarians into red-faced fits. Round the clock, the waiting room played host to a horde of reporters and photographers thick as the buffalo herds that used to run wild on the plains. And you ran about the same odds of being trampled, if you got between them and anything that smelled like a story.

On top of that the room endured the comings and goings of an equal number of shyster lawyers, plus an endless stream of angry spouses and delusional mothers, who drifted in and out on their various missions of justice and familial loyalty and to give the desk officers hell.

Jarboe looked better than I'd expected, considering he'd just done an all-nighter with Queenan and his blackjack. The worst mark I could see was from the tap Dusty had given him. The big bruise on his temple had turned a deep, mottled purple. Just looking at it made me happy all over. A cut lip and swelling under one eye were the only visible signs of the night he'd spent with Queenan. The copper knew how to hide his work.

An unsmiling uniform had ushered me into one of the jail's small, bare, visiting rooms. A table, two chairs, Jarboe and me. I sat down across from him.

"You asked for me. Here I am," I said. "I hope you aren't gonna waste my time trying to convince me you killed Dave Prince."

"No." He sat looking at his hands, folded on the tabletop.

"So why tell the cops a tall tale?"

"A fellow's kidneys can only take so much bruising." He rattled his handcuffs on the tabletop. "What the hell's the difference, anyway? If I'm looking to do life in prison, maybe I'd rather hang."

"Okay, at least we're agreed you didn't do it. So how come your gun's a match?"

"Could be somebody borrowed it." He looked up at me. "Could be. But that ain't what I wanted to talk to you about."

"Well, it's your nickel. What do you want?"

"I want to hire you."

I'd come in here with a handful of guesses why he'd ask to see me. That wasn't one of them.

"Hire me to do what?"

"I ain't givin' no particulars 'til I know you'll do it. Let's just say what I done, I done on behalf of a certain party who wanted *Stardust Trail* shut down. Why, I don't have no idea."

"So why'd you do it?"

"Paid to. Simple as that."

CHAPTER TWENTY-ONE

"And…?"

"And this party promised to manage any problems if I got caught. But now it turns out I'm being fed to the wolves. I'll pay for what I done—fair's fair, I guess—but I ought not to have to do it alone."

"What do you expect me to do?"

"I can give you this party's name. You ought to be able to find out the rest, get proof that it wasn't just me."

"What sort of proof?"

"This party keeps careful records. A ledger. It'll show payments to me." He paused. "Maybe some other payments that would interest you, too."

"Ed, I'm one of the chief witnesses against you. Hell, I'm the victim of one of your counts. I'll be giving testimony at your hearing."

"You ain't gonna have to testify. I'll plead guilty for shooting at you. So there won't be no…what do you call it? No conflict of interest."

"What about your murder confession?"

"That's horseshit. I had to tell 'em something." He snorted. "You come through and I can make a deal on the sabotage. On the Prince deal, I'll tell it how it was. That big cop bastard just sapped a confession out of me."

"Why don't you just tell the police who hired you?"

He shook his head. "This party's got friends. Some of 'em bound to be cops. Besides, those detectives are sure they got me dead to rights. They got no interest in chasing other trails."

He had me there. Queenan was probably plenty content to put this nice, tidy case behind him. Complications would only annoy him.

"What makes you think you can trust me?"

"Believe it or don't, I read the papers. I know you turned up your own boys. You're a straight shooter. You're a son of a bitch, but an honest one." He paused. "If it's money, I have the money."

"It's not that." I hadn't even thought about money. Jarboe's was probably no dirtier than anyone's. Clean money in Hollywood was as rare as virginity or good taste. "I need to think this over."

"All right," he said. "But don't think too long, amigo. My party ain't likely to let the grass grow, if you follow."

Chapter Twenty-Two

Next day I stayed in bed late. I was still in sore need of catching up on sleep after all my days of gallivanting around in the wilds. Just before lunch, I put a call in to Nesselroad in Dallas. It had slipped my mind to get in touch and call him off. The nasal, Eastern voice came on the line at the second ring.

"Nesselroad here."

"Mr. Nesselroad, Nate Ross."

"Nate Ross," he repeated, as though he had to remind himself of who I was. "Yeah." He gave the word three or four syllables. I heard papers rustling and realized that he was consulting notes.

"Ah, here we are," he said at last. Before I could stop him, he launched into a detailed recitation of the Maynard/Shandy case from their earlier crimes through their robbery conviction, the shootout on the train, Shandy's death, and Maynard's recapture and imprisonment.

"That's where the trail gets muddy," he said. "Some kind of hush-up by Uncle Sam, and believe me, I know how that game's played. Records lost or destroyed. Floods, fires, tornados. I've heard them all. But you can't wipe out all the tracks. Not while there are still people who know things firsthand. People will always talk. Maybe not today, or tomorrow, but eventually."

"Mr. Nesselroad," I broke in. "I hate to waste anybody's time. But I came across a source out here who's told me pretty much what you just did. So if you'll just bill me for—"

"Can't put the bulge on you California dicks, is that it?"

"Look, I didn't mean to offend you. I just don't think there's anything more on your end I need to know."

"I'm not offended. What I am is a specialist. And in a case like this, let me tell you, there's always more to know. For instance, does your source know Del Maynard was spotted in Oregon in 1912?"

I tried to remember what I'd read in Dusty's clippings. "Yeah, I think so."

"Breaking horses for a rancher in the Wasatch Mountains in 1915?"

"Uh, I'd have to look at my files."

"Does your source know," he said almost with glee, "that Cora Maynard was expecting when Del and his partner jumped that train?"

That checked me. "Expecting?"

"Ah, didn't get that tidbit, eh? This is why you hire a specialist." I could see he was going to enjoy the rest of this talk. "Now I'll admit I don't have the documents yet—those things take time. But here's what I pieced together. She was pregnant, had the child about four months after Del was ferried up the river. She left the baby with friends and moved away. A year or so later, probably when she thought the law had given up thinking she had Del's money, she sent for the child."

"The kid," I said. "Son or daughter?"

"Don't know that yet."

"Know where they went?"

"Not for certain. But I expect to have that information soon. Very soon"

I didn't say anything. I was rolling all this around in my skull.

"So," he said finally, "am I still on the job here, or no?"

"Yeah. I'd like to know the minute you have anything come in."

"Okie-doke, I'll wire you." We hung up.

I'd like to have run Nesselroad's information by Dusty, but he was still up at Vasquez Rocks. Thanks to Jarboe's stunt and the disruption it had caused, filming was half a day behind. I'd have to wait to brief him.

Meanwhile, I'd had time to think over Jarboe's proposition. Queenan wouldn't like it. As far as he was concerned, he had his killer in the bag. Downs would likely feel the same way, although I hadn't heard enough words come out of him to get a bead on what he did or didn't like. Regardless, it was probably worth my while to hear what Jarboe had to say. Nobody's more helpful than a crook looking after his own neck. Not that I had any interest in saving a guy who may have tried to murder me. But he was the one constant in all this business. If I wanted to get to the truth of it all, I needed to know what he knew.

+++

I swung by the office to check the mail and make a call or two, and to pick up Prince's photo. I may as well show it to Jarboe and see what he could tell me about it, if anything.

The mail was nothing that couldn't wait. I was looking over my notes and studying the photo one more time when I heard footsteps coming up the stairs. Female footsteps, probably headed to the dentist's next door. A young Hollywood hopeful getting a crown on her eye tooth, to give her that perfect cinematic smile.

The door swung open, and Val walked in. I laid down my magnifier and scooped the photo and other stuff into a desk drawer.

She stood there, a little uncertain. She played with her delicate little silver wristwatch, rotating it round and round her slim wrist.

"Hello," I said. Somebody had to speak.

"Hello, Nate." She had a strained expression. "I—I've come by a couple of times looking for you."

"I've been out of town a lot. Probably should have put a card on the door."

"Oh, maybe I ought to have called first."

"No, it's okay." I motioned to a chair. She sat. Primly, as if she was interviewing for a job.

I fished out my bourbon and a couple of glasses.

"Drink?"

"No. That is, yes."

I poured while she made up her mind which. She didn't move to touch hers. I clinked my glass against it. "Cheers." I sipped at the warm bourbon. She flashed a tentative smile, picked up her glass, and drained it. They grow them tough in Texas.

The drink seemed to ease her a little. "Were you gone on business?"

I nodded. "*Stardust Trail* business. You might like to know we caught our monkey wrench boy. Ed Jarboe."

One eyebrow lifted a fraction. That was all the surprise she showed. She slid her glass an inch or two toward me. I took the hint and refilled it.

"Did he say why he did it?"

"Not really. Not to me." It was as close to the truth as I needed to come right now.

"And…" She hesitated, her hand on the glass. "Did he kill Dave?"

"The cops think so. I don't."

Her eyes looked troubled. She sat the drink on the palm of one hand and rotated the glass with the other. "What'll happen to him?" She took a nibble at the drink. This one might last.

"Hard to say. Prison, no doubt. How long's probably up to him."

She nodded. It was clear Ed Jarboe's fate didn't particularly concern her. At least we had that much in common.

"How are you doing?" I asked. "Better?"

"I thought we should talk," she said, seeming not to have heard my question. "About the other night."

"At the Hackamore?"

"At my apartment."

I ought to have known this was coming. Just like a dame; there were things better left unsaid, and she was going to say them anyway.

"What about it?" I might as well feed her the straight lines.

"You were so kind to me," she said. "And I'm grateful. But…" Texans get to the point. She'd reached the "but" in record time. "But I'm still a little—I can't think of the right word. Jittery. Heartsick, maybe. You probably think I shouldn't be."

"That's not for me to say." I lit a cigarette to kill the sudden sour taste in my mouth.

"I knew what kind of fellow Dave was," she said. "I knew from the start. But he could be sweet in his way, too. Funny. Charming."

I poured another drink and tossed it off. If I was going to have to listen to her go on about what a swell guy Prince had been, it was my turn to start slugging them down.

"He treated my mother very kindly. Paid for the funeral when she passed on. Sat with me—helped me sort through her things. Helped me carry on." She took out a little flowered hanky and touched it to the corners of her eyes. "I guess when it comes down to it, Mother and I had the same taste in men." She looked at me. "I doubt any of this makes much sense to you."

"No, I get it." My voice sounded unnaturally loud. "Prince was a real champ. Just living up to his name."

She put the handkerchief away and stood up. "I can see I've upset you. I'm sorry. I guess it was a mistake coming here."

"Don't think twice about it. We all make our share. I've made a career of it lately."

Her eyes teared up, but she didn't bother dabbing at them. "I don't suppose you'll be coming back to the set?"

"No, the book's pretty much closed on *Stardust Trail*. For me, anyway."

She nodded. "Well, maybe I'll see you at the club sometime."

"Maybe," I said.

She tried a smile but couldn't quite manage it. "in case I don't..." She fished in her bag and came up with one of the copper cowboy hat ashtrays. "...I thought you might like this, you know, to remember..." Her voice trailed away. She set the ashtray on the desk, gave a little nod and went out, closing the door softly behind her. She didn't say goodbye. I was grateful for that much.

As I listened to her footsteps fade, it occurred to me that "maybe" and "maybe not" meant the same thing. Just to distract myself, I took out the photo and magnifying glass again.

Chapter Twenty-Three

I walked into the jail out of the bright afternoon sun and strained to adjust my eyes. The usual crowd of newshawks seemed unusually agitated today. The line at the pay phone was longer than a soup kitchen breadline, and excited knots of press boys held breathless, whispered conversations over their notebooks. It also seemed to me there were more cops moving around behind the scenes than usual. I wondered if another movie producer had been caught rumpling the sheets with an underage starlet. Maybe a councilman found with his mitt in the wrong cookie jar. Something had bled in the water and stirred up the sharks.

I eased up to the back of the phone line and nudged a skinny guy in a plaid suit that made my eyes swim, and a tie that looked like he'd shined his shoes with it. He scratched away furiously on a stenographer's pad.

"Hey, buddy," I said. "What's all the fun about?"

He scoffed without looking up. "Ha. Like you don't know."

"I don't, honest. Clue me in."

He stopped scribbling and squinted at me with suspicion. "You work for the *Daily News*, bub?"

"Not me. I'm a baker. Just dropped by to bring my granny a cake with a saw in it." I gave him my business card.

"Oh, one of the good guys." He leaned closer and lowered his voice. "Okay, cousin, I'll play." With a gnawed pencil stub he pointed to the barred gate that led to the jail's innards. "They found a guy hung himself in one of the cells back there."

"No kidding?" Jail suicides weren't exactly a novelty. Clearly something made this one different. "Somebody big time?"

"Nah. Just a bit player in the horse operas. They were holdin' him on some hushed-up movie-town murder. But it's slower than Christmas today and anything Hollywood's good for page two, at least."

It looked like I wasn't going to get my scoop today. Not from Ed Jarboe, anyway. The guy gave me such details as he knew. The jailer made a spot check of the cell block about two hours earlier, found Jarboe hanging from the crossbar above his cell door. He'd used his shirt. Nobody had seen or heard anything.

I wasn't buying. Sure, Jarboe had made some noise about preferring death to life in prison, but he'd seemed pretty certain he could avoid both if I acted on his information. He was waiting to hear if I'd go along. Unless something had changed his mind in the meantime, there was no reason for him to hop the midnight train just yet.

I went out to my car. In my glove compartment I kept a badge—one of the few items, apart from the .380 pistol I carried, that my father had left me. It was what city coppers called a "juice badge." For years, L.A. police chiefs had passed them out like lollipops to loyal supporters, Hollywood hotshots, and all manner of local business and political nabobs. It identified the bearer as a Detective Lieutenant, cagily omitting the word "police." My old man had probably confiscated it. I seldom used it, but it was a handy item now and then. I gave it a buff or two on my coat sleeve and dropped it into my pocket.

Back inside the teeming building I elbowed my way to the desk. I bypassed the visitor's window and went to the door the officers used. When I put knuckles to it the fresh-faced young copper on the phone behind the desk looked up. He wasn't the same kid who'd been working when I'd been here before, or I wouldn't have dared try this gag. I flashed the shield and he buzzed me in.

I leaned elbows on the counter as he hung up the phone. "Some bucket of worms, huh?"

He turned harried eyes on me. "You ain't just kiddin', mac. For once I was gonna to get out of this rat hole on time. Now I'll be lucky if the wife don't drop a rope around my neck. Something I can help you with?"

"Yeah, I just need to find out who this bird's called since he's been here. Trying to run down his next of kin."

"Sure, sure," the kid said. He flipped open the phone call register and laid it in front of me.

"Thanks," I said. "Visitor's log, too?"

The only person who'd signed in to see Jarboe was me. He'd only made one phone call, right after he was booked. A Hollywood number.

+++

Back at the office I dragged out my reverse directory and took a quick gander. The number Jarboe had called wasn't in it. That didn't surprise me. A couple of phone calls and one or two half-hearted promises later I had my answer. The unlisted number belonged to Joe Gowdy's private office line at the Hackamore Club.

Chapter Twenty-Four

The club was as quiet as I'd seen it yet. It was still pretty early. Couples occupied three or four of the tables, and a few barflies hunched over the horseshoe bar, drinking a late lunch or an early dinner. I didn't see any of Jarboe's cohorts on duty, but they'd hardly be needed yet. A bartender with a wet towel could keep order in this place right now.

None of the faces at the bar were familiar. The regulars were probably still out on one set or another. I made straight for the backstage door; I had a few questions for Joe Gowdy. I was curious how Jarboe knew he'd been "fed to the wolves" by his anonymous party and I was curious why after he talked to me, he ended up dead before we could meet again.

As I headed down the long corridor that led to the tooled leather door, I passed Val's dressing room. I wouldn't mind asking her a question or two about now, but hadn't expected to run into her here—not this early. But I heard a muffled sound from inside the room. Crying. A woman's crying.

I stood a moment, listening, then tapped on the door. No answer; the crying went on. I opened the door and sidled in. She sat at the dressing table with her back to me, her face buried in crossed forearms on the tabletop. Her shoulders bucked and heaved with rough sobs.

I felt like a window peeper just standing there watching. But I'd committed myself by coming in. As gently as I could I said, "Val."

It still startled her. She flinched, then shot to her feet, tipping over the little wire-back chair as she stood. She spun to face me. It wasn't Val. It was Maddie.

"What's going on?" I said. "Where's Val? And what's the matter with you?"

Her startled face changed in a heartbeat. In one graceful swoop she snatched up a hand mirror and slung it at me, sidearm, like a boomerang.

"You lousy bastard!" she screamed. The mirror missed scalping me by about half an inch. It smashed against the wall behind me, and silvery shards spattered the floor like hard rain. She crossed the room and was on me in an instant—punching, biting, slashing with her painted nails. Her cats' eyes looked big and round and crazed. Her voice went so shrill it must have set dogs barking for blocks around. She called me names her mother never taught her, unless her mother was a gunnery sergeant.

I'm normally gentle as can be with women. But she was a big girl, and after she landed a couple of sturdy lefts on my jaw, I got tired of this dance. I gave her a quick, two-hand shove and she reeled back a step and sat down hard on the carpet.

Then, just like that, she went from bloodthirsty to weepy. She threw open her huge maw until all I could see of her was tonsils, and wailed so loud I felt my eardrums kiss. After half a minute of that act, she just sat breathing hard and fast through her nose and trying to stab holes in me with her eyes.

Normally I'd have offered her a hand up, or a glass of water or something stronger. I wasn't ready yet to get that close.

"You want to tell me what's with the tomahawk attack?"

"He's dead," she said. The voice sounded calm and rational. It made me wonder whose voice it was; it didn't match the face at all. "He's dead, you son of a bitch, and it's your doing."

"Jarboe?"

She didn't answer. She might've blinked, but I doubt it.

"What makes you think I had anything to do with that?"

"I ain't sayin' you did it yourself. One of your policeman friends, no doubt. Just so you could put Dave Prince off on him."

She thought I had policeman friends. I had no time to explain how far that guess missed the mark.

"Ed never killed himself," she said. "That's nothing but a filthy lie."

"I'm with you, Maddie. Ed didn't kill himself. And I know damned well he didn't kill David Prince."

The hot, hard eyes went stupid. The big mouth worked up and down without a sound. She swapped her usual cunning expression for a blank mask. It's a shock when everything you thought you knew turns out to be wrong. I wasn't unfamiliar with the feeling.

"Who killed him?" she asked at last, in a tiny, far off voice.

"Where's Val?"

It took her a few seconds to realize I'd asked a question. She shook her head and started to stand up. I let her.

"I don't know," she said. She righted the little vanity chair and sat down.

"Listen, Maddie," I said. "Ed asked to see me yesterday. He wanted my help. I know that sounds nutty, but I guess he trusted me because he knew I didn't believe he killed Prince."

She dabbed at her face with a handkerchief and watched me in the mirror, with that intense look women give you when they're on the lookout for lies.

"He was going to give me some information today," I said, "about who hired him to torpedo *Stardust Trail*. He died before I could talk to him. If you know what it was—"

"I don't. I didn't know anything about that whole business."

"I need to know whatever you do know. Otherwise, they close the case on Ed Jarboe. As far as anyone's concerned it'll be he killed Prince, he killed a day player, then he killed himself."

"You just said he didn't kill Dave."

"But I need proof. If he didn't kill Prince, his gun did. The cops found it in his room."

She stiffened. "His gun? What kind of a gun?"

"A .45 automatic. Army Colt."

She put a fist to her mouth. Her eyes got back some of their usual feline slant. "I'll be damned," she breathed.

"What, Maddie? Tell me."

She turned around. "That gun wasn't Ed's. Well, it was, but he gave it to me. I had trouble with a couple of the boys here getting pushy. Following me home. Ed gave me the gun to protect myself."

"And?"

"It disappeared. A week or so before we heard Dave Prince was dead. Somebody took it from my dressing room."

"Any idea who?"

She gave me a long, searching look. She was weighing a decision.

"I need to know."

"Val." She looked down at the hanky in her hands. "I caught her coming out of my room one afternoon. She said she was returning some perfume she'd borrowed. But next morning I noticed the gun was gone."

"Did you ask her about it?"

She shook her head. "I told Ed. He said he'd handle it. He had some notion she gave the gun to Dave Prince, on account of some sort of trouble he was in."

"What trouble?"

"Ed wouldn't say. But he was plenty worried about the gun. We snuck into Dave's apartment and looked for it, but it wasn't there. Ed came in here looking for it and Val caught him." She looked up at me. "That was the night you and him had the row."

"Did he go to Prince's cabin looking for it?"

"I imagine so. He never said. But I know he never did find the gun."

"You're sure of that? It turned up in his room."

"He never found it."

There was a light, quick tap at the door and Jean started in. She stopped short at the sight of us. Even for her, she looked confused.

"I was lookin' for Val," she said. She gave me a tentative smile, then noticed Maddie's bedraggled state. "Oh, sweetheart, I heard." She wiggled over and threw her short arms around Maddie. "I'm so sorry."

They had a good cry together. I tried to give them time for it, but I had things that needed done.

"Jean, do you know where Val is?"

She broke the clinch and dried her eyes with her palms. "Well, since she's not here I guess they're still in the office."

"Gowdy's office? Why?"

"She came in a couple hours ago, all in a toot. Kinda scared, upset about something. Said something about needing to see Mr. Gowdy right away. She went down to his office. I ain't seen her since."

I left them and headed down the hallway again. No Deke or Ray guarding Gowdy's door today. The door was locked; I racked the horseshoe knocker and pounded my fist on the door, but nobody answered. It took me a good five minutes—this was no cheap hotel room door—but I got the lock to play nice and I was in. There was no one home.

I combed the desk, looking for any sign of where Gowdy or Val had gone. A few notes on the blotter pad—nothing helpful. A calendar book showed a meeting with a beer vendor this morning. That was of no interest. I was going through the drawers when the door swung open. Maddie and Jean were standing there.

"What in hell are you doing?" Maddie asked.

I waved them inside. "I don't have time to give you chapter and verse. Short answer is, your boss here killed Ed. Not personally, but I'm betting he paid the freight."

She turned sickly pale. Jean gasped and bit a knuckle.

"Is Val in danger?" she asked.

"Danger or trouble. Maybe both. You didn't see either of them leave? You're sure of that?"

She nodded. "But they probably went out that way." She pointed to a paneled door in the corner. "Mr. Gowdy comes and goes through there. He parks his car out behind the club."

The corner door led to a small storage room. It was nearly empty except for a few odd cases of whiskeys, some of the better stuff. At the back of that room was another door, a self-locker. I pushed it open. It gave onto an alley at the rear corner of the club. The alley's far end led in off Santa Monica Boulevard. The near end emptied out onto a little side street just off Western. There was no car in sight.

I propped open the door and stepped out to have a look. There were puddles of water here and there along the alley floor. There always were in alleys, even in the dog days. Wet tire tracks led from one large puddle between Gowdy's door and the side street exit. They were faint where they met the street. They hooked right.

A bum sat on a packing crate near the opposite end. He was trying, without much luck, to light a soggy cigar stub with a lipstick-smeared cigarette butt. Nobody else was around. I walked over.

"Hey, chief," I said. "You see a car parked here in the last half hour?"

He gave me a boozy stare. "Got a light?"

I dug out a Hackamore matchbook, and he snatched at it with grubby fingers. I held it out of reach. "A car?"

He sneered and went back to his task.

"You drive a tough bargain, chief." I took a couple of cigars out of my inside pocket. "How about a pair of virgin smokes? And I'll throw in the matches for free."

He took his time. After giving it a sufficient think, he tossed his butts back where he'd no doubt found them and held out a hand. "You first," he croaked.

The bums on my side of town weren't so damn choosy. In Hollywood they had airs, like everyone else. Any other time I'd have told him to go to hell and left him to his leftovers. I handed over the cigars but held on to the matchbook.

"Big blue Packard." He aimed a filthy forefinger down the alley. "Went that way." He made a vague gesture to the right. "Tall old boy driving it, had a big, grey mustache. Blonde girl with him." He gave me a slobbery leer. "Tidy little number."

I tossed the matches into the air. He made about three misses, picked them up off the asphalt as I walked away. "Come back any time you're in town, Senator," he called to my back.

The girls were still in the office when I got back. Maddie was pacing, and Jean was sitting in one of the horned contraptions, frowning like she was trying to figure the square root of pi.

I went back to searching Gowdy's desk. The top right drawer was locked. I got to work on it with a pen knife.

"Have you ever been to Gowdy's house?" I asked Maddie, mostly to get her to stop running laps.

"A time or two with Ed."

"Describe it." If I were going out there it wouldn't hurt to have some idea of the layout. She gave me a fair enough description. Two-story ranch house tucked into a little arroyo at the back of about seventy-five acres. Around half the property wooded. The usual outbuildings: a big horse barn, a tack shed, garage. A good-sized bunk house where the hands could stay including Ray and Deke and—until recently—Jarboe. She gave me directions. It was up in Placeritos Canyon, an hour's drive or more.

The drawer lock gave, and I pawed through the contents. A checkbook confirmed the guy was loaded, but was otherwise no help. The kind of payments I was interested in you don't write checks for. A thick, leather-bound journal, on the other hand, was well worth a look. Anxious as I was to get going, I spent a couple of minutes paging through it and studying the careful notations. Whatever Ed Jarboe was—and he wasn't much by anybody's measure—he wasn't a liar. Not this time, anyway.

I picked up the phone and dialed Phil Okel. Briefly as I could, I gave him a rundown on developments with Jarboe. Nothing with Phil was ever too brief.

"Holy hell," he said when I'd finished. "So much for keeping this mess out of the scandal rags. Yates is going to throw a rod."

"Better he hears it from you before he reads about it."

"Easy for you to say, bub. You're a hired hand. You just collect your fee and ride off into the sunset."

"Well, right now I'm riding off to Joe Gowdy's place and I could use some help. Dusty Vanner's still up at Vasquez Rocks with the *Stardust Trail* crew. Can you get a message to him?"

"They ain't at the Rocks. Mills wrapped up early and they've moved the whole shooting match back down to the Monogram Ranch."

"Even better. I'm going to be not ten miles from there, but I don't have time for detours. Can you get word to Dusty?"

"Will do."

I gave him directions and hung up. I wrote down Phil's name and number and gave it to Maddie.

"Go back to Val's dressing room and wait," I told her. "On the chance she shows back up, take her someplace safe and call this guy. He'll get in touch with me somehow."

She nodded, and she and Jean left. I collected Gowdy's journal and started out. As an afterthought, I went back to the phone.

"Gus's Diner," said the bright voice on the line. "Special today's the fried oyster sandwich with side salad and coffee. Two bits."

"Benjy. Nate Ross. I need a favor."

"Sure, Mr. Ross. Name it."

"Hot-foot up to my office and see if there's a telegram under my door. I can't wait, but I'll call you back in half an hour."

"Done, boss."

+++

Traffic was light on the San Fernando Road, and I made good time. I pulled off at a little roadside joint near the bottom of the pass. Their pay phone was broken, but a buck convinced the bartender to give me the house phone. Benjy answered on the third ring.

I cut him off; I already knew the special. "Any telegrams?"

"Uh huh. From a guy in Dallas. I'm not even gonna try the name. Funny kind of a message, though."

"Make me laugh, kid."

"Just one word. Muleshoe."

Chapter Twenty-Five

It was full dark by the time I reached the canyon road. It wasn't fast traveling now. The road was winding and narrow, with lots of sudden ups and downs, and there wasn't much moon yet. It's always amazed me how black the night can get once you're clear of the city. More than once I narrowly dodged rocks that had tumbled down the hillside onto the roadway.

The turnoff to Gowdy's ranch was about where Maddie had said it would be. It wasn't marked, but I knew it by the timbered arch straddling the path about fifty feet off the road. Logs lashed together, with a wagon wheel at the base. Real old West stuff, right down to the steer skull on the crossbeam.

The path that twisted down through the property was covered in gravel. It made the going easier. It was smoother and I could run along without headlights guiding by the scant moonlight on the light pebbles. But it made too much noise. I coasted along at not much over idle speed to keep the racket down.

I came up over a little rise, and far back against the base of the hills I could make out a dark shape that had to be the house. Amber light spilled out from a couple of windows. I'd have preferred to have Dusty along when I approached it but wasn't sure I could afford to wait. I pulled up at the side of the path and got out. I left the motor running; I didn't want the starter noise to give me away. I walked about ten steps ahead to have a look and a listen.

From here, the pathway led more or less straight on to the house. It was tough to gauge just how far away it was. When my eyes adjusted better, I could make out the barn off to the right of the house. Just left of the path, and a good deal closer than the house, was what must have been the bunkhouse. I'd have to pass it on my way in. I didn't see any lights there, but I'd better make it my first stop and be sure it was empty.

The only sound above the light breeze was the coyotes yipping and howling in the hills. They might have been a hundred yards off, or a mile, I couldn't be sure. First one, then three or four, then dozens, their shrill notes rising together in an eerie wail. My own personal Greek chorus, mocking me—maybe warning me—reminding me how far out of my natural habitat I'd strayed.

If I hadn't let them distract me, I might have heard him coming. He must have been hiding in the scrub oak that dotted both sides of the path. As I turned back to the car, I heard a swishing sound beside me. I didn't have time to register it, but I'd remember it later as the sound of a blackjack. The dim moonlight blinked out. Fade to black.

+++

When my eyes opened, I thought I was in the midst of another dream. I was sitting upright, straddling a dark horse. I was in no danger of falling off; a rope around my neck was stretched to a tree branch a few feet over my head. It kept me firmly in place. My hands were tied behind me. As my head cleared, I became conscious of other horses close by. Horses and people. Things came more into focus and I recognized Deke and Ray, and a couple of others I'd seen before, but whose names I didn't know. Jarboe's bunch.

They stood in a semi-circle in front of me. Their faces were half in shadow, half in the yellow glare of a kerosene lantern hanging from another tree. Deke held a pistol in his hand. The others all had rifles. Deke's face wore its perpetual jackass grin, while Ray was silent and stone-faced as ever. The others shifted their eyes between Deke and me, waiting for a cue.

Deke stepped forward. "Did you have a nice nap, Mr. Detective? You'll be having another one directly. A nice, long one."

That drew snickers from the no-name pair. Ray just stood there and stared.

"What game are we playing tonight, Deke?" My voice was a little strained, thanks to the rope.

"No games, friend. Games is all over with. This here's justice for Ed. Eye for an eye."

I knew now what the coyotes were trying to warn me about. Maybe next time I'd listen—if I were around for the next time.

"I had nothing to do with Jarboe's murder."

"So you admit somebody killed him. That's good. A man shouldn't make the jump with a lie on his lips."

"Somebody killed him. But it wasn't me."

"You or one of your cop friends, it's all the same."

Everybody seemed to think I was pals with the police. I wish someone would tell the police.

"This is a stupid play, Deke. People know I'm here."

"That don't matter. Ain't no one going to find you here. It's a mighty big desert, friend."

I was about to tell him he'd never get away with it. But that sounded too much like a line from a hundred gangster films, and I was no Jimmy Cagney. I was no Tom Mix either. I should have waited for Dusty; this was his sort of scene.

Deke looked at his friends and the half-circle parted. "If you want a minute to make your peace," he said, "I'll give you that. I'm willin' to bet it's more than Ed got."

I looked straight ahead. The moon was high now. I could see we were in a little sheltered pocket, with low hills on three sides. Down a slope from the open side I could see the house, closer now. Smoke curled from the chimney, and the light from the windows was soft and golden. It looked peaceful.

The whole scene was so dreamlike and unreal that I wasn't surprised at all to see several riders appear on the hilltop to my left, silhouetted against the moonlight. I half expected to see Perry Mills come rolling in behind them with a camera crew. I heard a quick, high-pitched whistle and braced myself as I felt my horse start to move.

But instead of surging forward, he went straight down. His legs buckled and he dropped beneath me until he rested on his belly. I went down with him and started to choke. My feet kicked in the air a couple of times as the big animal fell away, but then they found something firm and unyielding and scrambled to claim it. I stood on the horse's back and found that by standing on the highest parts of the saddle, I could maintain just enough slack in the rope to keep from strangling.

This kept me so occupied I was only half aware of the sudden activity erupting all around. The horsemen galloped down the hill, whooping and firing guns in the air. Deke and his boys were caught by surprise and stood transfixed, not believing what they saw. In seconds, the newcomers had crowded into our clearing and leveled their guns on the would-be hanging party. In the middle of the group was Dusty Vanner.

"Drop those weapons, boys," he barked. "Or we'll drop you."

Only Ray moved. He threw down his rifle, turned and ran. The thick brush and dense shadows swallowed him up. Deke and his two companions stood owl-eyed and motionless. Then another familiar voice rang out.

"You heard the man. He ain't gonna tell you twice." Duke Morrison edged forward into the light. He held a short Winchester upright, the butt resting on his knee. Without another word he gave the carbine a flip and spun it—spun it the way the old-time horse opera heroes spun their six-guns. As it rotated, the cocking mechanism made a deadly sound. He brought the muzzle around and centered it on Deke's chest.

Two rifles and a pistol hit the ground together. Deke and his boys looked punch-drunk and idiotic as they threw hands in the air. The riders dismounted. As they came into the light, I saw Mac and Reese, Joe Lopez, and Waldrop, the little one-armed stable keeper. A pretty motley rescue party.

Dusty and Mac saw to the prisoners, and Duke and Joe came over to me. Duke held me steady while Joe cut me loose. It was none too soon; I couldn't have kept up my balancing act much longer. When I had solid ground under my feet and they'd made sure I was okay, Joe swatted the horse's rump and made a clicking sound. The big animal scrambled to its feet.

"These boys should've been more careful what mounts they pulled," he said. He patted the horse's neck. "Good boy, Nero."

I rubbed some feeling back into my wrists and shook hands with both of them. "Usually," I said, "when you talk about somebody saving your neck it's just a figure of speech." I looked at Duke. "How did you get pulled into this?'

He shrugged. "I was at the ranch having some stills shot for the next Mesquiteers picture. I heard Dusty telling Reese what was going on, so I figured I'd ride along and see if I could lend a hand."

I nodded at the carbine dangling at his side. "Pretty neat trick with that thing," I said.

He grinned. "You like that, did you?" He held the gun out in both hands. It had been fitted with a big oval loop in place of its factory lever. "Yak and I have been working on it for the new picture. Wanted something flashy." He looked toward Deke and his pals. "Looks like it had the desired effect."

"You might have shot yourself with a stunt like that."

Joe snickered. "No chance of that." Duke glowered at him, and Joe led Nero away, grinning to himself.

"Don't tell me you guys rode in here shooting blanks?"

Duke gave me a half smile. "Have it your way, Nate. I won't tell you."

"Jesus, Duke." I tried not to think of all the other ways this could have played out. "I owe you for this. I owe you big."

He clapped me on the shoulder. "What say you pay me back right now, and we'll call it even?"

"Pay you back how?"

"Easy. I was never here. Pappy Ford would skin me alive if he knew about this little dido."

I assured him his secret was safe with me. He called to Joe, and the two of them mounted up. They waved a silent goodbye and disappeared back over the hill.

Deke and company were now sitting on the ground, legs outstretched, and their hands and ankles bound. Mac and Reese stood over them, guarding them with their own rifles. Waldrop had rigged a rope picket line between two trees and was securing all the horses.

My coat, hat and gun were in a pile at the base of the tree. I retrieved them. I was holstering the .380 when Dusty came over.

"That was a damned close thing," he said. "You'd have done better to wait for me."

"Wasn't sure I had the time. I didn't know if Phil Okel could reach you right away."

"No matter now," he said, looking towards the house. "If they didn't know somebody was comin' before, they sure as hell know now. What's your plan?"

"Well, we don't have surprise on our side anymore," I said. "But the idea's the same. Go down there and brace Gowdy."

"Fine by me. I'm looking forward to making the man's acquaintance."

"Or renewing it." He gave me a look. "Can we leave these three here to watch Deke and his chums?"

"They can manage it."

"Why did you bring him along?" I nodded towards Waldrop, who was tending the horses, and sucking on his unlit pipe.

Dusty chuckled. "Didn't have a choice. He was at the ranch dropping off horses. Only way he'd let us have these was if he could tag along."

Dusty explained to Mac and Reese and they agreed to keep watch over the three henchmen. Dusty and I set off toward the house.

+++

Once we reached the bottom of the slope and struck the gravel path, we followed alongside it. It was surer going since we didn't know the terrain and might miss our footing in the dark. Plus, I still wanted to check the bunkhouse. Ray may or may not be around yet, and we didn't know how many other hands Gowdy might have about the place. Down the path toward the road I could make out the shape of my car, sitting where I'd left it.

The bunkhouse looked as dark and deserted as before. As we drew closer, I could see that one side facing us had no doors or windows, while the side adjoining it had both. The window next to the door was covered by solid wood shutters. We approached from the blind side. When we reached the wall we stood and listened. Nothing. Dusty took up a position at the corner watching the door and window side. I tiptoed around the opposite way to look for other entrances. The remaining two sides had a window apiece, also secured with shutters. I tried them both gingerly. They seemed to be barred from the inside.

I backtracked my way toward Dusty. Just after I passed the second window,

I heard the squeak of a hinge and the unmistakable click of a hammer being drawn back. A soft voice said, "Don't move, Ross."

I raised my hands to my shoulders, pointing my .380 at the sky. "Hello, Ray," I said. I heard a light scuffling sound. He was climbing out the window.

I waited, and the instant I heard the thud of feet hitting the ground I dived to my right and rolled over. His shot went high, but it gave me what I needed. I fired twice at the muzzle flash. He yelped in pain and dropped.

I got to my feet and went toward Ray, ready to shoot again if need be. I stepped on his pistol where he'd dropped it. I rolled him over, turning his face up to the pale moonlight. There was dark froth on his lips, and a spreading stain on his shirt front.

He made a wet sound in his throat. "How'd you know it was me?"

"Simple. I didn't recognize the voice."

One corner of his mouth went up in a crooked smile. It remained there even after he was gone.

A shadow moved at my side, and Dusty said, "Easy. It's me." We slunk around to the front and pushed open the unlocked door. Nothing moved, nobody shot at us. We went cautiously in and found it one big empty room with cots along the walls.

We skirted the path from there up to the house, maybe thirty yards away. We circled around wide to the side of the house that faced the hills, where the shadows were deepest. A board porch wrapped all the way around, and we crossed it as quietly as we could. The only light visible now came from a ground floor window at a front corner of the house. Just around the opposite corner was a kitchen door. It was unlocked, so we slipped inside. Me first, then Dusty, keeping our heads low.

It was tombstone quiet inside. The only sound I could make out was the loud, hollow ticking of a clock. We moved through the kitchen into a wide hallway where lights burned in a couple of sconce lamps not visible from outside. A tall grandfather clock at the far end of the hallway was the source of the sound. A wide doorway off the hall to the left of the clock showed a brightly lit room beyond. As we moved toward it, the carpet runner muffled our footsteps and the occasional creek of a floorboard under our feet. Muffled them, but didn't deaden them.

We cat-footed it down the hall for what seemed like a day. When we were near enough to the doorway, I started shifting my position by degrees to get a view of the room beyond. Dusty inched up behind me. As we tensed ourselves, ready to make our move, a rich baritone voice called out from inside.

"Come on in, gents. It's about time we brought this little fandango to a close."

Chapter Twenty-Six

Dusty and I looked a question at each other. We button-hooked through the doorway, guns at the ready. Gowdy stood at the other end of the room behind a big, rustic desk. He held a pistol—a huge old thing that looked like it could lob cannon balls.

"Drop it, Gowdy," I said.

He slowly shook his head. He looked at us in turn with a sad, weary smile. "I'm wagering you gents didn't come all this way just to gun me down. If I'm wrong, open the ball, and may the better man win."

He held the big gun steady, while Dusty held his cowboy hogleg and I held my .380. We had a neat little standoff going. Gowdy could hardly shoot one of us without the other getting him, but that didn't mean he wouldn't try. He looked from Dusty to me and back again with a thin smile, like the villain with the girl tied to the tracks. I expected him to twirl his mustache. It was almost comical; I'd have felt silly as hell if not for the icy trickle running down my spine.

"Where's Val?" I asked him.

"Safe." His eyes flicked upward. "Upstairs. I gave her something to help her sleep."

I took my first look around the room. It might almost have been Dave Prince's cabin. Rough oak beams framed the ceiling and the doorway we'd come through. A bearskin rug with a head no bigger than a beer keg took up most of the floor. A varnished, half-timber stairway in the corner led to a loft above, with Navajo blankets draped over its peeled-log railing. Behind the railing, two closed doors were visible.

"What's your plan when she wakes up?" I asked Gowdy.

"Nothing sinister, if that's your concern. My idea was simply to relocate her someplace far away. Somewhere she could live a safe, happy life and be no threat to me. Now, I confess I'm not entirely sure what I ought to do. Much of it depends on you fellows."

"Meaning what?" I asked.

"I don't suppose financial considerations would tempt you to leave me in peace?"

"Not likely," I said. Dusty just made a contemptuous noise.

"Then I suppose it all comes down to which of us walks out of this room. Tell me first, Nate, what's your stake in this? What I mean is, apart from any fee you're getting from whomever, is there really any personal gain for you in seeing me pay for my past transgressions?"

"The past is my friend's bailiwick." I said, tipping my head towards Dusty. "I'm more interested in recent transgressions."

"Such as the murder of David Prince?"

"Well, that's recent enough. But I can't even claim a professional interest in that. I was hired to find him, and I did. Running down his killer's a matter for the police."

"No personal crusade on your part, then?"

"Somebody shot and killed a guy who by all accounts should have been shot at birth. I'm curious about it, but it's not keeping me up nights. Why? Are you telling me you killed him?"

"Supposing I am. What then?"

"Then that tells me something about you."

Gowdy nodded. "Yes, that I'm a fellow who's not afraid to drop a hammer if need be."

"No, it tells me you have a soft spot. That you'd lie to protect someone else. We both know you didn't kill Dave Prince."

Gowdy's smile faded. "Do we?"

"Val killed him. Out of what I'm sure she believed were good motives. She found out her old man wasn't dead, and her boyfriend was tapping him dry. Blood wins out. So they went for a horseback ride together and she came back alone. Then she burned his files on your case. She thought she was protecting you."

Gowdy's wistful smile returned. "She's inherited her father's impulsive temperament, I'm afraid."

"It's the same reason she bee-lined to you this afternoon when she saw this in my office." I took Prince's old photo out of my pocket. "She may have suspected I had it, but she wasn't sure until today. Then she knew I'd figured you out, or would soon."

"That damned photograph. How often over the long years I've regretted ever sitting for it."

I held it up at arm's length so that I could compare them side by side. "Funny thing is, it doesn't even look like you anymore. I'd never have made you from it, except for the watch charm."

Gowdy's free hand went to the chain on his vest.

"It's not all that distinct in the photo," I said. "But with a strong glass, it's clear enough."

His fingers felt for the Indian head. "A gift from a lady, long ago. The foolish risks a man will take for sentiment."

He stopped fondling the charm. The faraway expression dissolved, and he turned sharp eyes on Dusty. "And you, my friend; what's your play here? I can only guess you're some relic from the past, out for reward money or vengeance. Maybe a little of both?"

"I ought to be offended you don't know me," Dusty said. "But I'll admit I'd have never recognized you either. We've met. You and me took a long train ride together once."

Gowdy's eyes lit up with interest. "VanNeer," he said. "Walter VanNeer." He shook his head. "The years have played rough with us both, law dog."

"We're still standing, ain't we?" Dusty said.

"We are indeed. Which brings us back to our current quandary. It's clear you boys have your minds set. Now as for me, I have no desire to spend any more of my waning years penned up like cattle. So my proposal is this: in about two minutes that clock just outside the door is going to sound the hour. At the first chime we all turn loose and let the die fall as it will. The advantage is yours, as there are two of you. That's fair as fair can be, wouldn't you say?"

Dusty and I shot each other a quick look. The smart thing would have been for either or both of us to open up now. But that didn't guarantee he wouldn't get off a shot or two and take at least one of us down with him.

I rolled the dilemma over and over in my head and figured Dusty was doing the same. For that matter, no doubt so was Gowdy. My arm had already been growing tired from holding my gun level. Now I felt like there was an anvil at the end of it. It had grown dead quiet again. The only noises were the clock's relentless ticking and the sound of my heart drumming in my ears. Each fought to drown out the other. Just as the heartbeat was gaining ground, I heard something else. The faint squeak of a floorboard.

The tense silence was broken by a gunshot. Gowdy grunted and his big pistol thunked on the desktop. Dusty and I looked at one another, realized the shot had come from behind us. I flicked a look over my shoulder while Dusty moved to the side so he could both cover Gowdy and see the doorway.

Framed in the big oak-beamed passage, with another old cowboy six-shooter in his one hand, was Ike Waldrop. He walked through a black powder haze, his eyes burning and locked on Gowdy. He looked as though he didn't even realize Dusty and I were there. In one smooth motion, he tucked the pistol in his waistband and raised a sawed-off double-barreled shotgun, slung on a strap over his shoulder. He braced it on the stump of his right forearm and thumbed back a hammer with a lethal click. He leveled the boomer on Gowdy, who had a hand clamped over a wound in his left arm. It hadn't touched an artery; there wasn't enough blood.

Gowdy's dark face had turned a little pale, but he stayed upright. He gave the pistol on the desk a hungry look, but with three guns on him, he'd have to stay hungry for now. He turned his eyes on the newcomer.

"Who the hell are you?"

Waldrop took another step forward and flashed a bitter smile.

"I ain't surprised you don't know me. You never noticed nobody but you. People were just something you used to get from here to there, like doorknobs. After you've used one to pass through, why you wouldn't know that doorknob from any other. You never really looked at anybody, not even me. But you're looking at me now, ain't you, Del Maynard, you sorry son of a bitch!"

The old man's voice got higher and thinner as he spoke. This last part he said almost in a frenzy.

Gowdy turned half a shade paler and his eyes opened wide. "Abe?"

The one-armed man laughed. "Yessir, it's your old compadre come back from the grave to haunt you. Boo!" He cackled, and his wild eyes grew crazier. He did a quick pivot to cover the three of us in a short arc. "I'll ask you two to drop them pistols," he said to Dusty and me.

A stand against a handgun was one thing. Against a double load of buckshot at room range, it was something else. We dropped our guns and followed his direction to sit on the sofa.

"How," Gowdy said, his voice a dry croak. "How are you—"

"Alive? Yep, I ain't no specter; I'm flesh and blood all right. No harm in telling now, I suppose. After you and me...parted..." He chuckled at his joke. "I was overtook by sleep. When I come to it was morning and I was layin' in a wagon, my arm all bandaged up and wounds dressed. I thought the posse had took me, but it was a Mex truck farmer had come along on his way to town. He took me to a shack he lived in up a little arroyo, miles south. He nursed me there two, three weeks—I ain't entirely sure."

He looked from one to the other of us. He was enjoying his captive audience. Probably the first time he'd ever told this story.

"When I felt up to it, I figured I best get moving before the law come snoopin' about, or before that fella found out there was reward money. I was planning to skedaddle on his old mule while he was sleeping when I had an inspiration. That greaser was about my size, and not much older. When he come in from the field that evening, I waylaid him with the kindling axe. Dropped him dead. Then I used it to trim him a tad." He waggled his handless stump. "I put a couple or three bullets in him with his own pistol, then kicked over a lamp and touched off the kerosene. Figured the fire to bring someone around, but I'd be far and away by then. I knocked down the corral gate so's they'd figure the mule had done it, then off we rode. I buried the hand out in his fresh plowed field." He giggled. "I imagine it's there still."

He looked at Dusty and me. "You boys probably think that was an awful treacherous thing to do, but not this one." He nodded toward Gowdy. "He understands."

Neither Dusty nor I had moved but the old man gave us a suspicious glance. "Tell you what. What say you fellas clasp your hands behind your heads and keep 'em there for now?" He punctuated the request with a thrust of the shotgun. "That's better. Anyways, once I got my bearings, I headed for the spot. I wasn't going to take none but my share. Had me a hell of a time digging with only one hand, and it turned out it was for nothing."

Gowdy shifted uncomfortably. Waldrop took a half step and poked the shotgun at him. "What did I pull out of that mail sack we buried, Del? Tell these fellas what I pulled out of that hole!"

Gowdy's mouth made a gummy sound before he could get any noise out. His eyes were dead man's eyes. "Washers," he just more than whispered. "Washers and cut newspapers."

"Washers and cut newspapers," Waldrop repeated, his voice a lunatic trill. "But that ain't all, is it? There was a note. What did that say?" He looked black murder at Gowdy and fairly screamed. "What did it say?"

"Jesus, Abe," Gowdy whined. "It was near forty years ago. I don't remember."

"I do," Waldrop said. "I sure as hell do. It said 'Sorry, Abe. I needed it worse.'" He started pacing back and forth, careful to keep us all in the shotgun's sweep.

The clock chimed. Everyone flinched except Waldrop. He didn't seem to notice.

"I never wanted to jump that train, let alone kill a marshal. That was all you, you damn fool. You drug me along with you, left me shot up with a hand hacked off, bleedin' and dyin' for all you knew. Then I found out you'd already robbed me, even before we was caught."

"Maybe I'd have played you straight if you hadn't meddled with Cora." Gowdy's defensive tone turned angry.

"I never meant that to happen."

"Your pants just fall off, did they?"

"I'm talkin' about the child. That was pure accident."

"Accidents like that don't happen to fellows that sleep in their own beds."

Waldrop stopped pacing. His crazy tone turned almost conversational. "You ain't surprised. How'd you know she wasn't yours?"

"I had a dose of the clap that wouldn't turn loose. Cora and I hadn't fooled about for three or four months. But I saw her a couple of mornings out behind the chicken coops having a puke. So one day, I just up and asked her and she told me. She couldn't have hid it much longer anyway."

I'd had my fill of old home week by now. "Look," I said to Waldrop, "I understand. He stole your money, and you knocked up his wife. Or I guess it was the other way around. Either way, it sounds like a draw. Besides," I added, "if you were going to nurse a grudge, I'd think it would be for cutting your hand off."

A queer smile cracked open his face. "He never done that. I did."

I must have looked as surprised as Dusty. Waldrop seemed to enjoy the effect.

"I didn't expect I'd make it," he went on. "I thought one of us ought to look after Cora and her child. I figured if he could get to the money…" He turned venomous eyes on Gowdy. "Never crossed my mind he'd already done just that."

"I got the blame for your damn hand, just the same," Gowdy said. "They all took it for granted I'd done it."

Waldrop roared with laughter. "Who the hell would have believed anything but? You want me to feel guilty for it? Truth is, I'd have been all right with all of it, even you poaching the money, if you'd done right by Cora and the girl.

"You're one to talk," Gowdy said, a little fire coming back into his voice. "What did you ever do for her, or your daughter?"

"What could I do—broke, crippled, supposed to be dead? I was lucky just to make my way to Oklahoma. But work there was scarce, even for boys with two good wings. Doctor had to take another good-sized hunk of mine off just to keep me breathing. I scraped by on piss-ant jobs, muckin' stables and tendin' horses. I had nought to send Cora, even if I dared. But you." He punctuated his words with a jab of the shotgun barrels. "You had a fortune to do with as you pleased. And you did nothin'. I kept track of Cora, best I could. She lived in that ratty old shack in Muleshoe, not a nickel to her name, right up till she died."

"I had to stay on the run," Gowdy said. "I couldn't take the chance of anybody knowing where I was, what name I was using. It was no Sunday picnic for me, Abe."

"Yeah, sixty thousand dollars must have weighed you down something terrible."

"Is this about Cora and your girl, or the damned money, Abe? You can't have it both ways."

"I only ever cared about the money for her, and the kid. I tracked you for years. Followed hints and rumors here and there. Knew sooner or later I'd cut your trail. Then I'd bleed you slow—take it all from you, and more. But then I heard that Cora died, so plans changed. Figured then to just go on and kill you when I found you."

"What's been stopping you?"

"The girl. She come out here with that no-good Prince, and I got sidetracked. A man's bound to be curious about his own child. I kept my distance, but I watched. When I got wind of what Prince was pulling on you, I figured they was in it together. Good girl, I says to myself. It's only right. But that drunken bastard was no more true to her than you was to Cora. Served him right to go and get himself dead."

He started pacing again. He seemed lost in thought. He paused as he noticed for the first time the photo in my hand. I hadn't even realized I was still holding it.

"What's that there?" he demanded. I stretched my arm toward him, and he moved just close enough to peer at the photo.

"I'll be damned," he said, squinting at the faded image. His face seemed to grow a little younger. He regarded Gowdy with an almost friendly smile. "We was quite a dashing pair once, wasn't we, Del?"

Gowdy made no reply, and Waldrop's sudden dreaminess melted away. "The girl come to you, I guess," he said to Gowdy. "Told you who she was, ain't that right?"

Gowdy nodded.

"I expect she thinks you're her old man. Cora always had a funny sense of what was proper."

Gowdy nodded again.

"And you went ahead and let her believe that, did you?"

"I did. She reminds me of Cora—Cora in the good days. Anyway with things as they are, don't you think that's best?"

"Best for you, you mean. Aw, hell, maybe best for her, too. You're in the chips, so at least you can give her what you never gave your own wife."

Gowdy reddened. His eyes turned cold and hard. His bloody right hand lowered to his side and its fingers twitched. They moved an inch nearer to the gun on the desk. He locked eyes with Waldrop. His voice was even and calm when he spoke.

"Cora played me false," he said. "To hell with her."

He looked up as a door opened behind the loft railing above. Our eyes followed. Val stepped through the doorway, draped in a blue robe and carrying a water glass. She looked sleepy, but her eyes grew wide and frightened when she saw the scene below. She dropped the glass and retreated through the open door.

Gowdy looked back at Waldrop. "And to hell with you, too."

"No, sir," Waldrop answered, leveling the shotgun and cocking the other hammer. "To hell with you."

"Papa!" The scream came from the loft, followed by five quick shots. Waldrop dropped to the floor. One shotgun barrel discharged as he fell, and dust and plaster rained from the ceiling.

Dusty and I lunged for the guns on the carpet. Gowdy grabbed for the one on the desk. As we all came up, Gowdy's gun exploded and Dusty fell.

Gowdy swung the big pistol on me. I fired three shots, and he dropped his gun on the desk a second time. He crumpled all at once, like a marionette with its strings cut.

"Nooooo!" Val charged barefoot down the stairs, her little .32 in her hand. She looked down at the damp patch turning Gowdy's pale blue vest black, then turned on me. There was no green to soften her eyes tonight. They were ice blue and full of hate.

She raised the little revolver and pulled the trigger over and over. The hammer fell with a dry click on each spent cartridge. Dusty was back on his feet and holding a bandana to the side of his head. He clamped a hand over Val's pistol and forced her arm down. He pried the gun gently from her hand.

"It's over, girl," he said.

I checked the two downed men. Gowdy was dead. Waldrop wouldn't be far behind; his breathing was ragged and moist. His lips strained to form words. I knelt down and leaned an ear to him. The whispery voice seemed to come from somewhere else.

"Sh-she sure does look like Cora."

Chapter Twenty-Seven

"My job's pretty secure with you around, Ross," Queenan said. The last words slurred a little as he picked a flake of cigar tobacco off his tongue. "Better part of two weeks now all I've done is follow you around and pick up bodies."

"Always glad to help out a public servant," I said.

He cocked his head to one side and studied Joe Gowdy's inert form. He looked like an artist deciding whether the light was hitting the basket of fruit just right. "You could draw the line, though, at providing your own stiffs."

The quiet ranch house was now busy as a bus terminal. Cops and coroner's men swarmed around stone-faced, trying to get their own pieces of work done without tripping over ambulance crews, lab and photo boys, and one or two press hounds Queenan had allowed in because he owed them favors.

They'd already carried Waldrop's body out. The ambulance guys had sedated Val and bused her off to the receiving hospital. She'd been in pretty shaky condition. They'd also seen to Dusty, who now had to carry his big hat because he had about two pounds of cotton and gauze wrapped around his head. Swap the hat for a fife or drum and he could have been an artist's study himself. Bernal was busy taking his statement.

"So check me on this," Queenan said to me. "This frail..." he peered at his notebook. "Cady. She shoots Waldrop—or Shandy. Then Gowdy—Maynard—shoots Vanner, and you dump Gowdy. Kind of a Tinker-to-Evers-to-Chance play, and two men out. Have I got it right so far?"

"Just like that."

"Jeez, the coroner's jury's gonna need score cards and a couple bottles of aspirin to keep all them names straight." He licked his pencil point. "Now give me again how the Cady broad figures into this mess."

"She was Prince's girl, to start with."

"A fact you left out of all our conversations about Prince."

"I didn't know it to begin with."

"But you did know it." He gave me the fisheye. "Maybe you had other reasons." He let that hang, and when I didn't bite, he said, "All right, we'll skip that for now. How's she get from being Prince's girl to punching this one-armed bird all full of holes. He didn't kill Prince, right?"

I shook my head. "She thought her father was dead. Her mother always told her so. Prince figured out who Gowdy was and was draining him in exchange for keeping it quiet. Val—Miss Cady—learned what Prince was up to and put the pieces together. When she found out I knew, too, she went to Gowdy to warn him. He brought her here. He planned to ship her out of town to keep her safe and silent. When she walked in on our little parlor play and saw Waldrop about to settle his old score, she shot him. The rest you know."

"How did Prince know who this guy was?"

I showed him the photograph of the onetime train robbers. "Prince had this. Stole it from Cady's mother, or maybe she sold it to him—she was hard up. Either way, Prince had a writer's eye for detail. He knew Gowdy from the Hackamore, recognized him in the photo, and started squeezing him for money."

"So you think he squeezed too hard and Gowdy killed him."

"He as much as admitted to me he did." It wasn't much of a lie, as lies go. "I doubt he did it himself. I guess you were right all along about Ed Jarboe."

"So Jarboe hung himself to avoid the state doin' it for him?"

"I'll believe that if you will," I said.

"Which means what?"

I looked around us. There were too many ears in the room to suit me. "How about we take our conversation outside?"

He pocketed his notebook and swept his arm, maître d' style, toward the door. We passed by Bernal and Dusty on our way out.

"You manage things in here, Frankie?" Queenan made his voice louder than usual over the buzz of activity. "Ross wants to show me his handiwork out by the bunkhouse."

"Sure thing, Carl." Bernal gave him a curious look, shifted it to me. I shrugged and Queenan followed me out.

+++

When I came back to the house half an hour later, quiet had returned. The clock tick-tocked away in the hall, unaware that this night was any different from a thousand others. The dead had been hauled away, the uniforms had taken Gowdy's boys in for booking, the medical guys had gone back to their stations to wait for the next tragedy. Reese and Mac had told their stories and taken Dusty home to get some rest.

I stood in the big doorway to Gowdy's study, watching. The room was empty now except for Frank Bernal. He didn't notice I was there. He stood hunched over Gowdy's desk, sifting through papers, pulling out desk drawers, pawing around in cubby holes. He'd always been such a slow, methodical guy, it interested me to see him working at such a fevered pace. I was almost sorry to interrupt.

"If you're looking for the ledger, it's not here," I said.

If I'd fired a shot, Bernal couldn't have looked more startled. He forced a grin—a shade late, but he managed it.

"Hey, Nate. Just looking to tidy things up a little. See if we could help Downs out, find anything more to tie this guy in with the *Stardust Trail* business." He puffed his cheeks, blew out a breath with fake nonchalance. "Jarboe told you about the ledger, huh?"

"Yeah," I said. "That book would help a lot. Probably shows all the payments for Jarboe's extra services."

"That's what I'm thinking. Gowdy's blackmail payoffs to Prince, too. I'm betting Jarboe was the bagman for those."

"I don't know. I'm guessing Gowdy used somebody more reliable for that."

"You think? Like who?"

"Let me answer that with another question. When did Jarboe tell you about the ledger?"

He was good, but not good enough. I could see him struggling to come up with an answer I'd buy.

"Queenan questioned him," I said. "But he never mentioned a ledger to Queenan."

"No? That's funny, I…"

"I found it, Frank," I said. I'd lost my stomach for watching him squirm. "And it's got everything in it you're thinking it does. Everything."

He stood up straight. His intelligent eyes looked flat and dead.

"Payments to 'Frank Bernal' alongside every payout to Prince," I said. "Assorted others, too. The last one's dated Wednesday, the day before they found Jarboe doing the Texas Cakewalk in his cell. It's quite a bit bigger."

"What are you saying, here, gumshoe?"

"I'm saying Ed Jarboe didn't kill himself. Gowdy wanted him gone because he'd become a liability. And I'd think a guy as sharp as you would ask more than five grand for playing executioner."

The dead eyes studied me. "Where's the book?"

"I gave it to Queenan."

His face went as gray as his gabardine. All at once he looked older than Abe Shandy.

"You should have brought it to me," he said. "I'm sure we could have come to terms."

"I'd have been no better than Dave Prince, then. And I don't sell myself as cheap as either of you."

He was smooth and professional. The gun was in his hand like hocus pocus. "You sanctimonious son of a bitch. Just can't quit going after cops, can you?"

"I don't even try. They keep coming to me."

His eyes burned at me. Behind them, I could see he was figuring angles.

"You shoot me, then what?"

"I don't know. Lots of ways to play it. Maybe it was you gunned Prince in the first place."

"Why would I? And why with Jarboe's gun? And how did it get back in his room? How would any of that nix the ledger? Too many questions, Frank. You'll have to do better. And fast."

He shook his head with disgust. "Gowdy was a damned fool to rely on Jarboe, a chump who'd shoot a guy and leave the gun at the scene. I'd heard it was missing. I wish you'd found it out there, instead of me. This would all be simpler then."

"If wishes were horses, pal."

He smiled. "Yeah, if wishes were horses." He raised his gun.

"Okay, that's enough of that." Queenan's voice boomed down through the empty room. Bernal's eyes flicked around for the source. They settled on the loft above. Queenan stood there with the muzzle of Abe Shandy's stubby scattergun resting on the railing, angled down.

"Lay it on the desk nice and neat, brother," he said. Bernal didn't move. "I wouldn't like to do it, Frank, but don't kid yourself I won't."

Bernal hesitated. He looked uncertainly between Queenan and me.

"Don't be a sap, Frankie. This thing'll open you up like a meat piñata. Let's don't part that way."

Bernal let out a long, slow breath. He lowered his piece and slid it halfway across the desk. I covered him with my .380 as his partner came down the stairs.

"Jesus, Queenan," I said. "Don't you think you sliced that a little thin?"

With his free hand Queenan backhanded the air. "Blah."

Chapter Twenty-Eight

"It ain't bad," Dusty said. "Not exactly Texas brisket, but it ain't bad."

God deliver us from heathens. "Maybe they could put that in their ads," I said, a little peevish. "Try a Gotham Deli pastrami. It ain't bad."

Dusty shrugged as though he'd heard worse ideas. This was the thanks I got for trying to introduce a backwoods pal to a little culture and refinement. He took a slug of beer, leaving a mustard smudge on the mouth of his bottle. Refinement indeed.

Mac, Reese and Joe had politely declined my invitation with a limp excuse about working some new horses at the stables. I suspected it had more to do with native suspicion of an eatery with such a citified name. Their loss. I'd only wanted to offer them some small token of my gratitude. Maybe that should be my slogan: Nate Ross, Private Investigations. Save my keister and the sandwiches are on me.

Duke had been excluded from the offer, only because he was busy filming in Monument Valley. His thank-you pastrami would have to wait.

"What do you have in the works," I asked Dusty, "now that you're all done tracking down real wild West bad men? You going to stick with chasing the celluloid variety?"

"Might as well. Work's steady. Republic's got projects enough lined up to carry me to my rocking chair days. And if this Duke Wayne picture is anything like they say, the big studios are gonna have plenty more to go around. Who knows, maybe pay'll improve."

"You're a permanent Hollywoodian then?"

"There's nothing permanent in this burg." He finished his beer. "Or this world, for that matter."

"What name you planning to go by? Walter VanNeer or Dusty Vanner?"

"I wondered when you'd get around to asking about that."

"What's the story? Don't tell me you robbed trains yourself in your wild and wooly days."

"Ain't much story to tell. When I was in the rodeos, I got tired of announcers calling me Van Nee-ur so I went with Vanner."

"What about the Dusty part?"

He grinned. "I spent more time in the dust than on the horse. One reason I quit." He cocked an eyebrow. "And none of your smartass remarks. I can still ride rings around Autry eight days a week. Anyway, I've seen you in the saddle."

"Well, whatever name you go by, just remember your old friends when you're living in that mansion in the hills."

"The hell you say." He waggled his empty bottle. "Buy me another one." I signaled the waitress and she gave me a wink.

"How about you?" he asked. "How does a fellow in your line drum up trade?"

"He doesn't, much. It tends to find him. For now I can afford a little breather. Herb Yates cut me a pretty generous check."

"There's a line that was never spoken before."

"He even sent me a box of cigars." I pulled two out of my pocket. "Join me?"

We lit up and sat in silence for five minutes puffing our cigars like a couple of railroad barons.

"Seen the girl?" he asked at last. It was a touchy subject and he knew it. But if I'd learned anything about the cowboy breed, it was that tact wasn't in their kits.

"Not since she tried to perforate me."

"She was upset."

"Yeah. Try that excuse out on Dave Prince."

He couldn't say much to that. But it wasn't going to stop him talking. "Decent of you to keep her out of that."

"Decent of you to back my story."

He just shrugged. "You're going to leave things stand with her, then?"

"She hates my guts," I said. "If she knew the truth, she'd hate her own. It's better to let her hate mine."

"I expect you're right. Life is a damned sorry business sometimes."

"You only say that because you're an optimist."

+++

It had only been a few days, but it felt like I hadn't been to the office in months. I figured I'd better stop in and knock down the cobwebs.

The cobwebs were light—the spider's union must have been on strike. I was flipping through my normal assortment of uninteresting mail when I heard heavy steps in the hall. The door opened and a sheriff's deputy stepped in.

I didn't see a subpoena or handcuffs in his hand. That was a relief. He stepped up to my desk and stood at near attention. He was a splendid specimen. The dark green uniform was immaculate. His leather gear was buffed to a blinding sheen. The six-pointed star on his chest was polished to such brightness just looking at it made my head ache.

He was a youngster; his face scrubbed and pink and hairless. He'd have looked more natural in a letter jacket and dungarees than a cop suit.

"Are you Nathaniel Ross, sir?" he asked in that authoritative tone the academies teach you will melt bad guys like butter.

I shot to my feet and barked out, "I am he. And your name?" Two could play this game.

He looked a little hurt, and I felt guilty. I wished I had some licorice to offer him, or a puppy.

"I'm Deputy Spellman, sir," he said.

"You're not that Deputy Spellman, are you?"

That shook him a little. "Sir?"

"I'm sorry, buster," I said, sitting down again. "I've had one hell of a week and I'm feeling kind of mean. What can I help you with?"

He cleared his throat and readjusted his swagger. "I'm Sheriff Biscailuz's driver. I'm here to ask you to accompany me to his office." There was awe,

189

with an undertone of dread, in his voice. I understood it. For a slick-sleeve deputy, a call to the sheriff's office was like a summons to the throne of God. Except that God had mercy.

I was sympathetic, but not enough to roll over and play dead.

"What for?" I demanded.

"I'm not privy to that, sir. My orders are to deliver you ASAP, if not sooner."

I was about to tackle that last phrase, but I held my tongue. I'd already given him my normal dose of grief. He seemed like a nice, earnest kid and I didn't want to break his spirit. His job would do it soon enough.

May as well get it over with, whatever the hell it was. I knew they wouldn't leave me alone until I did. I grabbed my hat and swept it toward the door. "Lead on, garcon."

I followed the kid down the stairs and out into the hazy sunshine. A big, black county car sat not twenty feet from the door. It had to be the sheriff's own bus; it was freshly waxed, not a dent in it, and it had no bloodstains on the back seat. This last observation I made as the young deputy opened the rear door and stood waiting beside it like a limousine jockey.

"No thanks," I told him. "I have my own bucket."

"My orders are to transport you, sir. There and back."

"Not unless you plan to cuff me first."

He looked crestfallen. I don't imagine he'd ever failed an order yet.

"Don't worry, pal," I said. "I won't tell him if you don't. I know the way, but I'll follow you."

+++

Young Spellman marched me straight into Biscailuz's office, bypassing a gray coiffed, pugnacious secretary who looked like Wallace Beery in pearls. She was none too happy that she didn't get to use her intercom buzzer.

I hadn't been in this office in over three years and it hadn't changed. It wasn't just that the furnishings and décor were the same; everything was. The visitor's chairs sat canted at the same forty-five-degree angle to the glossy mahogany desk. The same glass ashtray, big and clean enough to eat soup from, sat on the same corner of the desk. The same three law books were neatly stacked in the same order on the opposite corner. A freshly

190

sharpened, unused pencil still lay centered exactly two inches behind the blotter pad. The same dove-gray fedora hung on the same hook of the corner hat stand.

In the midst of all this sameness, the high sheriff himself seemed least changed of all. Same stocky, compact frame. Same thick, seal-black hair. Same caterpillar eyebrows behind horn-rimmed glasses.

As I walked in, he stood and extended a hand. He flashed an oily, politician's smile. That hadn't changed either.

"Hello, Nate. Thanks for coming in."

Eugene Biscailuz came from old California stock on both sides. His paternal grandfather had grazed sheep in the Valley. His mother was descended from Spaniards who'd lived in the region since around the time the first mission bell tolled. Her father had been an L.A. city marshal, killed in the 1870s in a genuine old West gunfight, right about where city hall stands today. Biscailuz had the ideal pedigree for his job and everyone, including him, knew it. He was no less honest than the average L.A. politico, but that wasn't much to brag on.

I accepted the handshake. It was drier and firmer than I remembered, so at least one thing had changed. He dismissed Spellman and swept me into one of the perfectly angled chairs, then sat on the edge of the desk. It put his head well above mine, an advantage he couldn't claim if we were standing.

"Nate Ross," he said in a suave, soothing voice, like a doctor about to ram the needle home. "It's been how long—three years?"

"Three and change," I said. "What did you want to see me about?"

The unctuous smile returned. "Direct and to the point, just like your dad. One of the things I always liked about you." He reached behind him and toggled the intercom. "Miss Lehman, we're ready."

The door behind me opened and the old valkyrie clomped in followed by a ferrety looking guy with a camera the size of a steamer trunk. No one but a news hawk would wear white socks with a suit.

"This is Mr. Brant, of the *Times*," the sheriff said. He stood and adjusted his jacket and indicated I should do likewise. He spun me around beside him and trotted out his official voice. "Nathaniel Ross, on behalf of the County of Los Angeles and its grateful citizens, it is my distinct honor and privilege to present you with this Award for Meritorious Service."

The secretary handed him a big, gold frame. Behind the glass it held a document with more gilt and ribbons and wax seals on it than the Magna Carta. Somewhere in the midst I saw my name. He pushed the frame at me and turned his smile on the boy with the camera. All I could do was follow suit. The flashbulb the guy touched off left me sunburned for a week, and when I saw the photo later on in the *Times*, my smile looked like a death rictus.

The little sideshow concluded, Biscailuz hustled them both out of the room and we took up our former posts.

"Sorry to spring that on you," he said, "but there was just time to make the late edition." He offered me a cigarette from a snazzy gold case with the county star on it. He probably had the same emblem stitched in bullion on his pajamas. I politely declined.

"You're quite the man of the moment," he said. "Front page of every paper in town. It's not every private investigator who could close a case from before he was born, and clear up a homicide or two to boot, all in one fell swoop. The papers don't know the half of it, naturally. And that's just as well." He pointed to the framed award. "This sort of thing is just frippery, of course. You're savvy enough to know that. What counts is not what some piece of paper says you are, but what you've proven yourself to be."

I cut in. "With all due respect, Sheriff…" There was a phrase loaded with all sorts of interpretations. If he'd known me as well as he pretended to, he'd have realized it. "I went along with your request to come down here. Mostly out of curiosity, I'll admit. Maybe a little bit for old time's sake, too. But I'm sure you wanted me for something more than phony press snaps, so could we skip the palavering and just get to why I'm sitting here?"

He was unfazed. "Fair enough. I want you to come back to work for me." He reached into a desk drawer, then plunked a shiny gold star on the desk and pushed it across to me. "Sergeant Downs had excellent things to say about you." It was tough to picture Downs saying much about anything. "And our past differences aside, your prior record here is solid. Say the word and that badge is yours, along with an immediate assignment to Detective Division and a promotion to sergeant."

I hefted the badge and ran my thumb over its ball-tipped points and across the grizzly bear center seal. "This is a little surreal," I said. "The last time I saw a badge on your desk it was sliding the other direction."

"Winds change, Nate. And times change. Maybe it's time you and I forget the past and draw a bead on the future." He stood and thrust out a hand. "What do you say, son?"

I stood up and looked at him for a long moment. I laid the badge back on the desk. "Do you know, Sheriff," I said, "what's wrong with a star-shaped badge?"

Chapter Twenty-Nine

I was surprised to look up from my desk and see Queenan coming through the door.

"I didn't think I'd find you here, Ross. Slow day in the racket for L.A.'s number one gumshoe?" He dropped his big frame into a chair.

"What's on your mind today, Lieutenant?"

"Captain. Papers came through day before yesterday."

"Congratulations. Sorry, I'm fresh out of champagne."

He sat with his right ankle propped on his left knee. He ignored the Hackamore ashtray on the desk right in front of him—or didn't know that's what it was—and trimmed his cigar by shaving ash off against his shoe sole, letting it fall to the floor.

"Yeah, well, this *Stardust Trail* business scored me big brownie points with the chief. So I guess I owe the new badge partly to you."

"I'll bet that hurt to say."

"You have no idea. But I'm a fair guy; I believe in credit where credit's due. I owe you one. I won't forget it."

"Okay." I wouldn't forget it either. "But if I know you, that's not what you came down here for."

"Nah, I came to tell you Bernal's preliminary hearing's a week from Tuesday. You'll be needed."

"You could have phoned and told me that."

"You're right. Truth is, there was one more thing. I was curious about a rumor I heard." He leaned forward with his hands on his knees and thrust his big moon face at me. "Did you, honest to God, tell Gene Biscailuz to shove a badge up his ass?"

News travels fast in cop circles. "I don't remember my exact words," I said.

He threw back his head and cut loose with a hard, braying laugh. "Father God and Sonny Jesus, what I'd give to have seen the look on his puss!"

It only then occurred to me I'd left my framed commendation in the sheriff's office. It was probably in the trash bin five minutes after I cleared the building. It had served its purpose.

"Well, you'll want to watch yourself," he said, dabbing his eyes with a hairy wrist. "That old boy has a long shadow."

"Well, I wasn't winning any popularity polls over there to begin with."

"You're one for the books, Ross. I can't decide whether you're ballsy or just stupid."

"I guess one doesn't rule out the other, Cap."

I'd never seen a genuine smile cross his face before. I hope I never see another; it was hideous.

He stood up. "Well, crime don't sleep. Time to toddle off." He noticed my half-open desk drawer. Just before he came in, I'd stuck my .380 inside.

"Still packin' that pimp rod, huh?" He held out a hand. "You mind?"

I handed him the gun. He deftly broke the magazine, shucked out the chambered round, and sighted on my wall clock.

"It belonged to my father," I said, for no reason.

"I know," he said. "I seen it in action once, years ago." He turned his head toward me. "I never told you I met your old man, did I?"

"No." For once, he had my interest.

"Yeah, summer of '22. I was just a young beat copper, full of piss and vinegar. I knew who Jimmy Ross was, of course. Most every copper, and half the lawyers and judges in the county bought their hooch from him."

I lit a smoke. I wasn't sure I wanted to know the rest of this story.

"Anyway," he went on, "I bit off more than I could chew one evening, got cornered by four punks in a seventh street alley. They had the drop, and numbers, and were getting ready to put a serious hurt on yours truly. Then, out of nowhere there's a gunshot, and this bird holding a sawed-off on me drops it and starts howling and trying to stop up a hole in his gut. Two of his pals take off running. The other one just stands, kind of frozen-like, and watches Jimmy Ross come walking up the middle of the alley, dressed to the nines, this very piece in his hand." He held out the pistol to punctuate. "This guy's holding a gat of his own, but he seems to have forgot. Your dad just strolls up to him. Casual, like he was going to ask for a light. When he's close enough, whack! He bats the guy across the chops with his pistol and slaps the gun out of his hand. What does tough boy do? He pisses himself, and starts whining 'Please, Mr. Ross!' Jimmy screws his muzzle into the hood's ear. In his other ear he tells him, 'It's Sergeant Ross, shitbird. Now get your pal patched up, put on some dry britches, and the both of you get your candy asses out of my county. You ever come back, I'll hang your nuts off my watch chain.' You better believe those two beat feet pronto."

He reloaded the gun and laid it on the desk, almost reverently. "I live to be a thousand, I'll never forget that night." He looked around like he'd just remembered where he was. He shook his head. "Your old man was something."

"Yeah, he was something, all right."

"Different times, pal, different times. Talk about your wild West." He stubbed out his cigar in the copper cowboy hat—guess he did know what it was for. He started out, but stopped in the doorway. "I still don't like you, Ross."

"That's all right, Cap. I don't like you either."

He grinned and flicked his hat brim. "Stay pure, kid," he said, and went out. I put my gun back in the drawer.

Chapter Thirty

Republic never made *Stardust Trail*. The studio line was that with all the troubles that had beset the production, they were worried their film was more cursed than *Macbeth*. It made for snappy reading in *Variety* anyway. But the talk around town was that once Yates heard from a couple pals who'd seen early footage of *Stagecoach*, he realized there would be no competing with Ford's film. He shut down production that same day and went back to tilling more familiar ground.

The footage Perry Mills had already shot wasn't entirely wasted. For twenty years snippets showed up in one or another of Republic's trademark Westerns. Mills missed his big break; he spent the rest of his career on three-day soundstage shoots directing cheap science fiction films about little green men from Mars.

My own moment in the spotlight was nearly as brief. Hollywood scandals have about the lifespan of egg salad, so within two weeks of seeing my name in every rag from the Palisades to Pomona I was back to being Nate Ross, professional nobody.

One mixed blessing from the hoopla was that every movie outfit in town now wanted to hire me to make its private little problems go away. My feelings about studio work hadn't changed, but neither had my fondness for regular meals and a roof above me. I took as many of these jobs as my schedule and constitution would bear. For the first time since I'd left the county payroll, my bank account was flush. Not impressive, but flush.

Dusty's cowboy pals never did take me up on my lunch offer. Dusty himself was kept busy for a while lobbying—unsuccessfully—to collect the reward in the Maynard/Shandy train robbery. The railroad had changed hands more than once in thirty-six years, and the current ownership claimed to have no record of any such offer. Not such shabby bookkeepers, after all. In the end Dusty gave it up. He'd only fought as hard as he did because he'd planned on giving the money to Val. But she didn't need it. Once the courts finished untangling the various legal threads in re Delbert Maynard AKA Joseph Gowdy, it was determined that Valerie Myrla Cady was his soul and rightful heir. She sold the ranch and the Hackamore and left for parts unknown. Unknown to me, anyhow, and I planned to keep it that way.

Duke sent me a letter or two from Utah. Just notes, really—news from the set, how was I getting along, that sort of thing. I had heard he was back in town, but we hadn't been in touch. I was loafing around the office on a slow morning—a rarity lately—when the postman popped in with a special delivery letter. It read: *Dear Nate, Hope you can make it. I think you'll like this one. Duke.* It was folded around two tickets for the *Stagecoach* premier.

I owed it to Duke to go, but wasn't sure what to do with two tickets. It seemed a waste to go alone, but all the people I knew who might want to be there would already be there. Almost all.

+++

Duke was right. I liked the film—I liked it a lot. When he first showed up on the screen and did his Winchester flip, the awe-struck audience gasped in unison. The bit gave me chills for a couple of reasons. I felt like an insider when I recognized Yak Canutt in Indian garb and war paint, doing the gag under the stagecoach. I'd seen him do the same stunt in one of Duke's earlier films, but it hadn't looked half as spectacular then. When the cavalry rode in, the cowboys and college kids in the audience and the posh Hollywood folk alike cheered and stomped like football hooligans.

In the lobby afterwards, I thought I'd go deaf from the excited chatter. Nearly everybody was raving about the film, and about its star. I say nearly, because in the middle of the mob I bumped into Herb Yates. He was civil enough—even shook my hand—but he looked like somebody had spiked his martini with vinegar when I asked how he'd liked the picture.

"If its Westerns they want, they'd better let us make them." Without another word, he turned and melted back into the crowd.

Yates was welcome to his sour grapes. Maybe even entitled, considering all that *Stardust Trail* had cost him.

As if to make up for Yates, there was one person in the room who, above all the others, was absolutely over the moon about the movie. Mikey Galvin had been surprised when I'd stopped by and offered to bring him. He'd been a chatterbox the entire drive to Westwood, and had forced me to assure him more than once that yes, I really did know John Wayne. I'd had to shush him several times during the film; he couldn't keep the lid down on his excitement.

I had a tough time getting near Duke. He was the conquering hero, after all, and everyone wanted to slap him on the back and offer congratulations. When I finally maneuvered close enough to catch his eye, he politely disentangled himself from the knot of well-wishers and waded upstream to shake my hand. I didn't say anything he hadn't heard a hundred times already that night or wouldn't hear a hundred more. But there would be plenty of time later to tell him what I thought. For now, I had something else in mind.

Duke was a real sport. He shook Mikey's hand, signed an autograph (with a wink, he signed it "To Mr. Lindy") and told a story or two. He even waved one of the studio photographers over so they could pose for a photo together. I thought the poor kid's heart would fail him then and there.

+++

On the drive home Mikey must have thanked me a dozen times for bringing him to the premier. I was relieved when he nodded off; I could enjoy the drive in peace. It was a pleasant night, and with the kid dozing, I thought it couldn't hurt to take a little detour. I angled up Santa Monica and drove by the Hackamore. It had a different name these days, and a different look. Now it was just another middling night club catering less to the Hollywood crowd than to tourists and folks from the suburbs who wanted to dress up and play Hollywood.

It made me wonder where the cowboys were doing their drinking nowadays. They may not have much leisure time if the majors got back into the Westerns game. Duke Morrison—I still couldn't think of him as Wayne—would probably be the busiest of the bunch. I was still no expert, but my gut told me he might have a real future in show business.

About the Author

J.R. Sanders is a native Kansan and longtime denizen of the L.A. suburbs. His interest in Old West history stems from childhood visits to the Dalton Gang hideout, Abilene, and Dodge City. His interest in crime dates back to his days as a police officer and a private investigator. His nonfiction articles regularly appear in magazines such as *Law & Order* and *Wild West*, and he's authored books on topics as diverse as Southern California apple farms and Old West lawmen killed in the line of duty.

J.R. currently lives in Southern California with his wife, Rose, and their rescue dogs, Ruby and Marlowe.